The James Tiptree Award Anthology 2

The James Tiptree Award Anthology 2

EDITED BY

Karen Joy Fowler · Pat Murphy · Debbie Notkin · Jeffrey D. Smith

TACHYON PUBLICATIONS · SAN FRANCISCO

CRANSTON PUBLIC LIBRARY
AUBURN BRANCH

The James Tiptree Award Anthology 2

contents

introduction

Debbie Notkin

The James Tiptree Jr. Literary Award was started in 1991 by Karen Joy Fowler, now the best-selling author of *The Jane Austen Book Club*, and multiple Nebula Award-winning author Pat Murphy. It wasn't the James Tiptree Jr. Literary Award, then, but just the beginnings of an idea. I'm going to tell you a bit about the history of the award, talk about how it compares to other awards in the field of science fiction, and then mention some questions that the existence of the Tiptree Award has raised.

As I mentioned, the Tiptree Award was founded by Karen Fowler and Pat Murphy. Karen is an interesting combination: she's the world's nicest person, and she's also easily annoyed. She was, at that moment, annoyed that none of the science fiction awards were named after women — Hugo Gernsback, Philip K. Dick, and Mr. Nebula, I guess. Anyway, Karen was annoyed and Pat was impish (Pat is often impish), and somehow they decided that the best way to name an award after a woman was to name it after "James Tiptree Jr.," who was really a woman named Alice Sheldon writing under a male name for a variety of reasons.

Pat was guest of honor at WisCon that year. WisCon is the annual gathering of the feminist science fiction community; held once a year in Madison, Wisconsin. One thing WisCon does is invite guests of honor, and one thing the guests of honor do is give speeches to the whole membership. So Pat announced the award in her guest of honor speech.

Now Pat and Karen are more than smart enough to know that

there is more to an award than an announcement. Awards need goals, and rules, and some degree of process. Pat set the goal in her initial speech. This was to be an award for works of science fiction and fantasy that "explore and expand gender." That description is still the one we're using today. They wanted the award to have a money prize, so it was to be funded by bake sales: hence the slogan, "If you can't change the world with chocolate chip cookies, how can you change the world?" Chocolate is also an integral part of the award winner's prize — in response to an off-hand comment by Ursula K. Le Guin. (In the first year of the Tiptree Award, Le Guin suggested that the award itself should be edible, writing in a letter to Pat Murphy: "I have seen and even received some awards that would be far far better eaten.")

Now this could still have gone nowhere. I imagine that several great ideas for awards have been the subject of guest of honor speeches at SF conventions, and that's the last anyone has heard of them. But this was WisCon. When the WisCon crowd decides that something should happen, you can consider that something already finished and tied with a red ribbon. WisCon is, among many other things, a pretty unstoppable machine.

So, before anyone could say "James Tiptree Jr.," people were volunteering to do bake sales, to design logos, to do publicity, and generally to make the award happen. Apparently, it was an extremely exciting evening. (I wasn't there.)

Did you notice that I said up above that awards need rules and some degree of process? That's where I came in. Pat returned home from WisCon and called me up. (We knew each other socially, but we were not good friends.) She told me about WisCon, and the award, and I was suitably enthusiastic. Then she got to the point. "Karen and I want you to chair the first panel of judges."

"Really? What's involved?"

"We're counting on you to figure that out."

"Oh."

I don't think I even did the prudent thing, which would have been to say, "Let me think about it," and then call back the next day and say yes. I think I just said yes. Pat and Karen recruited four other judges: Vonda N. McIntyre, Suzy McKee Charnas, Sherry Coldsmith, and Bruce McAllister. Then Pat and Karen smiled at me and said, "Let us know if you need anything."

So the five of us read a lot of books. Pat and Karen wrote to publishers asking for copies of books or stories we wanted to check out. In the course of the year we figured out a bunch of stuff. First, we had to define what "explore and expand gender" meant to us, a process that each subsequent jury has also gone through. (If the definition sounds obvious to you, you might find that thinking about it some more makes it less obvious.) That helped develop one piece of the award philosophy, which is that the award administrators don't guide the jurors at all in what they choose, nor explain any of the terms. Each jury has to figure out the definitions and parameters for itself, which is one reason the award winners are so delightfully all over the map.

I'm pretty sure it was Vonda McIntyre who came up with another key characteristic of the award. "Listen," she said, "no matter how much they may say it's an honor to be nominated, if your book is on the ballot and doesn't win, you feel like you've lost." So the award doesn't have a set of nominees from which a winner is chosen. Instead, the judges announce not only a winner but also a "short list" of works they really like. That way, the short-listed authors get a nice note saying that their work was honored by the jurors, after the fact, instead of chewing their fingernails and wondering if they'll actually win.

So my jury plugged away, reading books and writing each other paper letters (this was 1991, remember!) about what we thought about them. At the end of the process, some jurors were actually spending money on Federal Express to make sure everyone else got to read their comments. One thing we decided was that it was essential for the jury process to be confidential — open discussion of difficult issues and the work of colleagues was, we felt, challenging enough among the five of us, without inviting the world in to watch.

Our first jury started learning about how juries bog down and what kind of disagreements we could expect. Can a book where the basically likable protagonist commits rape be considered a candidate? Should we consider how famous the author is in the mainstream world, or just think about the book? When it comes down to it, how are we going to turn our qualitative opinions into the quantitative naming of a winner? My jury solved these problems in our own way; the thirteen succeeding juries have each solved the problems in their own way. (However, all of them had some past precedent and advice to draw upon. I envy them that!)

While we were deliberating in relative obscurity, the WisCon/Tiptree Award machine was falling into place. Bake sales were happening and money was being collected. What the award should actually be was in discussion. As the jury came closer and closer to consensus, Pat and Karen were commissioning an original work of art, finding the source for a typewriter made of chocolate (!) and figuring out what size check they could write for the winner.

The first award was a tie (as several awards since have also been). The winners were Eleanor Arnason, for *A Woman of the Iron People*, and Gwyneth Jones, for *White Queen*. Eleanor's memorable response was that it was great to win an award which no one she disliked had ever won in the past! Gwyneth traveled from England (and Eleanor from Minnesota) to accept their awards at the 1992 WisCon, and thus the Tiptree Award ceremony was born. The ceremony is a movable feast, traveling to conventions that take place between April and July around the country, as well as once in England, returning to WisCon every other year.

Over the ensuing years, much has developed and much has stayed the same. Every year, a panel of five jurors reads a lot of books, discusses a lot of definitions, and comes up with a winner (or two) and a short list. Some juries have also chosen to come up with a "long list," usually of books that they liked enough to encourage people to read, but which do not treat with gender in important ways. Every year, an award (or two) is given with a ceremony, a check, some chocolate, and a piece of original art (each year by a different artist). The song aspect of the award ceremony, where a bunch of mostly unprofessional singers serenade the winner with a silly parody song in their honor, showed up early in the award's history and has become quite a tradition.

Bake sales still continue, but other fundraising activities have proven important from the award's beginning. Talented collage artist Freddie Baer has created silk-screened T-shirts and prints to commemorate each award, sales of which have helped fund the award. Volunteers working on behalf of the Tiptree organization have published two cookbooks, two anthologies, and a reprinted fanzine. Currently, there is no doubt that the central fundraising effort is the legendary Tiptree Auction, the key entertainment at Saturday night of WisCon. Our auctioneer, Ellen Klages, raises the bar for the definition of the word "irrepressible." Ellen has auctioneered in a chicken suit, in drag, and in spangles. She has auctioneered when she was so ill that she had to be taken to the hospital when she came offstage. She has sold a knitted uterus. Actually, she had the audience fill the knitted uterus with money donated to the award, and gave the knitted uterus to Pat Murphy, who wasn't at WisCon that year! Ellen has sold audience members a ride in her car, and the right to watch her shave her head.

The administration of the award has "grown up" as well. We are now a 501(c)(3) corporation, a tax-deductible public charity. We have a board of directors (yours truly is chair of the "Motherboard"). Aside from the award, we give out the occasional Fairy Godmother Award ("the fairy godmother strikes without warning") to someone doing work in areas of interest to the Tiptree Award whom we've been informed needs a little boost to the pocketbook. We have some formal volunteer roles: a procurer or procuress to get books from publishers, a publicity person, a website manager. We publicize our efforts and seek nominations for future Tiptree winners at our website, www.tiptree.org. (Visit us online for lists of winners, short lists, and other detailed information.)

That's the story of the Tiptree Award, a story that can be told with only the barest allusion to the role of gender in science fiction and fantasy.

I think it's also interesting to contrast the Tiptree Award with some of the science fiction and fantasy field's other awards. Science fiction and fantasy's leading awards are the Hugo Award, the Nebula Award, and the World Fantasy Award.

The Hugo Award is given out annually by the World Science Fiction Society. Everyone who joins the World Science Fiction Convention (or "Worldcon") for a given year and all members from the previous year are eligible to nominate and vote for the Hugo Awards, but in fact only a tiny fraction of the membership votes even for the most popular categories (Best Novel and Best Dramatic Presentation). The core voters join every Worldcon, some of them only to maintain their Hugo franchise. (The Worldcon is far too complicated to explain here; let's just say that anyone with a comparatively small amount of money can join, and the convention itself is a several thousand person extravaganza for readers, writers, editors, gamers, costumers, movie fans, and more.)

The only characteristic that defines a Hugo winner is "best," which is arguably more subjective than "work that best explores and expands gender," but subject to far less discussion and reification. For several years now, the same few authors and series have been winning year in and year out, implying perhaps a popularity contest, and at the very least a strong advantage for voter familiarity.

The Nebula Awards are selected by vote of the membership of the Science Fiction Writers of America, a group that you can only join if you've sold at least three short stories, one novel, or one dramatic script to a professional market. While some people join and some people leave this group every year, the core membership is much the same from year to year. The nominees are also selected by popular vote, except that two juries are selected every year — one jury reads all the eligible novels and the other reads all the eligible short fiction, and each is invited to add one work per category to the final ballot. "Best" is still the only criterion. The Nebula Awards go to a wider variety of authors and works than do the Hugo Awards. Because the SFWA membership is comparatively small, campaigning for nominations and awards is common practice. At the same time, the membership is large enough to preclude or at least interfere with substantive voter discussion of potential award winners and reasons to vote for or against.

The World Fantasy Award jury is comparable to the Tiptree jury: a five-person group with a mandate to read widely, including reading works nominated by convention members, and to choose a "best" work in each of several categories. That jury, however, is very closely overseen by the administrators of the convention, who put their stamp on the award winners as a whole. The World Fantasy Award winners are a very respectable and varied group of books, and the process, like the Hugo and Nebula Award processes, works well. Nonetheless, I believe it is easier to second-guess what books are likely contenders for the next World Fantasy Award for Best Novel than it is to have the vaguest clue what work will win the next Tiptree Award.

While stability and predictable process are important to other awards, fluidity, flexibility, and unpredictability are the hallmarks of the Tiptree Award. At the same time, the fact that the Tiptree Award has a subject matter guideline provides its jurors with something of a hook to hang their decisions on. Never having served as a juror on a "best" award, I'm hard put to know how the jury conversations go. I do know, however, that when I discuss the question of which book is better than another with friends and colleagues, we very frequently bog down into complete subjectivity. Perhaps we agree that one book is more skillfully crafted than the other, and the other is more intellectually challenging, or more emotionally gripping. Which is better? Is craft more important than impact? Tiptree jurors can, and do, also engage in these conversations, but they do have that one phrase to come back to: the work that best explores and expands gender. Thus, if a jury reads a book and feels that it "explores and contracts gender," as happened with one work, it can be ruled out quickly. A story that catches the hearts and minds of the judges but does not have gender as a core issue can still be saved for the long list.

Don't like what one jury thought was gender? Wait a year — next year's jury will undoubtedly see it differently. Hated the winner? That's fine with the award's administrators, especially if it made you think about why you hated it. See a trend in award winners that you don't care for? Get on the web and nominate some other options — missing some books is inevitable, so we rely on our supporters to keep their eyes open as well. Volunteer to be a juror.

Underlying all these questions of history and procedure is the central question: why have a Tiptree Award at all? Do science fiction and fantasy deal poorly with gender issues these days, or have we grown up? Is the award really a feminist award in a vaguely transparent disguise? If it isn't, should it be? Does the science fiction world need a feminist award? Has the field changed enough — has the award helped the field change enough — in the last fourteen years to render the award irrelevant or passé? And has everything that can be said on the subject of gender already been said?

We've had a lot of controversy swirl around the award over the years. Two of our biggest critics have been well-known writers, each with more than one Hugo and Nebula Award trophy on their mantelpiece. One, a woman, saw the Tiptree Award as part of the totalitarian feminist machine that wanted to control what she writes. One, a man, saw the Tiptree Award as somehow designed to exclude him personally from recognition and praise. (In the early years of the award, he wrote a book which he believed would either win or be proof positive that the award was unfair. The book made the long list, but it didn't win, so he believes he *de facto* demonstrated the basic injustice of the award's premise.)

A leading editor got very angry when a book from his list with a lesbian protagonist didn't get much attention from that year's jury. He wants the award to be a feminist award and doesn't understand (or agree with) the distinction between feminism and gender in this context. The jury's response was that having a lesbian protagonist is no longer an exploratory or expansive auctorial decision.

In the first four years, the question was, "Will a man ever win the Tiptree Award?" In the fifth year, Theodore Roszak shared the prize with Elizabeth Hand and that question went away. Now, we've had four male winners in a row (John Kessel, M. John Harrison, Matt Ruff, and Joe Haldeman). If Johanna Sinisalo hadn't also won this year, some people might be asking if a woman would ever win the award again...

Having fourteen juries struggle with the question of "what does 'exploring and expanding gender' mean?" has led to an awareness that we do not have a social consensus, even in the science fiction community, on what gender is, let alone how it relates to feminism. Over the years, the award has gone to at least one book that many readers consider anti-feminist. Many readers see at least one other winner as treating little if at all with gender. In that case, the judges were most interested in the book's treatment of celibacy in the characters' lives. The award has been given to a book which features a serial killer of women as a main character: can that overused and disturbing topic ever be a legitimate ground for exploring and expanding gender?

Another huge set of questions which the award raises are the questions of race, class, and other social divisions. What's so important about gender, that it has its own award? Should we be expanding our focus, becoming an "RCG" (the educators' term for Race/Class/Gender) award?

No one on the Tiptree Motherboard, and hardly anyone who's served on a jury, would deny that race and class are important questions that deserve comparable attention to gender. As the award has grown in scope and influence, the Motherboard has made an effort to ensure that at least one person of color serves on each jury. And at the same time, Tiptree/Sheldon herself wrote a great deal about gender, and a good deal less about race. Thinking about Tiptree's works as I write, I'd say that class is a factor in many of them. However, the American approach to class is to deny its existence and thus never call it by name, and the Tiptree (and Sheldon) bylined works generally followed that pattern.

And, of course, of race, class, and gender, gender is far and away the one that the "other side" is most motivated to consider. White people have very little obvious reason to really engage with the problems of people of color. Upper-class people have comparatively few obvious reasons to really engage with the problems of the poor. (Give yourself an extra point if you thought about public health risks when you read the previous sentence.) But men have very significant reasons to really engage with, or at least acknowledge, the problems of women, the most obvious being that all men have mothers and many men want women in their lives, as partners, wives, and the mothers of their children.

So the award concentrates on gender, while making more than token and less than equivalent efforts to acknowledge the issues of race and class. Is this a good decision? It was the one that we made when the award was founded — and one that might have been reconsidered. But the Tiptree Award is not the only group to grow out of the Wis-Con community. That same community has recently nurtured the Carl Brandon Society, a group dedicated to increasing the awareness and representation of people of color in the genres and in the community. This group recently announced plans to offer two awards focusing on issues of race and ethnicity, citing the Tiptree Award as an inspiration. Does that mean the Tiptree Award should not be concerned about these issues?

Over the years, we have realized the main point of the Tiptree Award is not to provide answers — but rather to raise questions. When a work wins the Tiptree Award, readers then proceed to argue about whether or not that work was really about gender. That's fine with us. These continuing arguments mean that people are reading the work, thinking about gender, and discussing it with others. And that's the point, after all.

So that's the Tiptree Award: eccentric, unpredictable, fluid, controversial, well-funded (as such things go), trying to struggle with hard questions while staying open-ended and open-minded. Take a look at the contents of this book. I think this work is worth doing, and I think the quality and range of the fiction and nonfiction you're holding is the evidence. I hope you agree.

The James Tiptree Award Anthology 2

Talking Too Much: About James Tiptree, Jr.

Julie Phillips

Julie Phillips writes:

I never met Alice Bradley Sheldon in person. But for the past nine years I have been writing her biography: *James Tiptree Jr.: A Life of Alice Sheldon* (St. Martin's Press, 2006). During those years, I spent long hours in the archives of various libraries, and sorting through boxes in the basement of Jeff Smith, Alice Sheldon's literary trustee.

In this essay, I have tried to show the woman I met in the archives: Alice Sheldon (Alli, to her friends), a.k.a. James Tiptree Jr. Since she had published under a pseudonym, you might expect a spooky, elusive Alli, fleeing down library corridors, slamming doors. Instead I found her sitting at a desk, early in the morning, drinking coffee, chain-smoking cigarettes, and talking about herself. Talking, by her own account, too much. In cartons and archives, I found an Alli who struggled to make sense of her experience and was determined to communicate it, because she thought her story might be of use to others — if not in her lifetime, then in the future.

Aside from her dates (born in Chicago in 1915, committed suicide in 1987), the easiest fact to learn about Alice Sheldon was that she had had an extremely public childhood. First there were her mother's books. Mary Hastings Bradley, novelist, explorer, and Chicago socialite, wrote five travel books about the family's journeys in Africa, three for adults and two for children. The children's books, *Alice in Jungleland* and *Alice in Elephantland*, are not only illustrated by her only child, they have her in the starring role. How public can you get? In Mary Bradley's scrapbooks, archived at the University of Illinois at Chicago, I found a photo from *The New York Times*. It showed Alice as a six-year-old in a white dress, with an enormous bow in her golden curls, just back from the Congo. It was captioned "First White Child Ever Seen by the Pigmy Tribes."

In Alice's own papers, I found more clippings. Many are from the society pages; they show a teenage Alice arriving at the opera in an ermine coat or leaning into a horse's neck as it goes over a fence. The captions talk about her as a child prodigy, a talented painter and illustrator. Or they call her "Miss Bradley, who has penetrated the interiors of Africa and India."

They show an Alice who was very beautiful; I suspect her looks helped make her public property. Those who knew her in high school and college describe her as one of the school stars: exciting, popular with boys, very much admired. Alli herself was vain about her looks, but said about these years only that she had been lonely. She was like Delphi/P. Burke in "The Girl Who Was Plugged In": lovely on the outside, but who wants to see the mind within? Who could ever love *that*?

As James Tiptree, Jr., Alli was a prolific correspondent. Alli kept carbons of her letters as Tiptree, so I found her, forty years later, talking about that same childhood as if it were a man's. In the fall of 1973, James Tiptree, Jr. started corresponding with the writer Joanna Russ. He wrote her a fan letter. She told him off for a sexist remark. He reacted with so much sympathy she asked him if he was gay. Then she started explaining feminism to him, and telling him what it had been like to grow up a girl.

Alli really wanted to talk about feminism with Russ — but how? In one letter, Tiptree answers one of Russ's questions about male behavior — did men think vampire movies were sexy? — while trying to convey his own childhood in disguise.

Maybe I had such a geographically aberrant youth I never connected with most of contemporary culture. I can't give you a clue, [vampire movies] leave me totally tepid. One of the problems may be that I grew up partly among people who actually were drinking blood. (That's the African part.) After you've heard somebody killed, butchered and eaten a hundred feet from your cot as a normal sort of lark you don't see many haloes around the process. My idea was to sort of avoid such scenes personally. […]

...Movie stars. Well, you say Movie Stars and something inside me still snuffles GRETA GARBO and goes *Uhhhhhh* [....] I
never wanted to *be* any of the exotic ones, I mean, where I came
from you had Humphrey Bogarts and White Hunters draped
all over the bar — what I wanted to be was an *utterly normal* USA
teen-aged jock who could drive a model A around to the early
version of McDonald's and didn't get looked at funny for talking different... And *too much*. Who knew sports scores instead
of the Italian forward seat, who played poker instead of chess.
[...] Who had been trained in the US speechless clonk style of
masculinity instead of the British talky style.

So I'm no help. And frankly, the material to be derived from
the "night-side of the traditional male culture" by *me* is a thin
vein, what I got mostly trained in was being polite to old ladies
and not running away if something charged.

This worry about talking too much recurs in some of Alli's private
writings, when she is thinking about growing up a girl. As a teenager,
she felt, she was always blurting out her opinions on Hegel or horses,
and never talking about dances, boys, things the other girls wanted to
hear. No matter how hard she tried, she was never quite like them.

As Tiptree, as a man, she could write about part of her problem:
the crushes she kept getting on classmates at her all-girls school. In
her papers is a draft of an essay on her unrequited loves, written as
Tiptree for one of Jeff Smith's fanzines. Tip never figured out how to
end it.

Alli did use her crushes on girls to make Tiptree look straight — a
condition she equated with not talking too much. Russ had asked if
Tiptree was gay. Two months later, in December 1973, Tip's young editor at Ace Books, Albert Dytch, said his sister had asked the same.

Tiptree answered, "I'm not gay so far as I know. [...] It's my bloody
talkiness." Yet he went on to say how much he wanted to talk — as
long as it wasn't too much.

I am damn touched about your sister's thinking I show feeling or sensitivity, tell her I try. To me, my stories do not show ENOUGH. I don't mean collapse-into-ooze-type "feeling," I mean finding some way of letting the long-suppressed real reactions hang out. Too many years of choking the mouth with tin. [...] As to gay, if I were I assure you I'd write it. Yea verily, I'd love nothing better. Imagine, all those toothsome asses, the great plots, some *originality*. But I can't seem to get the wavelength. No; my secret is elsewhere. What I really am, Albert, is a latent xenophile.

Oh, god, how I yearn for stars' arses, for the sexual capture of ALIEN flesh. No...maybe not really "flesh"...some deeper essence, alien-ness, the Other, the Never-Seen, the Other Reality... Of course, women are the closest things to Martians on earth. I used to keep falling totally and hopelessly in love with incredibly beautiful, hideously rich, doomed, and unscrewable girls. And I mean doomed. Spent years at it. Hopeless idiot, figure of fun. Someday I'm gonna write a piece on it... Xenosexual. Not so damn latent. [...]

Which is what hooks me about people. I love the alien in people, god I love the wildness, the wit, the lightning of the Other mind. A kind of sex-in-the-head, you know it's a rather Victorian affliction. Something to do with communication. I have had moments of *communication* with people, often totally unsuitable people, which had a truly unholy intensity... A sort of orgasmic meaningfulness and clarity, you know, all the old romantic stuff — two strangers stop and suddenly exchange glimpses of reality before moving on into the mists.

Communication is a recurring theme: Alice eloped with her first husband, William Davey, partly because he was the first person she ever met besides her father who got her jokes. She was nineteen, he twenty-one. She broke away from her parents and set out to become a promiscuous bohemian artist genius. All it got her is another starring role in someone else's book: Davey's 1941 novel *Dawn Breaks the Heart*. I found very little by or about Alice during this time: a few pages of journals and essays, a letter in which she appears to be lying to her parents, college transcripts full of incompletes.

Bill Davey, when I interviewed him in 1996, with his (I believe) eighth wife (though by then they had been married for thirty years), was charming, full of wild stories, and still nursing a grudge against the woman who hadn't loved him enough sixty years before. It made him particularly mad that she and not he was getting a biography.

In 1942, a year after their divorce, Alice joined the army. The society-page clippings describe

> Third Officer Alice Bradley Davey, Waac, looking better dressed in her G. I. uniform than any of a group of well-dressed women with whom she was lunching at the Arts Club. Blond-gold hair curling under her officer's cap, a new erectness to her shoulders under her olive-drab jacket, gray shirt matching the gray skirt, olive-drab tie.

In the army Alice started keeping a diary. She planned to write about women in the army. Among her papers I also found essays, short stories, and an outline for a novel. She published a story in *The New Yorker*, in 1946, based on her army service in Germany in 1945. By the time she left the army in 1946, at age thirty-one, she mostly wanted to write about her own life.

The next year, she and her new husband, Huntington "Ting" Sheldon, bought a chicken hatchery in New Jersey. They had been told they would only have to work half a year, and Alli wanted time to write. (She wrote that to her mother, who saved years' worth of her letters.) From this time, she saved draft after draft of science fiction stories, mysteries, and essays trying to figure out what it meant to be a woman.

In 1952 she and Ting sold the hatchery in disgust and went to work for the CIA. I tried filing a Freedom of Information Act request. I was told the CIA would "neither confirm nor deny" that Alli had worked there at all. (Instead I filed one on Ting, who had been publicly acknowledged by the Agency as an employee. Four or five years later I got a call from a nice man at Langley who said, "Well, we can send you many, many boxes of paper with almost every line blacked out. But I don't think you'll get much out of it." I gave up.) Once again, the best source was Alli's own files, where I found carbons of the papers she had written on African politics.

Alli quit the CIA in 1955 because she wanted time to write. She began studying experimental psychology because she wanted to write about perception and aesthetics: Why do we think a painting is beautiful? I suspect she wanted to defend her own perspective, to leave a record of herself that was not her mother's or her husband's, but hers alone.

Women often begin writing fiction later in life. I wonder if it doesn't take women longer sometimes to establish a solid sense of self — a self strong enough to sustain a writer's alter ego. At any rate, it was when Alli was fifty-one, just finishing her Ph.D. thesis (there's a copy of that in her papers too), and about to become Dr. Alice Sheldon that she began writing science fiction.

Tiptree wrote his letter to Albert Dytch in December 1973, the same month his most famous short story, "The Women Men Don't See," was published in *The Magazine of Fantasy & Science Fiction*. Everyone complimented Tip on how well he had understood the women. A few years later, Alli told Robert Silverberg, "If you could have known how much I craved to know if the *male* reactions were right! Shit, I knew Mrs. Parsons, all I had to do was keep her from talking too much."

Tiptree allowed Alli to write partly because he got her writing under control: he kept Ruth Parsons from talking too much. "The Women Men Don't See" is an angry story, but look how beautifully controlled it becomes when it's told in Don Fenton's voice. Tiptree's stories, from "The Last Flight of Doctor Ain" to "A Momentary Taste of Being," don't blurt out inappropriate opinions. They are controlled, held in check, like deadly weapons with a safety switch.

In Tiptree's epistolary friendships, too, Alli was in control, "exchanging glimpses of reality" before slipping back into the mists of her pseudonym. She wanted to hide and to tell the truth; for a little while, Tiptree let her do both.

A person who is afraid of talking too much doesn't want to stop talking. She wants someone to listen. In the summer of 1945, in a journal, Alice wrote,

> I find, in all the writings of women, a strange muffled quality, as if the living word, as it left the lips, had been hastily suppressed and another substituted, one which would conform to some pattern imposed from without. [...] I am trying, from the living urge of my own life, to force open channels of communication so far mostly closed. [...] To press out naked into the dark spaces of life is perhaps to build a small part of the path along which others like myself wish to travel.

This is the Alli I found among her papers — and the writer who is honored in the James Tiptree, Jr. Memorial Award. For forcing open the channels. For building paths. For, despite everything, talking about herself.

Letter to Rudolf Arnheim

James Tiptree, Jr.

Both as James Tiptree and as herself, Alice Sheldon was a prolific correspondent. Her letters — missives intended for individuals rather than a great anonymous audience of readers — provide a picture of her concerns and motivations.

Alice Sheldon met Rudolf Arnheim, a Gestalt psychologist interested in perception, in the 1950s, when she was embarking on her academic career. He became a friend and informal mentor. In this letter written in 1972 and uncovered by Julie Phillips during the research for her biography of Sheldon, she describes why she writes — a question often asked of writers.

> 11 Jan 72
> Leaving for Yucatan in
> the morning

Dearest Rudi —

My heart reproaches me for this sodden silence — believe, believe, to me it is as if we spoke yesterday, you are to me more living even though absent than all the speaking lumps brushing by — and *always* will be. Always — whether you like it or not!

It's just that I have been going through this — does one call it a transition period? — in all the external things of life, like a kaleidoscope slowly turning, and being a very slow metabolizer I haven't emerged yet. I won't bore you with all the pieces in the 'scope, probably the chief was realizing nobody wanted me in perceptual work, at least, that I should have to make heroic efforts — such as teaching monster courses in basic stat — to hold the official door open... ("We have too many women already...") And I had made all the efforts I could, no more in the barrel. Revolt!... And at this time the writing became so interesting — what you refer to as the galactic bargain basement, wicked Rudi — but the fact is I am a total sucker for *learning* any new thing, and it is such fun, such fun!... And I needed fun... So I've been doing that, and it being a wordy craft, it monopolized all my words and thoughts eventually, like the monkey with his fist in the date jar, only it was my head.

Add to that [her husband] Ting's retirement, and travels — My God, travels!!! I have been lost on avalanches, struck by coconuts, drenched in salt waves (cold)...and no end in sight. Yes, an end — we have rented a tiny beach house in the really wild wilds of Yucatan, where we went for a couple of short stays, and we'll be going down there for 2-3 months at a time particularly in winter. Utter peace.

Parenthesis — Listen, Rudi, one of the things I'm going to write you when I write is that you and Mary *must* plan to drop down there some nasty Jan-Feb-Mar. [...] There is *nobody* I'd love — we'd love — to see more. [...]

As to all the rest, the usual — some illness, and a thing fell on my head and cracked teeth, and Ting got cancer in his ear and got rid of it, and my mother went mad and recovered, and, and — the usual. And the stories sold and sold and now a little book will come out...all bargain basement, but Rudi — "Science fiction" has moved on, you know, with anthropologists and such writing it. Not many rockets now. *And* I've been able to say so much I had bottled up, to scream nasty things about the shittiness of, say, organized science, wars, man-the-polluter, the rape of the planet, all the things that were boiling up in me but had no place in my scientific work. So it has been good.

(Guiltily, that piece of research [Ph.D. thesis] is still drawing reprint requests from all over, long after I've run out of reprints, I should pay to have it xeroxed or something, but I'm too traumatized still — I just put everything in a shoebox.)

Also... do you know, the basic concealed secret of me is coming out — after all my posings and windy sighings, the truth is...I'm a comedian. Really a fundamental clown. Some fan magazine published an interview with me (conducted by mail) called "If you can't laugh at it what good is it?"... And I am finding a funny mean way to write that warms something inside me, the shameful secret at last out… A clown at heart.

All the blood, all the tears, all the wrongs and Death's fingers closing around all I love…and the gut reaction, the deepest noise is…a snort.

Can I do that in science?

Tried so long and hard to be *serious*… All I did was pile up a huge huge pile of faggots to which I have put a match to make a serious fire.

Look, Rudi, if I were Newton, or you, or Dostoyevsky, that's one thing, I should be serious. But I'm just me, a face on the flood, the flood of six billion, passing out of sight next breath…and I want to make faces, sing songs before I disappear. The songs will disappear with me, they are only small songs, but they are my size, and mine. I have ceased standing on the mighty shoulders of noble science, forming an atom in the human chain that hopes to be cumulative wisdom, I am responsible to no one, acknowledge no master, owe nobody, and need not even appear in the flesh in what I do now. Can you not see why?

What is that line… "I have taken my leave from the world of truth to sleep for a season and hear no word, only the song of a secret bird"?… That's all wrong, wait… "In the world of dreams I have chosen my part, To sleep for a season and hear no word Of true love's truth or light love's art, Only the song of a secret bird." That's more like it. (Some minor English idiot…even as me. [Swinburne])

Dearest Rudi & dear Mary — does this convince you that friendship never ends — *never* — that for what good I am, your disciple and devoted admirer and pal is here, is thinking of you — all letters treasured, all horrors sympathized with, news awaited (really, *please* drop a card saying if you live or…no, saying *that* you live) —

Only I trust too much to ESP.

You are one of the few great structures of my landscape, never forget it.

[no signature]

In his answer, on January 14, Arnheim wrote: "I have always thought of you as a great comic talent — you know that! What better mission could anybody have than playing the Shakespearean clown to this present world? And if you do that by invented fictitious worlds, that's certainly a time-honored device. Of course if there were some love left in you for your elderly friends you would have sent me copies of your books."

Congenital Agenesis of Gender Ideation by K.N. Sirsi and Sandra Botkin

Raphael Carter

This is the only short story ever to win the Tiptree Award as a solo winner. And it might be the most direct exploration and examination of gender in the entire Tiptree "canon." Raphael Carter uses the technique of an academic paper to background character, plot, and story, while focusing on undecorated ideas and concepts…ideas and concepts that take hold of your brain and never let go.

"What we call learning is really remembering," Socrates says in the *Phaedo*; for our ideas, in their abstract perfection, could not be formed by observation of this sloppy and imperfect world. For Descartes, too, such immutable ideas as "God," "mind," "body," and "triangle" could not be derived from the swirl of sense-impressions reaching our eyeballs and fingertips, but must be already present at our births. Locke, on the other hand, believed that ideas were derived from experience: "the natural and regular production of Things without us, really operating upon us."

The days are past when questions such as this were argued using reason and introspection; now we solve them by magnetic resonance imaging and DNA sequencing. The study of brain-damage patients and people with learning disabilities has been especially useful in wresting the great questions from philosophy. The two of us and our colleagues have now unlocked the answers Plato sought, and resoundingly confirmed Descartes's view of the mind.

THE PARABLE OF THE TELEVISION

To see what brain damage can teach us about the mind, imagine that you are trying to learn how television works by examining several broken television sets. Even without opening the sets, you could learn something about their workings by studying what happens when they break. Suppose, for example, that some sets work perfectly in all respects *except* that the faces are distorted and unrecognizable. You might guess that these sets have a problem with displaying flesh tones, or with shapes that are roughly oval. But if the sets displayed hands and eggs correctly while garbling even the green faces of midnight-movie aliens, you could deduce that faces are processed differently from other images. There must be some special function of the television just for faces — some face-generation circuitry.

No such disorder of televisions exists, or can exist. Faces on a TV screen are produced by arranging the same pixels as hands, or furniture, or any other object. But minds work differently. Lesions to certain parts of the brain produce an inability to recognize people by their faces, but do not affect any other brain function. This disorder, called prosopagnosia, leaves its victims perfectly able to read, to name objects they see, and to recognize voices; but present them with a photograph of a close friend, and they are at a loss. The real brain, like the imaginary television, must contain a special module for faces — a face-recognition organ.

Disorders like prosopagnosia help us decide between two basic views of the brain. In one, the brain is a universal computer with an all-purpose ability to perceive and reason; this ability is often called "general cognition." In the other, the brain is a toolbox full of instruments specialized for different tasks.

The existence of prosopagnosia shows that face recognition, at least, is a specialized tool. But this does not mean that general cognition does not exist. Most scientists believe that the brain has some specialized tools for common tasks, such as face recognition and grammar, but falls back on general cognition for everything else. In fact, most prosopagnosics use general cognition to partially overcome their disability: one patient identifies people by noting the length of their hair (but is confused anew every time a friend visits the beauty salon!).

A FAMILY IN RAJASTHAN

Our work on ideas began as a study of language. One of us (Sirsi), a neurologist, became interested in the work of the Canadian linguist Myrna Gopnik. Gopnik's research indicated that a single dominant gene could lead to an inability to apply basic grammatical rules that the rest of us take for granted ("Impairments of Tense in a Familial Language Disorder," *Journal of Neurolinguistics*, No. 8, 1994, pp. 109–133). Children with the gene could learn a present-tense verb such as "pray," but could not readily inflect it to get the past tense "prayed." Yet these children had no serious auditory impairment and seemed intellectually normal in other respects.

Follow-up studies (such as Ricci and Serafini, 1999; Leman and Lander, 2000; Acacia and Myrmidon, 2002) continued to show that other functions of the brain were unaffected by the disorder. In fact, many people with grammatical impairments were able to use general cognition to partially compensate for their disability: rather than conjugating verbs instinctively, they mentally recited a memorized rule, much as people do when learning a second language in adulthood. This strongly suggested that normal grammatical competence is produced by an inborn "grammar instinct."

But how, Sirsi wondered, does the language organ work? Is it a generalized instrument for recognizing patterns in sounds? Or is it specifically attuned to such basic features of language as verb tenses and grammatical gender?

To find out, Sirsi undertook that rarest of activities for a neurologist, fieldwork. While on an extended vacation in Jaipur, India, he visited schools to distribute small photocopied coloring books that he had designed with the help of a teacher of Hindi. Each page was divided into two panels. One panel illustrated a nonsense word, using it in a sentence. The other contained an incomplete sentence requiring the child to fill in an inflected form of the word. Some of the nonsense words were in Roman characters and sounded like English ("to wuzzle"), while others, in Devanagari script, had Hindi or Marwari endings. Sirsi offered a small packet of M&Ms for the return of completed coloring books. This plan nearly ended in disaster when more coloring books were returned than had been handed out — some teachers had traced them onto ditto masters and produced their own copies — and he ran out of candy. Luckily, the disgruntled parents that appeared at Sirsi's doorstep were pacified with tea, *churma*, and curd by a quick-witted servant, and analysis of the coloring books could begin.

Sirsi had hoped to find children who had trouble with the same grammatical rules in all three languages. At first he thought he had found many such cases, but it turned out these coloring books had been filled out by children younger than the eight-year-olds Sirsi had targeted. Other anomalies were due to children who spoke no English or no Marwari, or whose dialects of English simply lacked the features being tested. This left only one anomalous result: two children who apparently spoke no Marwari had incorrectly formed the feminine of adjectives in Hindi — a task that has no analogue in English. The children were evidently siblings; they had the same surname and lived at the same address. A dispirited Sirsi visited their home, assuming he would find a family fluent only in English and some other Indian language — perhaps Bengali, which lacks morphological gender distinctions. When he arrived at the door, however, he found himself unable to explain his purpose to the children's parents because both spoke fluent Hindi but no English!

Returning the next day with a servant (she of the *churma* and curd) as an interpreter, Sirsi showed the coloring books to various members of the children's extended family. Eight out of the seventeen family members that Sirsi tested had difficulty with the gender of adjectives. When such problems were presented, their answers were correct no more than half the time. Yet they correctly answered all the remaining questions in Sirsi's repertoire. Sirsi found no other indication of neurological impairment; school records showed IQ scores of 104 and 108 for the two children, along with a history of good grades. The oldest family member with the disorder was the children's maternal grandfather, who had passed it on to all of his daughters but none of his sons — a pattern that suggested dominant inheritance on the x chromosome.

Sirsi next obtained MRI images of the brains of six family members as they answered a second series of grammatical fill-in-the-blanks. As a control, he ran the same tests on two family members whose grammar was unimpaired.

As expected, the MRIs showed differences in brain activity between the affected and normal patients when they tried to inflect gendered adjectives. But the differences were nowhere near the areas of the brain usually associated with grammar. Instead they were in regions of the frontal lobe associated with higher cognition and memory. Despite this anomaly, Sirsi wrote up the results in the *Journal of Neurolinguistics* (No. 16, 2004, pp. 189–195). Partly on the strength of this publication, he was offered a non-tenure-track teaching position at the University of Toronto, and reluctantly set his plans for further fieldwork aside.

A few months after his article appeared, Sirsi received a letter from Dr. Sandra Botkin. Botkin, an occupational therapist, recalled working with a patient who had been admitted after an 8 mm. hole was bored diagonally through his brain during an archery competition. This patient had consistently referred to the male nurses on staff as "she." After hearing staff members grouse about the patient's sexism on three separate occasions, Botkin had begun to suspect that he really could not help himself. When she presented him with photographs cut from *People* magazine and Polaroid snapshots of obstetrics personnel, she found that he consistently identified short-haired women as men, and men in nurse's uniforms as women. She presented this finding to the patient's neurologist, who identified it as a limited form of prosopagnosia: the patient was unable to identify gender cues in faces. But Botkin, who had logged far more hours with the patient than the neurologist had, felt that the disorder went deeper than mere facial recognition.

Botkin's letter then called attention to one of the drawings that Sirsi had used to elicit gendered adjectives from his subjects. (A page from the coloring book had been reproduced with the article.) The first panel showed a very tall building and used the feminine form of a nonsense adjective. The second panel showed a very tall man and required the respondent to fill in the masculine form of the adjective. Did all the questions Sirsi had asked rely on pictures of men and women to elicit gendered adjectives, Botkin queried? If so, might his subjects — like her patient — simply have been unable to identify the drawing as a man rather than a woman? This would explain why they answered such questions incorrectly about half the time. It would also explain why the differences in brain activity were not in the expected regions. Perhaps her patient and Sirsi's subject shared the same disorder — one neither perceptual nor linguistic, but cognitive. Perhaps the misfired gene and the misfired arrow had abolished the power to distinguish the sexes of humankind.

"I know it sounds strange," she concluded, "but it's really no weirder than hemi-neglect or blind-sight." Blind-sight, a condition resulting from lesions to certain areas of the brain, results in apparently total blindness. Yet when asked to humor the researcher and guess where a light has been placed, the patient with blind-sight can point to it almost infallibly — all the while insisting that he cannot see a thing. Hemi-neglect is a loss of awareness of one half of the body; some victims wash only the right half of their bodies, and ardently deny ownership of their own left arms.

FINDING THE GENE

Sirsi was sufficiently intrigued by Botkin's hypothesis to contact his former servant in Rajasthan. After a frustrating and expensive series of international phone calls, he tried to ask her to talk to the family he had studied and report any curiosities in their use of pronouns. But no sooner had he made this request than the servant said that yes, of course, several members of that strange family had acted as if she were a man. She had not mentioned it because it didn't matter; hadn't the study been about language? Since he had been deliberately vague about his study's topic in order to keep her from accidentally influencing the results, Sirsi had to swallow his frustration.

Sirsi and Botkin could not immediately go to Rajasthan, so they used samples Sirsi had previously taken in an effort to identify the gene for agenesis of gender ideation, hoping to find it in families closer to home. A preliminary analysis found six candidate genes on the x chromosome that were present in all the affected family members but none of the others. Two of these genes had well-known functions and could be discarded, but Botkin had to find and interview people with each of the other four. Ten years ago this would have been an impossible task; the availability of genetic databases made it feasible, though not precisely easy (people are understandably alarmed when asked to come in for tests based on a cell sample taken five years ago).

Eventually Sirsi and Botkin did find an individual who sorted photographs of men and women with little better than chance accuracy. Though everyone in the family denied that anything was odd about their views of gender, three women and one man proved to have the condition (by this time dubbed *genagnosia*). The genagnosics seemed to compensate for their disability by not using gendered pronouns to refer to a person until they had managed to overhear some hint of his or her gender. This works fairly well in a language like English, in which only pronouns are gendered; it would be useless in Hindi.

To avoid unconscious bias in the selection of photographs, Sirsi and Botkin used DVD movies for their first experiment. A computer displayed random frames from the disks in a DVD-ROM carousel, and, using speech synthesis, asked a question from a randomized list. The genagnosics in this study were able to correctly answer "Where is the actress?" with "She is behind the plant," and "Where is the actor?" with "He is on the wing of the plane" — demonstrating that they could use pronouns correctly as long as they had a hint about the gender of the person referred to. However, when chance produced a reversal of pronouns — e.g., when a question asked for a description of "the actress" and the only person on screen was John Travolta — the subjects carried over the incorrect gender rather than substitute a correct pronoun. On questions that provided no clue to the actor's gender, at least forty percent of the time they referred to Arnold Schwarzenegger as "she" and Meryl Streep as "he." A control group achieved one hundred percent accuracy in this task.

In another experiment, Sirsi and Botkin asked genagnosics to choose photographs that showed potential mates. The objects of desire they chose were male and female at a ratio of almost exactly 1:1. It is a puzzle how three successive generations of genagnosics in this family managed to legally marry; perhaps they responded to encouragement or discouragement from unaffected friends and relatives, or perhaps they were guided by preferences for particular sex acts that even a genagnosic could not confuse. Sirsi tried to sound out one of the older family members on this subject, but determined that the topic was too sensitive to broach. He did, however, manage to determine by experiment that one young genagnosic who frequently expressed disdain for homosexuals was in fact unable to tell a same-sex couple from an opposite-sex one.

"I DON'T THINK IT'S ME"

Sometimes an experiment reveals more about the experimenters than the subjects. Initially, rather than having a computerized voice ask questions, Sirsi and Botkin used graduate students who had not been told what they were trying to prove. But these assistants had to be replaced, one after another, for arguing with the subjects about their answers. "There's something about this disease," Sirsi says. "When a prosopagnosic is trying to identify the picture, you watch in a kind of mute horror. When a genagnosic says Glenn Close is a man, your instincts tell you he's just being difficult."

Transcripts of these arguments were preserved, and they are in some ways more compelling than the experiments' official results. One first-time assistant, astonished that a subject had called Danny DeVito "the actress," kept asking the same question over and over in hope of getting a different answer. The subject repeated the same answer three times, growing more and more frustrated each time, and finally snapped "One of us is wrong here, and I don't think it's me."

Sirsi and Botkin eventually realized that the exact scope of their subjects' impairment would have to be teased out by interview, producing the following remarkable exchange:

Sirsi: "Do some people have breasts?"

X: "...Yes."

Sirsi: "Which people?"

X: "All people."

Sirsi [regrouping]: "Breasts larger than a teacup?"

X: "Some of them."

Sirsi: "And can some people bear children, out of their own bodies?"

X: "Some of them."

Sirsi [triumphantly]: "Now, those two kinds of people we just talked about, are they the same people?"

X thought about this for nearly fifteen seconds before answering, "Sometimes." When Sirsi repeated the question a few minutes later, X repeated his answer, annoyed; but when he asked it again during the next weekly session, X again had to think a long time before answering. X could not remember the association between breasts and childbirth from session to session. And no amount of badgering could convince him to combine individual observations about men and women into a unified concept of gender.

THE NUCLEATION MODEL

This result led Sirsi to the theory of innate ideas he presented in his famous paper, "Congenital Agenesis of Gender Ideation in a Midwestern Family" (*Journal of Neurolinguistics* No. 20, 2006, pp. 35–44). "X could understand correlations between the various traits that make up manhood or womanhood," Sirsi wrote, "but he could not retain the information — as if he had no mental file drawer to put it in."

Sirsi likens the mind to a fluid in which all the raw data of perception are dissolved. An innate concept, like a seed crystal, can cause ideas to solidify around it. Some perceptions will crystallize while others remain dissolved; a different seed could produce different ideas. But a seed will not produce crystal unless the right kind of perceptions are in solution — which helps keep innate concepts from producing mental models that are radically at odds with our experience.

Sirsi contrasts his nucleation model with the "mandation model" that the discovery of innate ideas might tempt us to adopt. We might suppose that the ideas we are born with directly control our understanding; but if that were true, we would not be able to change our minds or to learn anything. On the nucleation model, innate ideas merely help our perceptions to structure themselves. So transient and local information about the sexes, such as differences in clothing and hairstyle, can become part of our ideas of gender — like an impurity in the crystal — even though they are too variable to be directly programmed by our genes. Also, useful perceptions may languish in unconsciousness because there is no seed for them; but above a certain concentration, ideas may precipitate without seed. True, the idea of gender did not crystallize in X's mind even when Sirsi attempted to seed it with an elementary association. But other ideas, Sirsi hopes, may prove more plastic.

MINNESOTA TWINS

Botkin, still working as an occupational therapist at St. Eleggua Hospital in Minneapolis, received a phone call one day from a graduate student working in an ongoing identical-twin study. The researchers had found "her gene" in a pair of identical twins; the twins, however, displayed no obvious impairment of gender ideation. Would she be interested in interviewing them?

Botkin was. Again she applied the technique of asking the subjects to identify photographs, but this time she used only photos of doctors in surgical garb — reasoning that this epicene apparel would reveal even a well-hidden cognitive defect. The twins, however, effortlessly identified all the pictures as male or female — except one. That photograph — of Dr. Lisa D'Aout, a pediatric urologist — they refused to classify. When pressed, each twin independently produced the same word of a private language the two had shared as children, and declined to explain further.

Puzzled by this result, Botkin mused aloud in the hospital cafeteria as to just what trait of D'Aout's might have produced the twins' anomalous response. At last an RN with whom Botkin was dining explained what, seemingly, everyone on staff but Botkin knew. D'Aout was a female pseudohermaphrodite. She had been the plaintiff in a landmark 2001 case against the hospital, applying the Minnesota Human Rights Act's provisions for transgendered people to intersexuals.

Botkin explained her results to D'Aout, who responded with skepticism. But after being introduced to the twins, D'Aout agreed to put out a request for photographs in the newsletter of a national intersex organization. Not only did the twins correctly sort these photographs from the male and female controls, they distinguished accurately between such different intersexual conditions as true hermaphroditism, gonadal agenesis, and male and female pseudohermaphroditism. The most impressive result involved women with complete Androgen Insensitivity Syndrome, who have XY chromosomes. The twins distinguished these women from those with XX chromosomes with one hundred percent accuracy on the basis of head and shoulders photographs — a feat that no endocrinologist on staff could duplicate!

Although the twins had not been told what the study was trying to prove, by this point they clearly knew what was going on, so Botkin asked them if they could provide any further information about the control photographs. After some hesitation — which Botkin attributes not to the difficulty of the task, but to a crisis of trust — they picked up the pile of control photographs and sorted them into a total of 22 categories, each one corresponding to a word in their private language. Botkin numbered these categories and began to investigate what they might mean. Categories 9 and 21 proved to identify women born with clitoromegaly and men born with hypospadias, respectively, even though these are minor cosmetic conditions of the genitals with no known effect on clothed appearance. Category

6 comprised people with high scores on the Bem test of psychological androgyny. Again, it is not clear how this could be distinguished from a photograph, but the twins' identifications have proved to be repeatable. Number 18, whose exact biological meaning is unclear, includes a disproportionate number of people with a family history of osteoporosis; two women and one man in the category have since been diagnosed with bone loss themselves. Perhaps most strikingly, categories 4 and 9 identified men and women who took artificial sex hormones rather than producing them naturally, even when this was the result of hysterectomy or accidental castration rather than of a genetic difference.

Of the nine categories that still elude analysis, Botkin says: "I'm convinced that these identify real things too. There's a kind of a family resemblance among the people in each category. I've found myself meeting a person and thinking, 'I know he's an eight. He's got to be an eight.' I can *see* it. But I can't define it."

"The last straw," as Botkin puts it, came when she visited the twins after being told by her physician that she was entering an early menopause. Upon hearing this, the twins exchanged what Botkin calls "significant glances" and said: "Don't worry. Your sex won't be changing for another few years yet." It didn't.

These results led Botkin to propose a new model for the influence of genes on gender ideation. She suggests that patients with genagnosia are not impoverished by a lack of information, but bewildered by an overplus; the concepts "male" and "female" identify too great a range of variation to be understood. What the gene knocks out, then, is a filtering capacity that tells us what information to ignore. The twins Botkin studied were able to overcome this handicap — aided by their high intelligence and, perhaps, by their ability to compare notes.

Confirming this model of innate concepts will require more evidence than a single pair of twins, however. One of us (Sirsi) still prefers the nucleation model, which most of our colleagues have found more plausible. The twins' ability to tell men from women could be explained by variable penetration of the genagnosia gene. Their feats of identification might be duplicated by others with sufficient practice. Only further study will tell for sure.

THE VOICE OF THE WHIRLWIND

As we observed at the beginning of this essay, philosophers have been talking about innate ideas at least since Plato. Most have supposed that innate ideas were given by God, and therefore must be true. If we find instead that our innate ideas were formed by evolution, then they need not be correct at all, as long as they lead to the reproduction of the genes that produce them. Even modern thinkers that embrace the concept of innate ideas, such as Noam Chomsky, have often failed to come to grips with this possibility. As Geoffrey Sampson points out in his 1980 volume *Making Sense*: "Chomsky does not suggest that we might have innate predispositions to analyze the world in terms of inappropriate concepts or to hold false beliefs, although logically this should be equally compatible with the notion of innately limited minds" (p. 6).

Our findings provide no defense against this troubling suggestion. We may indeed cling to mistaken ideas because our mental organization requires them. We may reject plain facts because our minds cannot grasp them. Even science, for all its self-correcting mechanisms, may be permanently unable to arrive at certain truths. Dr. Anne Marlowe-Shilling, a noted critic of sex-differences research, pointed out to us that while many thousands of studies have been done to tease out sex-linked capabilities and personality traits, none, until our chance discovery, had been done to determine whether some people might be genetically predisposed to believe in "brain sex." Indeed, preliminary research indicates that the propensity to do brain sex studies is at least as strongly influenced by genetics as any of the traits such studies have analyzed. One of our graduate students is now trying to find a gene that determines whether the brain-sex researcher will find a positive result.

How, then, can we know whether we know anything? The very discovery that has raised this question may eventually provide an answer to it. Perhaps one day we will transcend the limits of human knowledge by consulting such people as Botkin's twins and the family in Rajasthan. Sirsi has now begun a series of studies designed to find out whether genagnosics' perceptions might not be *more* accurate in some respects than other humans'. For example, when genagnosics are asked to sort photographs of people into "short," "average," and "tall" without reference to sex, their choices correlate well with statistical norms. Most control subjects cannot discard gender from their considerations, even when they are admonished to do so.

Sirsi points out that other humans can match the genagnosics' accuracy at height-sorting if they are told the average height and shown photographs of people standing in front of a height scale, as in a police lineup. So perhaps general cognition can overcome the predispositions foisted on us by innate ideas. Sirsi cites a study in which a chimpanzee was allowed to choose between two stacks of candy, then was given the stack he did *not* choose (Boysen and Bernston, 1995). Although he clearly understood the rules of the game, he chose the larger stack every time — only to immediately cover his eyes in self-reproach, realizing he had once again been trapped by instinct. When the experimenters taught the chimpanzee Arabic numerals, however, could readily choose the smaller number to get the larger treat. Using numbers rather than real candy seemed to help the chimp overcome an instinctive response and use general cognition instead. Sirsi suggests that humans may prove "as smart as chimps" — we, too, may be able to use general cognition to overcome our innate ideas, if we cling fast to symbolic manipulation and quantification and try to ignore common sense.

Botkin, however, suspects that the problem may go even deeper. Rather than applying general cognition to a problem ordinarily handled by its own cognitive organ, Botkin sees the twins as using one specialized function to substitute for another. "Most people think that general cognition is a sort of fluid that sloshes in to fill any gaps between the innate ideas," she says. "I think the brain is more like a box full of specialized tools — but if your toolbox is missing a hammer, you can always pound nails with a screwdriver."

In particular, she suspects the twins have converted a brain function ordinarily used to recognize species of animal. Unlike the gender ideation organ, this faculty does not require a division into only two classes, so it does not filter out as much information. It filters enough, however, to keep the twins from having to avoid pronouns. "The twins are saying, 'suppose the sexes are like species.' They're not compensating with general cognition, they're compensating by metaphor.

"People want to believe in general cognition," she adds. "We want to believe that the brain is some sort of universal computing engine that can do anything — learn any possible fact, entertain any possible idea. So when we find something like a separate module for gender ideation, they just say that, well, that isn't a part of general cognition, but everything else still is. Maybe so. But what if we just keep carving away at general cognition until there's nothing left?"

If Botkin is right, then we can never be completely free of our innate ideas. By applying several metaphors successively we may be able to limit their effects, but even if we overcame all of them, we could never be sure that we had. Our knowledge of the world, although not totally illusory, is filtered through an unreliable narrator whose biases deny us direct access to the truth.

"It's easy to act as if nothing has changed," Botkin muses. "Most days I don't even think about the implications of what we've found. And then I'll meet someone, and I'll start thinking, 'He's a twelve. I know he's a twelve. How do I know he's a man?'"

The Gift

L. Timmel Duchamp

L. Timmel Duchamp is one of the most frequently short-listed authors in the history of the award. Since this year's jurors short-listed her collection, *Love's Body, Dancing in Time*, we had three stories to choose among: two that this year's panel of jurors mentioned and one that was short-listed in the year it was originally published. The decision was not easy. In "The Gift," Duchamp takes the belief that sexuality is "culturally mediated" — that what sex means and what it implies can vary from culture to culture — to a very intense, and moving, extreme.

[1]

"I don't know what bug's gotten up your ass," Stavros said when he saw the new piece. "But your choice of words is bound to piss off all those tourists who might find the penitential ritual fascinating and gross out all the rest. GTI would bounce it if I sent it to them as is."

Florentine couldn't remember the last time Stavros had asked her to make changes in a piece. But she knew he was right. The section in question featured a stand-up in the Plaza of Penitence, with her POV showing some poor down-in-the-mouth slob creeping on bleeding hands into the Plaza, his nose a virtual geyser of blood. Her voice-over ran:

Blue Downs is the kind of place where you're likely to see people crawling on their hands and knees down the main drag a couple of days a week. Many tourists will, I'm sure, find this a fascinating, even thrilling sight. I found it irritating in the extreme, myself, to the point of being tempted to join those who take righteous civic pleasure in kicking the damned fools and otherwise jeering them on their way, but for my far more powerful urge to kick those doing the kicking. Blue Downs suffers a raging thirst for public humiliation of its truants, miscreants, and trespassers, a thirst no amount of sleazy quaff-ing can slake. For that reason alone I'd rate the penitential ritual as one of the most significant characteristics of this city, however widely known Blue Downs is for the superior graphic arts displayed in its churches, market district, and more affluent homes.

Galactic Tours, Inc., made a bundle off Florentine's travelogues and always paid her well in the expectation that every piece she produced would bring the big spenders running. But she knew that Stavros was probably right when he warned that they wouldn't see the point of her presenting a "darker view" of a city known for its cultural brilliance. As he put it, "That kind of thing is fine for pieces on places known for their sin and sleaze. But Blue Downs practically stands for purity of spirit in an atmosphere of high corporate profit."

Fixing the piece would be easy: splice in an old bit on the lack of beggars, pushers, and prostitutes in the street; remove all references to penitential exercises; and dig through her files for fully sun-lit rather than shadowed shots, which she'd favored throughout. She wouldn't, though, delete any of the material about the Blue Downs musical scene. Stavros agreed that all of that was "interesting, if a bit disturbing." Absent any reference to the penitents, it shouldn't have the "sullying effect" he apparently feared could dim the city's lustrous reputation for purity.

That reputation now seriously galled Florentine. If she could, she'd let the rest of the galaxy in on the secret. "The Custodian of Human Arts," Big Blue was usually called, and many people considered it simply one grand all-encompassing museum.

Oh Alain, my Alain. My heart, my love. My loss.

Florentine found her loss an unbearably lonely one. How could anyone who didn't really know Blue Downs ever understand? And how could she burden even one of the few souls she could confidently call *friend* with the story of such a loss? Time-dilation was the mother of discretion. Florentine's every friend traveled, too. A momentous change in their lives never failed to break apart old friendships, which, depending on an even, smooth semblance of continuity for their long-term maintenance, could not sustain major upheaval.

Worse, she knew that the story of her loss would make sense to no one to whom what happened to her might matter. *How could you have been so foolish?* she could already hear any possible listener say. Merely telling the story — unless she told it lightly, ironically, as a little cautionary tale at her own expense — would have exposed her to the charge of *whining*.

Some day, no doubt, she would discover and appreciate the irony in her story. But that day lay so far in her subjective future that she found it difficult to believe in.

[2]

When Stavros had said he thought it was about time for Florentine to do another tour of Blue Downs and reminded her that GTI had said it would finance as many tours of the place as she cared to produce, her initial reaction was *been there, done that*, maximum yawn. Her Blue Downs tours were top sellers that appealed especially to people who had never before traveled. GTI liked this attractiveness to an audience of non-travelers because her pieces on Blue Downs tended to draw a significant number of them into taking the tour. GTI also liked the numbers showing that each time Florentine made an additional tour of a place she'd previously covered, a significant number of travelers who had done the previous tour signed up for the new one. Stavros worked on the basis of royalties rather than fees; not surprisingly, his advice typically addressed the bottom line.

Blue Downs had always been special for Florentine; it had launched her travelogue career, and she counted the day GTI accepted her first proposal to tour that city as one of the most exciting moments of her life. It had been shortly after that that Stavros, though he professed to be gloomy with the conviction that Florentine was likely to fail since her knowledge of Blue Downs was strictly academic and her life experience "almost nil," contracted to be her agent. His attitude had only spurred her determination to bring her academic love for Blue Downs into her work, to seduce all who viewed the tour with every tone and nuance of its many and wondrous beauties. And Flo-

rentine's first two visits to Blue Downs in the flesh had in fact con-
summated her adoration — more profoundly the second time even
than the first.

She hadn't had the faintest idea that she had grown jaded with
the very idea of Blue Downs until Stavros suggested the third tour.
Hearing herself tell him *been there, done that* shocked her as much as
it amused him. Looking back, she supposed that that reaction must
have been an effect of her having done so very many tours around the
galaxy for GTI — or an effect of age.

Still, months after Stavros had first made the suggestion, as she
prepared to leave the starship to shuttle down to the surface of Big
Blue, she enjoyed a pleasant sense of anticipating known delights
and meeting up with company already proven to be comfortably congenial. The feeling held even through the unpleasant shuttle flight
and surged when she stepped out onto the planet's surface, reeling
with fatigue and the lingering traces of nausea.

Her positive mood dissipated, though, and just the slightest undercurrent of something griped her — not cynicism, not boredom,
and certainly not anxiety — when she found Magdalene awaiting her
as she exited the shuttleport's Public Safety intake center.

They kissed one another twice on both cheeks in the grand Blue
Downs style and frankly examined the marks of age and other
changes on one another's faces. Florentine hadn't expected Magdalene to meet her; she hadn't even let Magdalene know that she was
coming. She told herself that she should feel flattered to be met,
but instead felt nagged and stifled even before Magdalene told her
she had reserved a suite for Florentine at one of the more elaborate
B&Bs, where she had on her previous visit agreed — in theory — that
she should stay her next time in Blue Downs. GTI had, as usual, reserved palatial quarters for Florentine in one of the city's most luxe
hotels. Florentine knew enough about Blue Downs mores to take this
presumption — like her meeting Florentine before she'd had a chance
to recover from the grueling shuttle trip and decon — as a gesture of
warm affection. And so she smiled widely and thanked Magdalene
for the intended courtesy. Why not stay at the B&B, she thought as the

undercurrent erupted into something verging on recklessness. Why not make this tour something off the beaten path. She could still take up the aesthetic delicacies due to be featured in tour number three. But she could also include a few touches of "local color" while she was at it — something more than the charming interview with the master glassblower in tour number two; not anything "folksy" or anthropological, but something revealing the apparently sophisticated though largely unexamined personality and character of Blue Downs itself — something that would show Blue Downs as more than a mere repository for brilliant fine and applied arts.

Magdalene was apparently little better off financially than she had been in her student days, when Florentine had last seen her, for she said, when Florentine introduced the subject of transport, that she had trained out to the shuttleport. Her eyes lit up when Florentine said that GTI had arranged to lease an air car with driver. "It so reminds me of when you were last here," she said, almost sighing. "It makes me nostalgic for those days, which I've thought about so often, you know."

The expression in her eyes — gleaming, melting, wistful — made Florentine uncomfortably aware of how differently they regarded the "old times" they had shared. Florentine could see that for Magdalene they had been a taste of glamour and sophistication, furnished by all the fine dining and first-class theater tickets Florentine had at her disposal and spiced by tales of her galactic travels. For Florentine, though, it had been the delight of a set of young companions — Magdalene among several — open to experiencing all that they could, loathing cliché, engaged and intelligent and fresh: a pleasant interval, in retrospect, recalled only in fragments and therefore lacking the cohesion of emotional significance.

Florentine enjoyed the aerial view of Big Blue as greatly as she had the first time she had seen it. Sky, water, and grass glistened in every shade of blue imaginable. Across the 100 kilometers that lay between the shuttleport and Blue Downs rolled softly mounded hills that made her think of velvet and silk and jewelers' display windows. "It still doesn't look real to me," she said to Magdalene.

"You used to say that nothing about Blue Downs ever felt real to you," Magdalene replied.

"True." Florentine suppressed a surge of irritation at the reminder. She knew that Magdalene was only being polite and friendly in letting her know how much she remembered of those old days. But she detested any suggestion of sentimentality from someone who really only barely knew her.

Since Florentine had reviewed Magdalene's most recent communication to her shortly before boarding the shuttle, she was able to ask the right sorts of questions about her family and work life and so occupy the remaining conversational space until their arrival in Blue Downs. Though she no longer found Magdalene's eagerness charming and delightful, she had no difficulty keeping their interaction running smoothly. Magdalene, never having traveled off Big Blue, could have no notion of the effort this cost Florentine. Tired to death with the exigencies of travel, Florentine was eager to bathe and desperate to sleep. But this she managed, somehow, to conceal from Magdalene.

[3]

That first afternoon Florentine sent Magdalene away with the promise that they'd meet for lunch the next day and the remark that she was interested in getting into more of the music scene than the concert attendance of her previous tours. Magdalene's son, she knew, was a concert vocalist. He seemed the logical way in to an area of Blue Downs society previously inaccessible to her.

Big Blue was one of those fortunate worlds where water was abundant, and the B&B, as luxe as any of Blue Downs' hotels, included a large whirlpool bath in its accommodations. That first evening Florentine spent more than an hour in the tub as she considered her plan to make full use of Magdalene's local insights and connections. Florentine felt confident that Magdalene would enjoy being used — enjoy alternating the role of guide with that of sidekick, enjoy introducing her family and friends to someone she thought of as "famous."

Florentine went to bed early that night and slept an opaque, heavy fourteen hours. Despite the enormous physical fatigue from the shuttle trip and the additional stress on her body of diurnal-phase adjusters, she woke full of energy and ready, if not eager, to take on the challenge of making the stale fresh. Her outlook that morning as she went down to the breakfast room was strictly professional. She sampled and evaluated the B&B's morning cuisine in full work mode, with nothing more on her mind than making this third tour the most interesting yet of her pieces. Though she did not always include in her travelogues reports on all the places at which she ate, GTI paid her a fixed fee per meal reported separately (with a maximum of two meals per restaurant), since they used such reports in their accommodations directories.

After breakfast she wandered about the market district recording pieces of public art not covered in her previous tours. Magdalene had arranged to meet her at exactly one hour after noon, for what in Blue Downs culture was the main meal of the day. At the time of making the arrangements she had also informed Florentine that she would have a particularly interesting surprise for her there. In many places in the galaxy, "surprises" are not polite and are usually unwelcome. No doubt it was the prospect of a surprise that made Florentine grumble (silently) about badly named restaurants as she approached the Singing Orchard at the time appointed.

Her bad mood vanished the instant she set foot inside the restaurant. The entire place, a full square city block, was apparently open-air and thus basked under the constantly cobalt sky that granted the clarity and crispness of vision the planet, with its slightly oxygen-thin mixture of air, was famous for. A cool, moist breeze carried the scents of the fruit adorning the orchard's many trees and wafted tantalizing snatches of music unlike anything Florentine had ever before heard. She fell, almost at once, under a spell of enchantment. (How else explain what followed, except by reference to the most ancient of fairy tales?) Standing just inside the entrance, she abandoned herself so entirely to her senses that the maitre d' had to speak sharply to get her attention.

A robotic cart carried her through the trees to the table where Magdalene had already been seated. Clear cermet platforms, elevated perhaps two meters off the ground, were set discreetly among the trees. At the horizon Florentine made out a succession of the city's splendid bell towers, which she had no trouble identifying — first that of the Church of Christ the Redeemer, followed by those of the Jesus Died Christian Church, Holy Cross Catholic Church, the Church of Repentance, the Church of Mount Olives, Holy Spirit Pentecostal, Make A Joyful Noise unto the Lord Church of Christ — at which point Florentine halted her identifications. She knew that they couldn't all be simultaneously visible. The bell towers must, she thought, be magnificent holographs.

Which made her wonder, for a moment, whether any of the trees were real.

Magdalene waved gaily down at Florentine from one of the elevated platforms, and the cart halted. As the platform lowered slowly to ground level, Florentine waded through a shallow sea of ferns, lichen, and ivy to the nearest tree — a relatively lofty pear — and touched its trunk. It had to be real. Its bark scraped her knuckles when she knocked on it.

The platform waited as Florentine finished checking out more of the trees. (All were real.) When she had finally seated herself and the platform began its ascent, the table informed the women that though the menu at the Singing Orchard varied daily, it was fixed, assembled in accord with the finest Matrix Aesthetics principles, ensuring that the component parts of the meal achieved a unique aesthetic experience beyond their mere sum. Typically, the table said, even the best restaurants concentrated their efforts on providing very fine components without regard for their total aesthetic effect. The art of the Singing Orchard, it assured them, did not aim so low.

Her eyes brimming with excitement and mirth, Magdalene watched Florentine closely. Florentine knew, even then, that this visit to the Singing Orchard would probably be the centerpiece of the tour. She had discussed Matrix Aesthetics in both of her previous tours but had always concentrated on its architectural and graphic exemplars.

It had never occurred to her that the pleasures of the palate, throat, and gut could fall under its sway, too.

The service began not with the customary Blue Downs bread, but with a few morsels of a sweetly tender, spiced shellfish over which a thin, tartly fruited sauce had been drizzled. A half-glass of a very dry wine with a delicate pear aftertaste accompanied this dish, which was followed immediately by long slivers of avocado, red pepper, and snow peas dressed with a cumin-pecan vinaigrette. The shapes, textures, colors, and play of light in the two arrangements offered as much a feast for the eyes as the flavors provided a piquant delight to the palate. *Then* came the bread, a small round that could be eaten in a single bite, fragrantly warm and textured and crusty.

The music arrived with the shellfish, along with a wash of light and shadows that played in the leaves and fruit of the trees surrounding them. Though Florentine's implant recorded the mix of sound and visual images during the meal, she later found that the recording proved inadequate to the experience for the simple reason that it recorded only what she directly focused on — which could not be the whole, but merely the components, superb as they were.

So many subtle, not-fully-perceived sensory inputs surrounded and overwhelmed her with ecstatic sensations that she thought that only sexual orgasm could begin to approximate such physical and emotional intensity. The cuisine itself included many, many courses of maddeningly small portions, each teasing and flattering her palate, piquing her appetite — with increasingly longer intervals between courses. After only a few of the innumerable courses, she began to feel suspended outside the time-space continuum. Soon her entire body grew inflamed with the longing to gorge on any one of the excellent dishes set before her. Gorging, at least, would have given her the satisfaction of bludgeoning into submission so much that was elusive. Set outside time, overstimulated by an abundance of sensory inputs, she couldn't help but compare it to extended sexual foreplay — and began, finally, to wonder (almost anxiously!) whether, at the rate they were teasing her carnal desires, she would ever attain climax and satiation. Still, however maddening she found the experience, she never ceased to be thrilled by the awareness that she had never before been so overtaken by perfection and beauty — and would probably never be again.

Neither of the women used words for the duration of the meal. They exchanged speaking glances that acknowledged a shared — though separate — pleasure; but neither could bear to interrupt such beauty with the all too ordinary and banal blather of their own speech. Several times, glimpsing a certain expression in Magdalene's eyes, Florentine recollected memories of a Magdalene thirty years younger caught up in moments of wondrously naive pleasure that Florentine herself had long since forgotten. Yet for all the intensity of her pleasure, Florentine never once lost her professional awareness, which analyzed and intellectually appreciated the aesthetics of the experience in a way that heightened her sensual pleasure.

Her greatest delight — even greater than that of the palate, though the whole was indeed beyond the sum of its magnificent parts — fell in the realm of the aural. During the initial courses the music — which she at first thought wholly instrumental and canned — seemed to emanate from the trees, which she assumed held the speakers that were presumably disseminating it. But as they sipped a fiery gazpacho, a movement glimpsed over Magdalene's shoulder caught and drew Florentine's eye to the silvery shimmer of an olive tree a few yards from the base of the platform, where she spotted the first of the singers that she soon discovered were surrounding them (arranged, naturally, according to some arcane principle of Matrix Aesthetics). Perhaps it was the influence of Blue Downs working on her imagination, but in that first moment he looked to Florentine exactly like the incarnation of a depiction of an angel such as could be found in any of the city's churches. He stood — quite deliberately, without doubt, given the operation of the matrix — in a pool of sunlight, a muscular blond Adonis with a powerful diaphragm and magnificent posture that looked as though it could easily support a pair of wings should they have suddenly been inspired to sprout from his back. His voice soared powerfully, its tone rich and buttery, even as it sliced through the air as cleanly and purely as a polished and honed silver blade might cleave a block of hard, crystalline ice.

Infatuation, fascination, obsession teased and tempted her. And yet, what she felt wasn't simply lust — anymore than her appreciation of the meal's aesthetics was driven simply by gluttony. A grandly aspiring, yearning emotion suffused her, filling her with elation that such joy-in-fleshliness even existed. Never had she so appreciated the embodiedness of humanity, never had she so recognized the power that lay in that aspect of human existence — as opposed to the unending, crude efforts humans collectively put forward their every conscious (and unconscious) moment to transcend the animal status that their every cultural and intellectual achievement sought to deny.

Ecstatic, she felt she had achieved the single most perfect moment possible for someone lacking the extraordinary talents and abilities that only artists and athletes were given to know. The ecstasy became nearly unbearable when that moment continued long past what she felt she could sustain. It came as an unexpected relief, then, when this near-angel stepped into shadow and fell silent and a new moment of wonder took hold of her.

The musicians also included instrumentalists. Though the lot of them shifted position throughout the meal, they remained always around the women, a sonic matrix that integrated perfectly with the food and light and images. Even during the silences interpolating the music, Florentine's ears registered a pressure, a presence surrounding and impacting her much in the same way the intervals between courses did. Later, she learned that the matrices were overlapping, conceptualized as sited on intersecting planes. "The visible and audible," her informant would tell her, "is contingent on a layer of inaudibility and invisibility, which it makes present as a certain absence." Every aesthetic experience, he claimed, depended on something that was never directly perceived, an axis grounding all perception and cognition. In Matrix Aesthetics, the artists were not only conscious of this imperceptible axis, but deliberately determined its location, whether for subtle or maximum effects.

Some of the time Florentine felt as though the meal were taking an eternity, and she had the thought that one would never be able to bear an eternity of bliss, even as she lingered at the edge of exhaustion and overstimulation and being tired of not being *full*, not being *finished* with an experience and intensity that must, must, must have limits. Interestingly, it was at the very moment she was thinking about the human need for limits that the denouement suddenly arrived. Florentine was looking at the fleshly angel, as aware of his physical presence as she was of the food, when the table presented them with a serving so large, of food so filling, that eating a mere fraction of it made Florentine's stomach ache with the wickedly wonderful pain of gluttony.

She gave up on the food after five chewy, satisfying bites, as though her body suddenly recognized that it had consumed more than an entire day's allowance of alimentation. She wasn't in the least surprised when the table removed their plates and replaced them with small bowls of brilliantly colored and artfully carved ices gaily festooned with small, delicate flowers complemented by ethereally light and frothily aerial music. Her gaze met Magdalene's in a smile both content and gratified — as though they had proven their mettle in a test of their endurance, wits, and taste and not simply been passively receptive of this orchard's aesthetic bounty. Blue Downs' sky never looked so blue to Florentine, its air so pure as it did in that moment.

This odd sense of triumph — which she suspected must be in some way deliberately cultivated as the appropriate emotion with which to finish such an indescribable experience — prevented her from feeling any sort of post-coital *triste* as the platform descended and a robotic cart arrived to remove the women from paradise.

"Well?" Magdalene asked after Florentine had thumbprinted the voucher demanding a small fortune for the afternoon's pleasure and they stepped back into the city. Florentine exulted in the thought of GTI's paying such a price, which by itself exceeded the entire cost of her last tour on the relatively cheap planet of Siliconia. The priciness alone would be enough to make the backwater wealthy who aspired to the heights of Taste swarm into Blue Downs determined to claim the very best (and most expensive meal) their riches could buy. And GTI would certainly have no trouble cutting a lucrative deal for adding the Singing Orchard to its Exclusive Private Listing. Magdalene touched Florentine's arm. "Have you ever experienced such a meal before in your life?"

This touch on her arm, this explicit demand that they speak without time to reflect about the ineffable, grated on Florentine, abrading the pleasurable aftertaste and the sense of having experienced a delight few people in the galaxy would ever be privileged to know. She had enjoyed sharing the experience with Magdalene, who had surely appreciated it at least as fully (and perhaps even more) than herself, and who had never once throughout the meal said or done anything likely to break the wonderful spell. And yet Florentine found herself resenting Magdalene for intruding on what felt private. Florentine knew her reaction was unwarranted. Certainly she would never have wanted to partake of such a meal alone, for dining at the Singing Orchard without a companion would have been tantamount to masturbating in public.

Florentine barely tolerated the brief touch on her arm; unable to look at the other woman, she kept her gaze straight before her. "The Singing Orchard is unique," she said shortly, hoping that would satisfy the other woman. Why, why, why, she wondered, must people insist on simplifying and degrading an experience with words before it's properly been allowed its due? People often did that with sex, wanting to make a running mutual commendation as though there couldn't possibly be any pleasure in it but that expressed in words, which always, to Florentine's mind, cheapened the pleasure and stripped the embodiedness of the experience to render it abstract and thus lessen its power.

Magdalene said, quickly, "I need to be heading back to the studio now. But I wanted to tell you that my son is meeting with a few other musicians tonight at the Cafe Bellona and said you would be welcome to join them if you liked."

At the moment, all Florentine wanted was some time alone, to digest the meal in peace. But professional sense dictated that she seize on an invitation that might not be offered another time, and so they parted with the understanding that they would meet again in only a few hours.

As Florentine strode rapidly through the streets, her senses nearly closed to the world about her, she thought how sad it was that she now found herself resenting having shared such an experience with Magdalene. The rest of the afternoon passed slowly, uncomfortably, even anxiously. Florentine felt guilty for her resentment and annoyed at herself for the shadow this resentment cast on the meal. But though her resentment made her feel like a creep, she could not shake the belief that she was justified in not wanting to reduce something so wonderful to mere, banal *words*.

[4]

The Cafe Bellona looked exactly as it had the last time Florentine had been there. The popular music it used for background sounded harsher to her ear, but in fact it was simply an evolution of the old music, no darker or angrier or more angst-ridden than its antecedents. In planet years the place was three decades older, but for Florentine, its clientele, style of decor, and edginess remained the same. Sometimes, she thought, time dilation didn't matter at all.

But seeing Magdalene in this setting, her eye now perceived that *she* had altered greatly, for Magdalene no longer looked as if she really belonged there. In the few hours since they'd parted, Magdalene had changed into slinky silky lounge-wear and acquired shiny beads and very thin ribboned braids in her hair, numerous earrings and bracelets, and interesting face paint; but something about her looked out of place, as though she were a seeker trying too obviously hard to surface.

Florentine had no trouble spotting her in the jam of close to a hundred vibrating, socializing bodies. Before she could get a good look at the other people squeezed around Magdalene's table, the two of them kissed in the Blue Downs fashion and asked one another the ritual questions of greeting. When they finished, and Florentine glanced around at the others as Magdalene launched into introductions, she saw that the singer in the Orchard, the one who had made her body burn — the one whose back and shoulders looked as if they could carry a magnificent pair of wings effortlessly — was present. Caught in the blur of a total body flush, Florentine missed all the other introductions, but did not miss *his* name — though she *was* sufficiently distracted that she didn't at first match her angel with the Alain she knew to be Magdalene's musician son.

Up close, Florentine saw that his angel-like form was in every way earthy and sensual rather than ethereal. She was suddenly reminded of Magdalene's former warmth and sensuality — recalling how the younger Magdalene had always pressed herself close, had lain whenever she could with her head in Florentine's lap, had twined her arm around Florentine's waist, simply because it was her nature to be physically close to anyone for whom she felt the least bit of affection. Florentine realized, then, that this Alain must be her son Alain. Everything about him — even his gaze and speaking voice, as buttery and graceful as his powerful singing voice — seemed tactile in its warmth. His hair reminded her of honey — as Magdalene's used to — while his skin (unlike Magdalene's olive complexion) made her think of peaches — of a wonderfully soft, golden fruit blushed with a pleasing, glowing pink. Looking straight at her, out of his appraising yet caressing green eyes, his earthiness surrounded Florentine like an embrace, and for a moment it was as though the two of them were the only consciousnesses inhabiting the known universe.

"My mother talks often about your earlier visit to Blue Downs," he said, and Florentine observed that sometimes time dilation did make a difference.

Caught up in the fascination of Alain's presence, Florentine missed the first bits of general conversation and only tuned in when Alain spoke, to tell her that if she was interested, they could show her the "score" for the meal that afternoon at the Singing Orchard. This "score" included not only the notation of the music that had been performed during the meal but also a choreography of the musicians' placement and the visuals, and of course, the cuisine itself.

"Do you understand the basic operating principles of Matrix Aesthetics?" asked Souhlema, who was seated on Alain's immediate right.

"I know it as a philosophy of art." Florentine sipped the thick, fragrant liqueur everyone drank at the Cafe Bellona. "My impression is that there are only two basic principles — the first that form is the matrix of creativity and the second that the deliberate production of matrices generates the maximum possibility for artistic expression." She had that straight out of Rudinov, the basic art history text for interpreting the art of Blue Downs. She had laid these principles out in the first chapter of her thesis, so many years past; and more recently — namely not long after parting from Magdalene that afternoon — she had brushed up on Matrix theory, precisely so that she would be ready to make intelligent conversation with these musicians.

"The notation of the music is only of its fundamental structure and does not denote a specific execution," Jarrow, seated on Alain's immediate left, said.

"The most obvious difference, in Matrix Aesthetics, is what is left out," Alain said, drawing Florentine's eyes to his soft, plush, stunningly shapely lips.

Jarrow said, "In the case of the performance this afternoon, the extradiegetic element was a poem, which only the performers could hear read, a driving, physical presence to us that was an inaudible — but felt — element for *you*."

"What was the poem?" Florentine asked to take her mind off the element of *Alain's* all too driving, physical presence.

Souhlema answered. "A particularly hard piece of rhythmic poetry by Sark Ali, titled *Why don't you see what you're looking at straight on, Brother Jonas?*, the performance of which lasted twenty-five minutes and was repeated exactly four times at carefully spaced intervals."

Everything about Souhlema grated on Florentine's nerves. But then she was wanting badly, even then, to get Alain away so that she could have him and his attention all to herself.

Jarrow leaned most of the way across the table, as though anxious to make sure Florentine could hear him in the general hubbub of the

cafe. She found him physically peculiar — his features oddly, dispro-
portionately large, his hands and wrists strangely doughy, looking
as if they were made of flesh that had been denied the infrastructure
of bone. "Matrix theory is an extrapolation of the old theory that in
every act of vision there remains something unseen, the invisibility
of which is required to make an objectively real world that exists independent of perception and cognition possible." While Alain's voice
was buttery, Jarrow's had the thick, smooth texture of syrup. Jarrow,
like Alain, was a singer. Both Souhlema and Joseph, a brooding, depressed type, were percussionists. All four of them had been in the
group that had performed that afternoon at the Singing Orchard.

Florentine undertook to play the devil's advocate. She needed some
argument for her piece, and this scene in the cafe would provide some
Bohemian color that would go a long way to amusing those viewers
who would be bored or confused by the discussion itself. Careful not
to look at Alain, she smiled at Jarrow and said, "But isn't the so-called
missing element — in this case the poem you mention — inessential?
One might almost call its offstage recitation an affectation, given its
lack of overall importance."

Alain answered before Jarrow could get one word in. His eyes
gleamed with excitement, and his voice grew thick with passion even
as it soared with exuberance. "Surely you know that the missing element is an essential factor in the visual works produced through
Matrix Aesthetics! The final product excludes this element, but in
every case the excluded element has helped to determine the final
product. Can you begin to imagine what it is like to make music while
a piece of rhythmic poetry is beating hard into one's ears?"

Florentine said, "Like trying to make music while sitting in this
cafe, maybe?" And she smiled a little wryly at her consciousness that
she wasn't as tolerant of a loud musical ambience as she had once
been.

Though she hadn't intended it, Florentine wasn't surprised when
this remark led Souhlema and Jarrow into a certain kind of earnestly
"playful" discussion of how art in general and music in particular was
contingent on its definition and production of context rather than

its originating intention. Florentine established an interestingly intense eye contact with Alain somewhere in the middle of this "playful discussion." Magdalene finally broke into their riff to ask if it weren't possible for Florentine to sample some Matrix production first without and then with the missing element.

Florentine smiled warmly, right into Alain's eyes. "Would it be possible?" she asked him. "Because I'm confident I'd find that both helpful and fascinating."

The musicians assured Florentine that not only would it be possible, but that they were also certain they could arrange for her to be present in the Singing Orchard while they were performing.

"They arranged that for me," Magdalene said. "Contingent on my promise to keep out of sight of the audience."

Florentine realized that Magdalene had some kind of special place with this group, as a sort of a maternal sidekick who routinely hung with them. She was her son's best buddy, too, Florentine decided — and didn't much like the thought.

She told them she definitely wanted to take them up on their offer, and the musicians promised to arrange it. Grateful to be spared any further discussion of Matrix Aesthetics until she was "better informed" on the subject, Florentine settled in to ask the usual sorts of questions. What training had they had? And why had they decided to make music for a living, rather than merely for pleasure? Was it easy to make such a living on Big Blue? And how did a commerce-oriented society such as that which dominated Blue Downs regard professional artists?

The evening passed pleasantly for Florentine and gave her some wonderful material for use in the piece. More interestingly, it made Alain personally and vividly real to her — and made her certain, in her very bones and belly, that he was as attracted to her as she was to him.

Only Magdalene's presence kept Florentine from openly pursuing him. She didn't know how Magdalene would take such a development, but she suspected that the other woman would not like it at all.

[5]

Florentine rated sitting in on their gig at the Singing Orchard a smashing success. Her access to the "score" choreographing the performance/meal she watched enhanced her understanding of Matrix Aesthetics enormously as well as provided an interesting ground for thinking about her own experience of such a meal. More importantly, the contact with Alain proved to be the turning point in moving them from amiable acquaintances to passionately engaged…not lovers, yet, but something more than friends. Through constantly recurring eye-contact, small touches, and a series of private asides, they established the fact of a powerful mutual attraction, an attraction that Florentine understood Alain was as eager as she to pursue.

Neither of them, of course, was given any food at the Singing Orchard, and Florentine had, in any case, to check out another restaurant for the evening meal, so she invited Alain — and only Alain — to join her. If the other musicians were disappointed, they had the good manners not to show it.

Since it was far too early for supper, Alain agreed to accompany Florentine to one of the smaller churches on her list, one she hadn't seen on her previous visits to Blue Downs. The Church of the One True God sat literally in the shadow of the cathedral. For that reason, perhaps, it made use of only artificial light, something one saw in few pieces of architecture on a planet with the kind of radiance Big Blue's sun bestowed upon it. In the nave and especially over the altar and on the enormous symbol of death hanging over it, narrow shafts of light descended from a lacily ornate strutwork that obscured their sources, as though beamed down straight from heaven. While the nave seemed almost unnaturally still and their footsteps flat and muted though the wood planks they trod were uncarpeted, when one stood in one of these shafts of light, equally thin shafts of music pierced the silence, resonating with an almost eerie spirituality that would have been more suited to corporate glass and marble than the visually warm wood and silk of this church.

Alain stood in one of those flushes of light, his smooth young skin flattered by the illumination, his eyes swimming with pride and pleasure as he listened to the music his presence on that spot had triggered. "Jarrow and I are the singers in this bit," he said. "Ponsonby, whom you haven't met, wrote it." He stopped speaking, and Florentine could feel him listening. Suddenly the light began pulsing with harshly powerful bursts like showers of diamonds, blinding yet rich, that made her vision go dark and then stamped it with dots of colored lights that bounced in patterns she was convinced were deliberately synchronized with the music. The flow of the music itself swelled into a cascade of shimmering sound, sparkling in the brilliance of the moment. Alain, standing motionless in the light, became two-dimensional to Florentine's eyes, like a flat black-and-white photograph in the sharpest focus and of the highest resolution.

And then the moment passed, and Alain stepped out of the light and the music was just music and Alain merely ordinary flesh and blood, and a smile passed between him and Florentine, a smile of knowledge that would not be spoken, perhaps because it could not be. Then Alain showed her the rest of the church's treasure, and they left. A don't-miss sight, she rated the little church. Later, she thought of it as the place where she and Alain first began to love one another.

[6]

Florentine nearly asked Alain to stay that night with her. His warmth and eagerness and her excitement made physical consummation seem inevitable, but in the end, she hesitated at the brink, wary of a gentle but firm reserve in him that she did not feel she understood well enough to risk disregarding. Before meeting Alain, she would have stated, as a fact, that twenty-five-year-old males were invariably shallow and callow and depthless, however socially adept and sophisticated they might be. Alain was different. Though he showed no signs of true depression, she sensed, lurking beneath his warm, easy presentation, a profound, thoroughgoing sadness. This sadness seemed so *natural* to him that she found herself thinking that he must have been born sad and had carried this sadness with him for all the years of his short, talented life. She hadn't known many artists. She thought that perhaps the sadness was linked with his music, that it was its source, or perhaps its primary vector for expression. Since she was consumed with him, she wanted to know all about his sadness, not out of idle or voyeuristic curiosity, but because everything about him mattered deeply to her.

After that night, she wooed him, gently, lightly, with all the restraint her years of experience allowed her. She planned very little strategy and operated chiefly on intuitive impulse. It was a matter, she thought, of working to get from P to Q and not being sure how to accomplish it. Nights, alone, she lay awake fantasizing the detailed possibilities of exactly what Q might be. Days and evenings, she spent every possible minute with Alain — sitting in on his practice sessions, watching his performances, and taking him away from his colleagues as often as possible.

The third evening they spent together — this time following an informal performance given in a cafe that was a more serious intelligentsia venue than the Bellona Cafe — they talked, in Florentine's room, drinking wine, until four in the morning. Despite her excitement, her body began to scream for sleep long before that hour. But she didn't want to let him go, didn't want to let him leave. Through the night, Alain talked at length about his personal philosophy, his friendships, his childhood. Florentine thought she understood him. She felt close to him, as if the touch of their bodies would take her inside his skin and merge them bone to bone, soul to soul. She really, really, really wanted to fuck him. As, over the hours, they talked, sitting on the rug, drinking, they had moved closer and closer, until their knees were all but touching, their heads, constantly leaning closer, only inches apart. Her body grew wild for him. His penis, she found herself thinking, was in very easy reach. Only a touch, she thought, only a touch and everything else would follow, since nature would simply have to take its course.

Nature! That's how much *she* knew. Later she would bitterly ask herself if anything in Blue Downs could ever be *natural*, and answer: only as "natural" as the light in the Church of the One True God, where access to the sun was blighted by the cathedral looming over it.

Having decided her move, she lingered on the verge of making it, simply for the pleasure of anticipation. The possibility of being refused never entered her head. Her sole care was for sparing them the little awkwardnesses that commonly attended sexual scenes with the inexperienced, awkwardnesses that smooth orchestration by the experienced party could mute, if not eliminate altogether.

On and on Alain talked. Seriously, rather than garrulously, carefully rather than pretentiously. He was talking about how his grandparents were musicians, particularly about his grandmother, Sheridan, who had been born into an affluent merchant family and been expelled when she chose to become a composer of mixed electronic and live music rather than serve as high priestess of the family's business and fortune. At last, unable to wait a single moment longer, Florentine brushed her fingers over his knee and slid them along the inside of his coarse cloth-clad thigh. Her heart pounded, and her breath caught in her throat as the thrill of the touch coursed through her body. She looked into Alain's eyes, which first widened with surprise and then frowned with perplexity as her fingers moved on to the artistic little codpiece, an item of Big Blue fashion that was de rigueur for males of all classes and ages. His perplexity took Florentine by surprise — at the same moment that her fingers discovered what felt like a less than full erection beneath the codpiece.

"Um, Florentine?" Alain said, as though to inquire what possible reason she might have for stroking his genitals.

His response confused her. How could anyone not know the meaning of one person — whose face and neck is flushed, breath fast and short, fingers trembling — stroking another person's genitals? As she watched her angel's face dance its way through a series of swift, rapid changes of expression as elusive as a sequence of fleeting shadows, her confusion slipped over the border into the fascinated precincts of wonder. She saw astonishment, gratification, doubt, and pleasure pass across his face, to be succeeded, with heartbreaking finality, by sadness and firmness of resolution. As she watched, his face tilted slightly, bringing the light to shine in such a way as to bounce with a glare off the suddenly glazed surface of his eyeballs; she shivered a little, for something about that trick of the light sent a shaft of icy wind down her bones. She recognized the sadness, of course, for she'd been catching glimpses of it lurking around the edges of Alain's social self all along.

His hand settled over hers, which was searching for the Velcro seam that she presumed must be securing the codpiece's closure. "Florentine," he said tenderly, urgently, "It never crossed my mind that you didn't *know*. You comprehend so much about everything, and you're something of an expert, for a foreigner, anyway, about Blue Downs. So I just assumed you knew that...." He blushed, running up against the internalized constrictions of speech that so limited open verbal acknowledgment of what was assumed to be obvious in his culture. For the first time since Florentine had met him, he looked uncomfortable and embarrassed.

There followed a strange jumble of medical jargon and awkward euphemistic evasions, but Florentine took in only the painful, basic outlines of the story he told. Alain had stood out, virtually from infancy, as a musical prodigy with an exceptionally gifted voice. Much — oh much, much, *much* — had been made of it. He learned, very early, to identify himself with his voice. He had hardly even known how to be a boy, much less a child. His father, like his mother, was a dancer. They eked out a living with difficulty. And then Magdalene had her accident, which had resulted in a broken ankle and virtually ended her days dancing. Though as a moderately successful dancer she had been a frequent soloist, she hadn't reached the stratospheric level of success and so did not command even halfway decent fees for teaching. The family's income grew marginal, its existence hand-to-mouth, with expulsion to a workfare camp for indigents just one short illness of either parent away.

When Alain began the early stages of puberty, the Blue Downs Arts Foundation approached Alain's parents and offered them a small grant and the full funding for Alain's entire musical education if they agreed to have Alain's puberty interrupted during the fourth stage, to prevent the usual changes to his vocal chords. It would be simple and painless, they were assured. The gonadostat, a regulatory center in the hypothalamus, modulates gonadotrophin secretion. Increasing serotonin and particularly melatonin levels in the blood plasma was sufficient to cause the gonadostat to decrease gonadotrophin secretion. Maintained long enough, this treatment would eventually arrest puberty — permanently.

Alain, in other words, was a new form of that archaic creature historically known as a *castrato*. Oh, he still had his testicles. His penis, larger than a child's though quite a bit smaller than a normal adult's, was capable of erections and ejaculations. But his sexuality was thwarted.

Although Florentine was shocked and indignant to learn that his parents had allowed this to be done to him — and that a respected institution of the arts had actually *promoted* it — she said at once that she didn't care if he wasn't a mature adult male sexually, that she still wanted him, still desired him, still burned for him, and that it didn't matter a jot to her what kind of sex they had, so long as he wanted, desired, and burned for her, too.

"I didn't know," he said. "Florentine, I didn't know it was possible for anyone to *desire* me — that way. Everyone said, the counselors, especially, that since I can't produce sperm, I don't have the right pheromones to attract partners. They said that would make it easier on me. To keep chaste, I mean."

"Chaste?"

Florentine didn't know the word and didn't particularly care to. Her focus at that moment was on his not answering her implicit question — whether *he* wanted *her*. Sexually. But this word, *chaste*, as she soon was forced to learn, was one of the big ones in Blue Downs. It mattered tremendously to Alain, particularly at that moment. It was a word she soon came to loathe and detest, even if she never did manage to understand its importance to her beloved.

[7]

"Chaste," said Alain, his hand still over Florentine's, lying against his codpiece and the small treasure within, "means not ever having any kind of sexual contact with anyone, including with oneself. It means being sexually pure of mind, thought, and deed. Which not only has religious significance, but makes one a more powerful artist."

It took Florentine the better part of a minute to think through his explanation — which included, as part of the definition of *chaste*, the rationalization he had been given for why he needed to apply it to himself.

"Obviously, if you believe being *chaste* makes you a more powerful artist, this matters," she said carefully, trying not to betray the irony she felt toward the very idea in the tone of her voice. "I don't quite see how that would work, except by way of a crude model of sublimating your libido. Do you also find the religious significance — this *purity* you talk about — important to you as well?" Religion was not something that had arisen in any of their conversations, so naturally Florentine imagined she was posing a rhetorical question.

"It's all connected," he said. Florentine's heart sank. "I have to admit I'm not especially *devout* in my practice — I hardly go to church, except to perform. But...although I'm *lax*, there's no question that it matters to me. I mean, my Voice is a gift — a really special gift. Unlike other musicians, who have nonanimate instruments they can rely on and only have to worry about technique, *my* instrument — what makes me the musician I am — is produced through my body — a special gift from God. It could be taken from me at any time." Blushing, as though only now noticing that he had been pressing Florentine's hand against his penis, he pulled her hand away from his codpiece and held it between both of his. His eyes looked as intense as she'd yet seen them. Passionately, he said, "It's only by God's grace that I possess such an instrument at all. Which is something, Florentine, I never, never forget."

Florentine placed her other hand over the top one of Alain's, making a quadruple-deck sandwich of their hands. "How terrible, to have to worry about losing your voice," she said. "Is this fear typical of singers?"

The question launched Alain into a lengthy spiel about how there had never been a serious singer in the history of the species who hadn't suffered, constantly, from this fear. Why a simple cold or allergy could completely disable a singer! A cough! Anemia! Hiccoughs! A lengthy litany of health complaints poured out of Alain with such force that Florentine found herself concluding that all singers — including Alain — must harbor a fierce tendency to hypochondria.

If Alain's vehement diatribe wasn't the focus of passion she was interested in, at least it got him off the subject of religion. And it allowed her an opening from a different direction when, commiserating with him about the fragility of his gift and his dependence, as a musician, on his good health and well-being, she gently embraced him in a lingering hug of empathy, then nuzzled his cheek and softly kissed his lips — "chastely." He did not retreat in alarm. So Florentine's second kiss, deployed in a masterful stealth attack, resulted in a quivering, timid response that soon grew interesting.... Inevitably, though, as his excitement mounted and their caresses became bolder and more intimate, Alain pulled back, gasping, troubled, breathless, and trembling. "Oh God," he whispered. "Oh God. Now I've done it." Slowly the color drained from his passion-flushed face. He pressed his hands to his mouth as though he'd just learned he'd made the worst mistake of his life.

"What is it, darling, what is it?" Florentine's hand moved to stroke his hair, but he seized it and shoved it away.

"You can't understand," he said miserably. "I know all of this is as incomprehensible to you as Matrix Aesthetics."

She pressed him, of course, and coaxed him and gentled him until he revealed, halting and stuttering, that he'd had an orgasm. Which was something, it turned out, he'd never before experienced while awake. At first she thought he feared he'd never be able to sing again (by way of some bizarre superstition about ejaculation), but a stranger story than that emerged, and his halting embarrassment shifted to tearful anxiety. It seemed that when they'd arrested his puberty, he'd taken a "solemn vow" never to use his penis sexually. According to the terms of his vow, his voluntary violation of it — by having sexually ejaculated while awake — would entail his expulsion from Blue Downs' professional association of musicians, upon which hinged his employability as a singer.

Florentine was incredulous. She couldn't believe such a ridiculous entailment could possibly be legal, and she said so.

"You don't understand Blue Downs," Alain said sadly. "The courts would never interfere with the enforcement of such a vow. Vows are as binding as any mutual contract."

Florentine was nonplussed. "Well then you must simply never *tell* anyone. *I* certainly won't."

He swallowed and looked away as the tears standing in his eyes threatened to overflow. "There's no way I can't tell. To stay in good standing in my church, even if I don't attend Sunday services regularly, I do need to attend a monthly community confession group. While nocturnal emissions aren't violations of my vow, they are sins that I have to confess, sins that remind me that castration is no safeguard of my chastity. What I'm saying is, that even such petty sins, as embarrassing and humiliating as they are to confess, always come out in group, even if I'd rather not publicly admit to them. Because people often try to hide their sins from themselves, not to mention their neighbors, we all have to take a drug that makes us volunteer the truth." He stared bitterly down at his hands. "I won't have any choice but to tell the whole sorry story."

Sorry story — how these words stung Florentine, like one of the penitentials' lashes flicking at her breast. The only thing sorry about their heretofore lovely evening, she thought, was the way these barbarians were holding her love's sexuality hostage. As though it weren't his own private business to use or not as he wished! As though it were some precious community possession more important than the wonderful music he made with his exceptionally powerful voice! As though he weren't a fully embodied human being made of flesh and bone.

"Well let me tell you something, Alain." Florentine grabbed his hands and made him look at her. "If they don't want your gift on *this* world, there's a whole galaxy out there that's just yours for the plucking. Where this chastity stuff is *irrelevant*." Listening to her own words, she suddenly caught fire. The possibilities thronged her imagination. She had no doubt that Alain had the potential for becoming a performance god. Talent, beauty, presence — what more did it take? The rest, *she* could provide! The connections, the organization, the strategizing.... Shit, she was *tired* of being a travel critic. She'd done that. She was jaded. She was ready for something new, something different.

Eagerly she shared her vision with Alain; magically, it swept away his blues. So they didn't want him? He'd just leave! As for sinful unchastity.... Well. He had already broken his vow. He had no reason to hold himself back from total, full engagement in adult, sexual love.

And the rest of the night — what little remained of it — was bliss.

[8]

Though she had begun the evening under the influence of a powerful sexual infatuation, by morning Florentine discovered herself in total, overwhelming, mindfucking love. It might have been the vision she had of the trail Alain and she would together blaze across the galaxy that moved her from a traveler's indulgence in a momentary seduction to major emotional — and financial — commitment. For now she saw herself dedicating her own talents and resources to creating a brilliant career for him; she saw her life changed at a stroke.

When, finally, Alain fell into exhausted sleep and Florentine, too excited, lay for another half hour awake, she entertained the possibility that in a more civilized world, Alain could probably enjoy the effects of a completed puberty without sacrificing the fineness and wonder of his prepubescent vocal chords — *not* that the sex they'd had hadn't been everything delicious and satisfying, but because it made sense to her that he should be made whole, if possible, and that the sadness always lurking in his eyes, even when he was happiest, be made to vanish.

In that wakeful half hour, Florentine became convinced that they could have it all, provided only that she put everything she had into making it happen. If, after the long march of years, she had never given her heart to any of her many lovers, she did so now, as if she were an innocent young thing, unaware of the pain doing so necessarily risked.

Although Florentine had a schedule to follow, although Alain had a rehearsal in the morning and a gig in late afternoon, they slept, entwined, well into midafternoon. Florentine woke with a feeling of pleasure, of something wonderful having happened, a feeling that she hadn't known since childhood. She lay still for a few minutes, listening to Alain's breathing, watching his face, so young and perfect, his lashes long and thick against the downy curve of his cheekbone, free of all care and concern, unaware of the power he already commanded. Just the touch of his hand, where it lay in sleep with its edge lightly brushing her hip, made Florentine feel so warm, so loving, that quietly getting up and going into the bath for a shower felt something like a rupture of her flesh.

Florentine knew well the pull of obsessive sexual passion, but this was entirely new to her. She was enchanted rather than addicted. She felt something being born rather than blotted out. Standing under the hot, needle-point shower, she remembered how embodiment-positive she had first found Alain's voice. She knew it was right to take him away. Every creative fiber of that man knew the joy of embodiment. The bullshit about purity and chastity was ideological nonsense. It had to be a contradiction eating away at his soul. Once liberated from his awful world, he would realize that and be at peace, in the way he had not been when they'd finally called it a night.

Florentine found it impossible to think he was anything but an unwilling captive to his religion, caught up in its legalistic coils, its brainwashing methods, its terrorizing auto-surveillance system. All he needed, she believed, was freedom, and his life would open before him as he had never before imagined it could.

But the substantiality of Alain's internalization of this ideological terrorism confronted her directly on her finishing in the bathroom.

Alain had woken in a state. As he rushed into his clothes, he made a point of avoiding eye contact. And he muttered. "What have I done, what have I done? I'm ruined!" When Florentine tried to take him in her arms, he resisted almost violently. It was as though all the hours of talk had been idle fantasizing. In the light of day, he could no longer believe in even one word of it.

He no longer believed she loved him. Her assurances failed. He said he knew he was a freak, scarcely half a man. He said that she had made a fool of him — because he had been weak and foolish enough to let her.

Florentine hardly knew how to counter what seemed to her like madness. All she could think to do was to get him to wash his face and have a cup of coffee before rushing off. She made him believe she'd judge him rude if he did not.

Somehow she got him to settle down and look at her. She showed him the love in her eyes, she reminded him of the promises they had made in the hour before dawn. And then Alain reminded himself of the stark, plain fact that he had burned all his bridges and was finished as a singer if he did not leave the planet with her.

Still, he was stiff, and sore, and grieving. He might be gaining a life, but he had lost his world. Florentine felt, in her heart, that he was back to secretly thinking of their relationship as a "sorry story" rather than a grand passionate tale of love. But she was certain his heart would open to her again. Such harsh, painful ambivalence was to be expected. The stakes were so terribly high — for both of them.

[9]

The next few days flew by like a golden, shimmering dream. Florentine resumed her schedule, and Alain resumed his. They spent every moment in which their schedules didn't conflict together. Alain filed an application for an offworld passport. He was told that it would take ten or so days to be processed. Florentine canceled her reservations and left her tickets open. She could not book tickets for Alain until he had been assigned a passport number.

Everything seemed to be going just fine, but on the third night, when they were out to supper after a concert Alain had done with a small chamber ensemble, he began to get that haunted look back in his eyes, the look that Florentine associated with his "sorry story" state of mind. It came, she thought, from exposure to his mother, who had sat beside Florentine during the concert and had looked disturbed when Florentine indicated that she wasn't interested in joining Magdalene and Alain's musician friends at the Cafe Bellona afterwards. Florentine had no fear that Magdalene suspected anything. (Her plan was to keep everyone in the dark until an hour or two before departure.) But Magdalene made it plain she thought it peculiar that Alain chose a private over a social evening.

"Darling," Florentine said after she'd told him how riveting his voice had been that night. "What you're doing takes an enormous degree of will and courage. I know it must be terribly difficult to think of leaving your family and friends, and frightening to leave the only world you've ever known. But you owe it to your voice, you owe it to yourself, and you owe it to your manhood to do it." She tried to pour out, through her eyes, her immense confidence in his courage. And she told him again about the city-state of Celestia, on Gray's World, the very heart of the transgalactic music industry, and reminded him of some of the artists he himself admired, who lived there.

"My manhood?" Alain said faintly, as though he had no idea what Florentine could possibly mean by the word. "I'm not really a man," he said, frowning. "I don't think — "

"Of course you're a man!" Florentine thought of his arrested puberty and his beardless face and unmanly vocal chords and suppressed the impatience his doubt provoked in her. "Whatever people have been telling you, you're not to doubt *that!*"

He did not argue the point, but something in his expression made her think he didn't agree. He said, instead, "I wonder just how much courage I have. God knows that I owe a great deal to my Voice."

They drank champagne and ate bread and paté and fruit and agreed to talk instead about the chamber group he had performed with. Alain was terribly fragile, Florentine thought. Her big bold plan could fall apart at any moment with just the right kind of push from someone wanting to thwart it. Somehow she had to get them through the days remaining without that happening. Her primary strategy must be to keep him as occupied as possible. It was Magdalene's interference, not Alain's lack of resolution, that worried her.

Quite correctly, as it turned out.

[10]

Magdalene took Florentine by surprise two days later. Florentine was off guard, sipping wine on the terrace of a restaurant on the Plaza of Glory, reviewing the list of hotels prior to determining which one should receive her patronage when her contracted time ran out and she would have to start paying her own way. Some mildly pleasant, if canned, lute music played in the background. The place was new, but showed all the signs of being attractive to tourists. Since Alain had promised to join her for the midday meal, when she heard the scrape of the chair on the flagstones, she assumed his arrival. "A few seconds, darling, and I'll be done," she said, making the universal gesture indicating her engagement on-line.

"Darling," Magdalene said in a tone of disgust.

Florentine disengaged and faced a Magdalene she did not know. The usual display of deference, admiration, and the eager desire to please had been replaced with coldness and determination. She had squeezed Alain, Florentine thought, and he had told her. "I was expecting Alain," she said, imagining that a reminder of Magdalene's rudeness at joining her without an invitation would bother her.

"Alain asked me to come in his place."

"Oh really. Then shall we order?"

Magdalene's mouth twisted. "Do so, if you like. I want nothing more than water."

She appeared to be too upset to eat — a place Florentine was heading for fast, herself. But she had no intention of letting Magdalene see that. So she did order, only a far lighter meal than she had originally intended.

To put Magdalene on the defensive, Florentine said, "So if you don't intend to eat, why is it that you felt it necessary to come in Alain's place?"

Magdalene folded her hands on the table before her. Though her voice sounded cool and unstressed, her knuckles were blanched. "Alain came to see me this morning, before his rehearsal. He said he'd ruined his life. And that faced with that ruin, he had agreed to run away from Blue Downs, with you. I had no idea what he meant by *ruined*. Then he explained. It seems he thought that because he'd soiled his specialness, he'd no longer be able to perform in Blue Downs. I told him I doubted that was true. Granted, he'd forfeited his special position, but with church-guided penitence and reparation, cleansing his sin and restoring one part at least of his specialness, the Association will certainly agree to let him perform again. I've heard of such cases in the past. In Blue Downs, no one is held to be permanently beyond the pale. Our society is very forgiving to the *truly* penitent. It was only because Alain was so overwhelmed by the enormity of breaking his vow that he thought he was beyond forgiveness."

She paused to sip from her water glass, then continued in that same calm and quiet voice. "He was so upset, when he came to me, convinced he had to choose between working as a musician, using his gift, and his life and loved ones in Blue Downs. He cursed his own weakness — unable to resist ejaculating, he said, when he touched your breasts. He wept bitterly at his having allowed his sexual desire full consciousness. It was fitting, he said, that he be forced into exile as the price of continuing to use a gift he had betrayed. And I saw that my son was utterly crushed at the prospect. When I explained that such a choice would not be demanded of him, it was as though an intolerable burden had been lifted from his heart."

She paused to take several more swallows of water, and Florentine stared at the hard determination in her face. "Which was such a relief to me, since he almost instantaneously became himself again. As though nothing could ever be so terrible as the moments, hours, and days he had spent convinced he was facing exile." Magdalene lightly cleared her throat. "Of course, free of that burden, his next concern was for your feelings." Magdalene's expression was now *pitying*.

"*My* feelings!" Florentine felt outraged that this woman dared even *mention* them. She had intruded into a private relationship that was really none of her business. "My *feelings*," Florentine said sharply, "are not up for discussion in this conversation. At least not my feelings for *Alain*."

The first course arrived; carefully Florentine focused on it and the service in case she decided to use the recording she was making of it for the travelogue, or in case GTI wanted to use it in their Blue Downs restaurant guide.

Magdalene continued. "My son said you know so little about Blue Downs that he didn't think he could make you understand, himself, how important it is for him to stay. Important for his music, important for his identity, important for his *soul*."

Florentine picked up the narrow, two-tined fork, glanced briefly at Magdalene, and dug into the dish of lightly-sauced shellfish. She had a fair idea of what was going on. Magdalene had browbeaten Alain into disavowing his feelings for Florentine and now he was afraid to tell her himself, knowing, as he did, that she would not accept the triumph of his mother's will in the face of his moral weakness. Magdalene had put him in an unforgivably humiliating position. Florentine could not blame him for wanting to avoid putting that humiliation on display.

The shellfish was delicious, and Florentine was careful to give it her best recording gaze. "His *identity?*" She scoffed openly at the word. "It seems a full, mature identity is the last thing he's likely to find if he stays in Blue Downs. No thanks to the parents who have allowed him only a partial manhood totally unnecessarily." Florentine had checked a good medical source and confirmed her suspicion that it was perfectly feasible to prevent the thickening of the vocal chords without sacrificing genital maturity. "Any competent endocrinologist could have saved his prepubertal voice without arresting the full development of his virility, Magdalene." Though her throat was tight with distress, she swallowed another tender morsel, then looked directly at Magdalene. "I can't begin to understand how parents claiming to love their son would choose to mutilate him. No matter how much money they were offered to do it."

That brought some garishly hectic color into the smooth, olive-skinned cheeks. Now, Florentine thought, her coolness would dissolve into anger and outrage at the older woman of the world seducing her innocent young son. She would resort to clichés, and Florentine would find it easy to show her her shallowness for doing so.

Magdalene said, "You keep talking about manhood. Obviously you have some idea of making him into a *full, mature, adult male*. You may be a sophisticated galactic traveler, Florentine, but it's obvious you have a pretty simplistic idea about gender. What you fail to understand is that no matter what his sexual physiology might be made to be, Alain will never be a *man*. That isn't his identity. Which you apparently don't recognize, much less acknowledge. As I pointed out to Alain, it's unlikely anyone would recognize his gender anywhere off this planet. It doesn't exist elsewhere. So always he'd have to be pretending — while never feeling recognized for who he is." She nodded. "I see from your face that you have no idea what I'm talking about. You imagine that he is a man — a *partial* man — that needs only a little correction to be made *full*. You don't see Alain for what he is, under the skin."

The second course arrived, and though Florentine was distracted, she tried to do her focus on it justice. But before she took even one bite of it, she had to look at Magdalene and say, "You claim he isn't a man and never will be. But if he's not a man, what is he, Magdalene? A neuter? A drone? An *it*? Or an eternally pubescent *boy*?" Keeping her son eternally a boy would suit a woman like Magdalene just fine, Florentine thought as she picked up her soup spoon.

Magdalene took her time replying. "Florentine, you make me really, really sad. I would have thought someone so little interested in family life as yourself would be able to imagine there are other paths the human being can take than the sexual and reproductive." She leaned back in her chair. "You will scoff, but in Blue Downs we call those who do not finish puberty 'earthly angels.' They are respected and admired and envied in ways you could not begin to comprehend.

The specialness of Alain's kind lies in their being exempted from the ordinary duties and concerns and messy entanglements of the body and spirit that any kind of sexual relationship entails. The *reason* most religions consider sexuality problematical is because, unregulated, it throws the individual off-balance, at the mercy of illusions, hormones, and persistent misunderstanding. Alain was to have been spared all that. Devoted to art, he would never have known such loss of self, loss of control, loss of certainty. He's fallen now. And though he'll recover, he'll never be the same. He'll always have a tendency to wonder if it would have been better had he become a man. And people will know that he violated his sacred trust and is not quite as special as he was. Which is why his act of penitence must be correspondingly severe. His submission will be proof that though altered, he is still special. A fallen angel, perhaps, but an angel nevertheless."

"An angel!" Florentine shoved the barely-tasted cup of soup away from her. "It's like a mass psychosis! You're all fucking brainwashed!"

Somehow she got through the rest of the meal while Magdalene droned on and on about Alain's "specialness." Magdalene said that Florentine was disrespectful of Blue Downs mores. Florentine pointed out that a society's mores are not always deserving of respect and demanded that Magdalene admit that she agreed with her about *that*. Surely she wouldn't respect a society that ritually ate other humans, would she?

When Florentine had finished sampling a bite or two from every course she had ordered, Magdalene insisted that she accompany her to the Plaza of Penitence. She said she wanted to show her something. Statues faced the Plaza of Penitence on three sides, Florentine knew, and so she expected to be shown one whose significance she had missed — presumably a glorification of the "specialness" of Blue Downs's "earthly angels." She agreed to Magdalene's demand because she thought it the best way to get out onto the street and positioned for a fast getaway.

In fact, Magdalene's object was a good deal uglier.

Florentine heard the sounds of a mean, nasty crowd when they were only a block from the Plaza — jeering catcalls and angry invective, scary with the visceral overtone of a mob on the verge of losing the last vestige of civilized constraint. She pulled up short and glared at Magdalene. "I'm really not in the mood to watch some unfortunate wretch who's suffered a reversal of material fortunes get beaten up by a mob prior to being tossed out into the scrublands. Public beatings are disgusting enough, but the fear and loathing of failure in your society makes such beatings positively barbaric."

Magdalene's lips pressed tightly together as her suddenly angry, narrow gaze scoured Florentine's face. Until their exchange at lunch about Blue Downs's mores, Florentine had always gone out of her way to be tactful about the uglier aspects of Blue Downs. Naturally, this unaccustomed criticism infuriated Magdalene. "An elder of the Church of Repentance and head of one of the most important merchant families in the city is making a major act of penitence in the Plaza. I want you to see at least a few minutes of it, so that you can have some small idea of how brave and determined Alain must be to submit himself to the same process. Some people do prefer to run away, to accept exile off-planet rather than commit themselves to the pain and humiliation of public repentance. You will never have even the glimmering of an understanding of what's at stake for Alain unless you see what he is willing to undertake to retain his specialness."

Florentine was sickened at the thought of what must be happening in the Plaza, but given Magdalene's argument, could not refuse her demand.

They walked the remaining block to the Plaza and joined the fringe of the violent, jeering mob. And then Florentine watched with revulsion and disgust, recording every ugly abuse she saw. It wasn't the most brutal thing she had ever watched, but the stress Magdalene laid on its voluntary performance by the victim made it, hands down, the most nauseating. The man being beaten and defiled would, Magdalene said, survive, though it would take him months to heal physically.

Florentine knew the man would never be the same and that the ordeal would surely stamp his spirit with its inhuman savagery forever.

The last thing Magdalene said to Florentine, when they parted, was that Alain intended to visit her in her suite at the B&B early that evening. *Good*, Florentine thought. *Because I'm not going to let Magdalene do all his talking for him, as though he's some scared young boy hiding behind his mother's skirts.* But the cold, metallic thought that he had already decided he would prefer to go through with such an ordeal rather than leave the planet with her pierced Florentine like a spike being driven into her heart. She no longer believed that she could counter the brainwashing that shaped and distorted his every emotion and idea. She understood that she wasn't up against just his mother, but the entire horror of a society he'd been born and raised in.

[11]

Her one thought while waiting for Alain was to assert the reality of who they were together, of who he was to *her*, with her — of who they would be in the future, together. The key to this lay in their bodies, in their very embodiment, which was what in their designation of Alain's "specialness" Blue Downs sought to deny above all.

Alain, however, when he arrived at Florentine's door, would not allow her to touch him, not even to exchange the ritual double kiss. When he was safely over the threshold, she made the door close and said, "You're afraid of acknowledging what you really want."

In his lovely face — an angel's, indeed, she thought bitterly — Florentine confronted a pain so harsh that she nearly cried with vexation at its utter gratuitousness. "I'm afraid of a lot of things, Florentine. That is true." His voice was as buttery and steady as ever, but lacked its usual lilt and buoyancy. "I'm sorry for all the hurt I'm causing you," he said. "But I've come to say goodbye."

Desperation made her reckless. "Your loyalties are misplaced. Do you realize how unnecessary it was for them to deprive you of a completed puberty? You could *have* your voice *and* mature sexuality *both!* The sacrifice they demanded of you was totally artificial! And it still is!"

His eyes — reminding Florentine, so wrenchingly now, of Magdalene's — pitied her. "What lifts a species beyond the merely instinctual is the exercise of intentionality, Florentine. That's why art is the pinnacle of all that is best in human beings. It uses natural materials but is entirely, consciously artificial as it does so. That's what you still haven't grasped about Matrix Aesthetics. If anything exemplifies how Matrix Aesthetics works, it's my gift and the terms which frame my use of it." His hands swept into a graceful arc, turned palm up, and lifted slowly to the level of his eyes. "To you it's merely philosophy, isn't it."

"Religion, philosophy," she said despairingly. "It's sick to mutilate oneself for an abstraction."

He forced a strained, wry smile. "As if you and every other human in the galaxy don't do that *every day* of your existence in one way or another. The difference is that I'm aware of doing it, while you are not. And I'm therefore intentionally choosing." He dropped his arms to his sides, then folded them across his chest. "Think of me as being selfish in choosing for myself rather than for you, Florentine, if that will help. Out there, off-planet, I'd never fit in no matter what I did. I need the context of a world of artists practicing Matrix Aesthetics. I need an audience that understands the emotional, spiritual, and social significance of my Voice. Not people who think my Voice is 'riveting' or 'ravishing' or just plain 'pretty.' And I can't get that anywhere but in Blue Downs."

What could Florentine answer to that? Tell him he'd carve out a new niche for himself? He didn't want to be an exception — a "freak" as he had more than once worried to her he would become off-planet. In the context he had forced onto her, their love could only be a "selfish" intrusion of hers, not something equally important to both of them.

Florentine bowed her head in defeat. She had lost. Blue Downs' ideological terrorism, Blue Downs's artistic glory, had triumphed. The pleasures of the flesh posed a feeble opposition indeed. She knew when she was beaten.

[12]

Florentine devoted the remainder of her stay in Blue Downs to documenting the ugly underside that usually went unnoticed and unremarked by tourists. She haunted the Plaza of Penitence, she interviewed priests and ministers and counselors about group confession and acts of penitence. She even tried to schedule a trip out to the scrubs, to get a look at the city's dumping place for the homeless (where she expected to find merely piles of bones, since the people dumped there were usually bloody and broken from their *involuntary* acts of penitence), but ran out of time before it could be arranged. Because she could not bear to see Alain again or be reminded of what they had lost, she avoided all the arts venues she had previously haunted and the neighborhood in which Alain and all his friends lived.

Images of her "earthly angel" haunted her third and final tour of Blue Downs. She would never love anyone as she loved him. She knew she could never bear to love anyone so desperately again. She told herself that perhaps some day he would tire of his "specialness," tire of his immaturity, and choose at last to step down from his perversely proud pedestal. If that day were to come, she vowed, she would be there, still, for him — waiting for her fallen angel, waiting for the man he had so far refused to allow himself to become, waiting for the perfection of deep and total love that few people in any world were ever given to know.

[excerpts from]
Camouflage

Joe Haldeman

The jury for the 2004 Tiptree Award chose two winners: a science fiction novel and a fantasy novel, one by a man (with a female — sort of, eventually — protagonist) and one by a woman (with a male protagonist), one by an American and one by a European.

Camouflage by Joe Haldeman tells several stories, among them those of two shape-shifting aliens whose impersonations of humans involve having to choose gender. (What would Raphael Carter's genagnosics make of these creatures?)

Joe Haldeman describes *Troll: A Love Story* by Johanna Sinisalo as an "alternate taxonomy" novel. Sinisalo combines (among other elements) male homoerotic imagery, contemporary "mail-order bride" slavery, and Finnish folklore to examine the line between urban and feral life — and the role both play in our world.

These selections from *Camouflage* are the beginnings of the three intertwined stories: the efforts to raise an unknown object from the bottom of the ocean, and the two aliens' early contacts with humans. Rather than a continuous section of the novel, we chose the first four chapters and two from a little further along.

Similarly, from *Troll: A Love Story* (published in Finland in 2000, first translated into English in 2003 as *Not Before Sundown*) we have included selections from the beginning of the novel. To get as far into it as we wanted, we omitted some of the legends, stories, and natural history essays about trolls; you'll see the pieces of the *Kalevala* that Mikael reads on the internet, but when you read the whole book you'll see how Sinisalo uses many more of these, to excellent effect.

Although these two novels are as different as can be, they share commonalities. In both, the Other is living among us, non-human entities that help us define what it means to be human. They are both (unconventional) love stories. And the endings — which we won't reveal — parallel each other in very interesting ways.

The monster came from a swarm of stars that humans call Messier 22, a globular cluster ten thousand light-years distant. A million stars with ten million planets — all but one of them devoid of significant life.

It's not a part of space where life could flourish. All of those planets are in unstable orbits, the stars swinging so close to one another that they steal planets, or pass them around, or eat them.

This makes for ferocious geological and climatic changes; most of the planets are sterile billiard balls or massive Jovian gasbags. But on the one world where life has managed a toehold, that life is *tough*.

And adaptable. What kind of organisms can live on a world as hot as Mercury, which then is suddenly as distant from its sun as Pluto within the course of a few years?

Most of that life survives by simplicity — lying dormant until the proper conditions return. The dominant form of life, though, thrives on change. It's a creature that can force its own evolution — not by natural selection, but by unnatural mutation, changing itself as conditions vary. It becomes whatever it needs to be — and after millions of swifter and swifter changes, it becomes something that can never die.

The price of eternal life had been a life with no meaning beyond simple existence. With its planet swinging wildly through the cluster, the creatures' days were spent crawling through deserts gnawing on rocks, scrabbling across ice, or diving into muck — in search of any food that couldn't get away.

The world spun this way and that, until random forces finally tossed it to the edge of the cluster, away from the constant glare of a million suns — into a stable orbit: a world that was only half day and half night; a world where clement seas welcomed diversity. Dozens of species became millions, and animals crawled up from the warm sea onto land grown green, buzzing with life.

The immortal creatures relaxed, life suddenly easy. They looked up at night, and saw stars.

They developed curiosity, then philosophy, and then science. During the day, they would squint into a sky with a thousand sparks of sun. In the night's dark, across an ocean of space, the cool billowing oval of our Milky Way Galaxy beckoned.

Some of them built vessels, and hurled themselves into the night.

It would be a voyage of a million years, but they'd lived longer than that, and had patience.

A million years before man is born and its story begins, one such vessel splashes into the Pacific Ocean. It goes deep, following an instinct to hide. The creature that it carried to Earth emerges, assesses the situation, and becomes something appropriate for survival.

For a long time it lives on the dark bottom, under miles of water, large and invincible, studying its situation. Eventually, it abandons its anaerobic hugeness and takes the form of a great white shark, the top of the food chain, and goes exploring, while most of its essence stays safe inside the vessel.

For a long time, it remembers where the vessel is, and remembers where it came from, and why. As centuries go by, though, it remembers less. After dozens of millennia, it simply lives, and observes, and changes.

It encounters humanity and notes their acquired superiority — their placement, however temporary, at the top of every food chain. It becomes a killer whale, and then a porpoise, and then a swimmer, and wades ashore naked and ignorant.

But eager to learn.

BAJA CALIFORNIA, 2019

Russell Sutton had done his stint with the US government around the turn of the century, a frustrating middle-management job in two Mars exploration programs. When the second one crashed, he had said good-bye to Uncle Sam and space in general, returning to his first love, marine biology.

He was still a manager and still an engineer, heading up the small firm Poseidon Projects. He had twelve employees, half of them Ph.D.s. They only worked on two or three projects at a time, esoteric engineering problems in marine resource management and exploration. They had a reputation for being wizards, and for keeping both promises and secrets. They could turn down most contracts — anything not sufficiently interesting; anything from the government.

So Russ was not excited when the door to his office eased open and the man who rapped his knuckles on the jamb was wearing an admiral's uniform. His first thought was that they really could afford a receptionist; his second was how to frame a refusal so that the guy would just leave, and not take up any more of his morning.

"Dr. Sutton, I'm Jack Halliburton."

That was interesting. "I read your book in graduate school. Didn't know you were in the military." The man's face was vaguely familiar from his memory of the picture on the back of *Bathyspheric Measurements and Computation*; no beard now, and a little less hair. He still looked like Don Quixote on a diet.

"Have a seat." Russ waved at the only chair not supporting stacks of paper and books. "But let me tell you right off that we don't do government work."

"I know that." He eased himself into the chair and set his hat on the floor. "That's one reason I'm here." He unzipped a blue portfolio and took out a sealed plastic folder. He turned it sideways and pressed his thumb to the corner; it read his print and popped open. He tossed it onto Russell's desk.

The first page had no title but TOP SECRET — FOR YOUR EYES ONLY, in red block letters.

"I can't open this. And as I said — "

"It's not really classified, not yet. No one in the government, outside of my small research group, even knows it exists."

"But you're here as a representative of the government, no? I assume you do own some clothes without stars on the shoulders."

"Protective coloration. I'll explain. Just look at it."

Russ hesitated, then opened the folder. The first page was a picture of a vague cigar shape looming out of a rectangle of gray smears. "That's the discovery picture. We were doing a positron radar map of the Tonga-Kermadec Trench — "

"Why on earth?"

"That part *is* classified. And irrelevant."

Russ had the feeling that his life was on a cusp, and he didn't like it.

He spun around slowly in his chair, taking in the comfortable clutter, the pictures and the charts on the wall. The picture window looking down on the Sea of Cortez, currently calm.

With his back to Halliburton, he said, "I don't suppose this is something we could do from here."

"No. We've chosen a place in Samoa."

"Now, that's attractive. Heat and humidity and lousy food."

"I tend to think pretty girls and no winter." He pushed his glasses back on his nose. "Food's not bad if you don't mind American."

Russ turned back around and studied the picture. "You have to tell me something about why you were there. Did the Navy lose something?"

"Yes."

"Did it have people in it?"

"I can't answer that."

"You just did." He turned to the second page. It was a sharper view of the object. "This isn't from positrons."

"Well, it is. But it's a composite from various angles, noise removed."

Good job, he thought. "How far down is this thing?"

"The trench is seven miles deep there. The artifact is under another forty feet of sand."

"Earthquake?"

He nodded. "A quarter of a million years ago."

Russ stared at him for a long moment. "Didn't I read about this in an old Stephen King novel?"

"Look at the next page."

It was a regular color photograph. The object lay at the bottom of a deep hole. Russ thought about the size of that digging job; the expense of it. "The Navy doesn't know about this?"

"No. We did use their equipment, of course."

"You found the thing they lost?"

"We will next week." He stared out the window. "I'll have to trust you."

"I won't turn you in to the Navy."

He nodded slowly and chose his words. "The submarine that was lost is in the trench, too. Not thirty miles from this…object."

"You didn't report it. Because?"

"I've been in the Navy for almost twenty years. Twenty years next month. I was going to retire anyhow."

"Disillusioned?"

"I never was 'illusioned.' Twenty years ago, I wanted to leave academia, and the Navy made me an interesting offer. It has been a fascinating second career. But it hasn't led me to trust the military, or the government.

"Over the past decade I've assembled a crew of like-minded men and women. I was going to take some of them with me when I retired — to set up an outfit like yours, frankly."

Russ went to the coffee machine and refreshed his cup. He offered one to Halliburton, who declined.

"I think I see what you're getting at."

"Tell me."

"You want to retire with your group and set up shop. But if you suddenly 'discover' this thing, the government might notice the co-incidence."

"That's a good approximation. Take a look at the next page."

It was a close-up of the thing. Its curved surface mirrored perfectly the probe that was taking its picture.

"We tried to get a sample of the metal for analysis. It broke every drill bit we tried on it."

"Diamond?"

"It's harder than diamond. And massive. We can't estimate its density, because we haven't been able to budge it, let alone lift it."

"Good God."

"If it were an atomic submarine, we could have hauled it up. It's not even a tenth that size.

"If it were made of lead, we could have raised it. If it were solid uranium. It's denser than that."

"I see," Russ said. "Because we raised the *Titanic*…."

"May I be blunt?"

"Always."

"We could bring it up with some version of your flotation techniques. And keep all the profit, which may be considerable. But there would be hell to pay when the Navy connection was made."

"So what's your plan?"

"Simple." He took a chart out of his portfolio and rolled it out on Russ's desk. It snapped flat. "You're going to be doing a job in Samoa...."

SAN GUILLERMO, CALIFORNIA, 1931

Before it came out of the water, it formed clothes on the outside of its body. It had observed more sailors than fishermen, so that was what it chose. It waded out of the surf wearing white utilities, not dripping wet because they were not cloth. They had a sheen like the skin of a porpoise. Its internal organs were more porpoise than human.

It was sundown, almost dark. The beach was deserted except for one man, who came running up to the changeling.

"Holy cow, man. Where'd you swim from?"

The changeling looked at him. The man was almost two heads taller than it, with prominent musculature, wearing a black bathing suit.

"Cat got your tongue, little guy?"

Mammals can be killed easily with a blow to the brain. The changeling grabbed his wrist and pulled him down and smashed his skull with one blow.

When the body stopped twitching, the changeling pinched open the thorax and studied the disposition of organs and muscles. It reconfigured itself to match, a slow and painful process. It needed to gain about 30 percent body mass, so it removed both arms, after studying them, and held them to its body until they were absorbed. It added a few handfuls of cooling entrails.

It pulled down the bathing suit and duplicated the reproductive structure that it concealed, and then stepped into the suit. Then it carried the gutted body out to deep water and abandoned it to the fishes.

It walked down the beach toward the lights of San Guillermo, a strapping handsome young man, duplicated down to the fingerprints, a process that had taken no thought, but an hour and a half of agony.

But it couldn't speak any human language and its bathing suit was on backward. It walked with a rolling sailor's gait; except for the one it had just killed, every man it had seen for the past century had been walking on board a ship or boat.

It walked toward light. Before it reached the small resort town, the sky was completely dark, moonless, and spangled with stars. Something made it stop and look at them for a long time.

The town was festive with Christmas decorations. It noticed that other people were almost completely covered in clothing. It could form more clothing on its skin, or kill another one, if it could find one the right size alone. But it didn't get the chance.

Five teenagers came out of a burger joint with a bag of hamburgers. They were laughing, but suddenly stopped dead.

"Jimmy?" a pretty girl said. "What are you doing?"

"Ain't it a little cool for that?" a boy said. "Jim?"

They began to approach it. It stayed calm, knowing it could easily kill all of them. But there was no need. They kept making noises.

"Something's wrong," an older one said. "Did you have an accident, Jim?"

"He drove out with his surfing board after lunch," the pretty girl said, and looked down the road. "I don't see his car."

It didn't remember what language was, but it knew how whales communicated. It tried to repeat the sound they had been making. "Zhim."

"Oh my God," the girl said. "Maybe he hit his head." She approached it and reached toward its face. It swatted her arms away.

"Ow! My God, Jim." She felt her forearm where it had almost fractured it.

"Mike odd," it said, trying to duplicate her facial expression.

One of the boys pulled the girl back. "Somethin' crazy's goin' on. Watch out for him."

"Officer!" the older girl shouted. "Officer Sherman!"

A big man in a blue uniform hustled across the street. "Jim Berry? What the hell?"

"He hit me," the pretty one said. "He's acting crazy."

"My God, Jim," it said, duplicating her intonation.

"Where're your clothes, buddy?" Sherman said, unbuttoning his holster.

It realized that it was in a complex and dangerous situation. It knew these were social creatures, and they were obviously communicating. Best try to learn how.

"Where're your clothes, buddy," it said in a deep bass growl.

"He might have hit his head surfing," the girl who was cradling her arm said. "You know he's not a mean guy."

"I don't know whether to take him home or to the hospital," the officer said.

"The hospital," it said.

"Probably a good idea," he said.

"Good idea," it said. When the officer touched its elbow it didn't kill him.

MID-PACIFIC, 2019

It worked like this: Poseidon Projects landed a contract from a Sea World affiliate — actually a dummy corporation that Jack Halliburton had built out of money and imagination — to raise up a Spanish-American War-era relic, a sunken destroyer, from Samoa. But no sooner had they their equipment in place than they got an urgent summons from the US Navy — there was a nuclear submarine down in the Tonga Trench, and the Navy couldn't lift it as fast as Poseidon could. There might be men still alive in it. They covered the five hundred miles as fast as they could.

Of course Jack Halliburton knew that the sub had ruptured and there was no chance of survivors. But it made it possible for Russell Sutton to ply down the length of the Tonga and Kermadec Trenches. He made routine soundings as he went, and discovered a mysterious wreck not far from the sub.

There was plenty of respectful news coverage of the two crews' efforts — Sutton's working out of professional courtesy and patriotism. Raising the *Titanic* had given them visibility and credibility. With all the derring-do and pathos and technological fascination of the submarine story, it was barely a footnote that Russ's team had seen something interesting on the way, and had claimed salvage rights.

It was an impressive sight when the sub came surging out of the depths, buoyed up by the house-sized orange balloons that Russ had brought to the task. The cameras shut down for the grisly business of removing and identifying the sailors' remains. They all came on again for the 121 flag-draped caskets on the deck of the carrier that wallowed in the sea next to the floating hulk of the sub.

Then the newspeople went home, and the actual story began.

SAN GUILLERMO, CALIFORNIA, 1931

They put a white hospital robe on it and sat it down in an examination room. It continued the safe course of imitative behavior with the doctors and nurses and with the man and woman who were the real Jimmy's father and mother, even duplicating the mother's tears.

The father and mother followed the family doctor to a room out of earshot.

"I don't know what to tell you," Dr. Farben said. "There's no evidence of any injury. He looks to be in excellent health."

"A stroke or a seizure?" the father asked.

"Maybe. Most likely. We'll keep him under observation for a few days. It might clear up. If not, you'll have to make some decisions."

"I don't want to send him to an institution," the mother said. "We can take care of this."

"Let's wait until we know more," the doctor said, patting her hand but looking at the father. "A specialist will look at him tomorrow."

They put it in a ward, where it was observant of the other patients' behavior, even to the extent of using a urinal correctly. The chemistry of the fluid it produced might have puzzled a scientist. The nurse remarked on the fishy odor, not knowing that some of it was left over from a porpoise's bladder.

It spent the night in some pain as its internal organs sorted themselves out. It kept the same external appearance. It reviewed in its mind everything it had observed about human behavior, knowing that it would be some time before it could convincingly interact.

It also reflected back about itself. It was no more a human than it had been a porpoise, a killer whale, or a great white shark. Although its memory faded over millennia, past vagueness into darkness, it had a feeling that most of it was waiting, back there in the sea. Maybe it could go back, as a human, and find the rest of itself.

A couple enjoying the salt air at dawn found a body the tide had left in a rocky pool. It had been clothed only in feasting crabs. There was nothing left of the face or any soft parts, but by its stature, the coroner could tell it had been male. A shark or something had taken both its arms, and all its viscera had been eaten away.

No locals or tourists were missing. A reporter suggested a mob murder, the arms chopped off to get rid of fingerprints. The coroner led him back to show him the remains, to explain why he thought the arms had been pulled off — twisted away — rather than chopped or sawed, but the reporter bolted halfway through the demonstration.

The coroner's report noted that from the state of decomposition of the remaining flesh, he felt the body had been immersed for no more than twelve hours. Sacramento said there were no appropriate missing persons reports. Just another out-of-work drifter. The countryside was full of them, these days, and sometimes they went for a swim with no intention of returning to shore.

Over the next two days, three brain specialists examined Jimmy, and they were perplexed and frustrated. His symptoms resembled a stroke in some ways; in others, profound amnesia from head trauma, for which there was no physical evidence. There might be a tumor involved, but the parents wouldn't give permission for x rays. This was fortunate for the changeling, because the thing in its skull was as much a porpoise brain as it was a human's, and various parts of it were nonhuman crystal and metal.

A psychiatrist spent a couple of hours with Jimmy, and got very little that was useful. His response to the word association test was interesting: he parroted back each word, mocking the doctor's German accent. In later years the doctor might classify the behavior as passive-aggressive, but what he told the parents was that at some level the boy probably had all or most of his faculties, but he had regressed to an infantile state. He suggested that the boy be sent to an asylum, where modern treatment would be available.

The mother insisted on taking him home, but first allowed the doctor to try fever therapy, injecting Jimmy with blood from a tertian malaria patient. Jimmy sat smiling for several days, his temperature unchanging — the body of the changeling consuming the malarial parasites along with other hospital food — and he was finally released to them after a week of fruitless observation.

They had retained both a male and a female nurse; their home overlooking the sea had plenty of room for both employees to stay in residence.

Both of them had worked with retarded children and adults, but within a few days they could see that Jimmy was something totally unrelated to that frustrating experience. He was completely passive but never acted bored. In fact, he seemed to be studying them with intensity.

(The female, Deborah, was used to being studied with intensity: she was pretty and voluptuous. Jimmy's intensity puzzled her because it didn't seem to be at all sexual, and a boy his age and condition ought to be brimming with sexual energy and curiosity. But her "accidental" exposures and touches provoked no response at all. He never had an erection, never tried to look down her blouse, never left any evidence of having masturbated. At this stage in its development, the changeling could only mimic behavior it had seen.)

It was learning how to read. Deborah spent an hour after dinner reading to Jimmy from children's books, tracing the words with her finger. Then she would give Jimmy the book, and he would repeat it, word for word — but in *her* voice.

She had the male nurse, Lowell, read to him, and then of course he would mimic Lowell. That made the feat less impressive, as reading. But his memory was astonishing. If Deborah held up any book he had read and pointed to it, he could recite the whole thing.

Jimmy's mother was encouraged by his progress, but his father wasn't sure, and when Jimmy's psychiatrist, Dr. Grossbaum, made his weekly visit, he sided with the father. Jimmy parroted the list of facial nerves that every medical student memorizes, and then a poem by Schiller, in faultless German.

"Unless he's secretly studied German and medicine," Grossbaum said, "he's not remembering anything from before." He told them about idiots savants, who had astonishing mental powers in some narrow specialty, but otherwise couldn't function normally. But he'd never heard of anyone changing from a normal person into an idiot savant; he promised to look into it.

Jimmy's progress in less intellectual realms was fast. He no longer was clumsy walking around the house and grounds — at first he hadn't seemed to know what doors and windows were. Lowell and Deborah taught him badminton, and after initial confusion he had a natural talent for it — not surprising, since he'd been the best tennis player in his class. They were amazed at what he could do in the swimming pool — when he first jumped in, he did two rapid lengths underwater, using a stroke neither of them could identify. When they demonstrated the Australian crawl, breast stroke, and backstroke, he "remembered" them immediately.

By the second week, he was taking his meals with the family, not only manipulating the complex dinner service flawlessly, but also communicating his desires clearly to the servants, even though he couldn't carry on a simple conversation.

His mother invited Dr. Grossbaum to dinner, so he could see how well Jimmy was getting along with the help. The psychiatrist was impressed, but not because he saw it as evidence of growth. It was like the facial nerves and German poetry; like badminton and swimming. The boy could imitate anybody perfectly. When he was thirsty, he pointed at his glass, and it was filled. That was what his mother did, too.

His parents had evidently not noticed that every time a servant made a noise at Jimmy, he nodded and smiled. When the servant's action was completed, he nodded and smiled again. That did get him a lot of food, but he was a growing boy.

Interesting that the nurses' records showed no change in weight. Exercise?

It was unscientific, but Grossbaum admitted to himself that he didn't like this boy, and for some reason was afraid of him. Maybe it was his psychiatric residency in the penal system — maybe he was projecting from that unsettling time. But he always felt that Jimmy was studying him intently, the way the intelligent prisoners had: *what can I get out of this man?*

A better psychiatrist might have noticed that the changeling treated everyone that way.

The changeling began to construct sentences on its own just after New Year's, but nothing complex, and often it was nonsense or weirdly encoded. It still "wasn't quite right," as Jimmy's mother nervously said.

The changeling didn't have to acquire intelligence, which it had in abundance, but it had to understand intelligence in a human way. That was a long stretch from any of the aquatic creatures it had successfully mimicked.

It came from a race with a high degree of social organization, but had forgotten all of that millennia ago. On Earth, it had lived as a colony of individual creatures in the dark hot depths; it had lived as a simple mat of protoplasm before that. It had lived in schools of fish, briefly, but most of its recent experience, tens of thousands of years, had been as a lone predator.

It had seen that predation was modified in these creatures; they were at the top of the food chain, but animal food had long since been killed by the time they consumed it. It naturally tried to understand the way society was organized in those terms: food was killed in some hidden or distant location, and prepared and distributed by means of mysterious processes.

The family unit was organized around food presentation and consumption, though it had other functions. The changeling recognized protection and training of the young from its aquatic associations, but was ignorant about sex and mating — when another large predator approached, it had always interpreted that as aggression, and attacked. Its kind hadn't reproduced in millions of years; that anachronism had gone the way of death. It didn't know the facts of life.

At least one woman was more than willing to provide lessons.

When it knew it would be alone for a period, the changeling practiced changing its appearance, using the people it observed as models. Changing its facial features was not too difficult; cartilage and subcutaneous fat could be moved around in a few minutes, a relatively painless process. Changing the underlying skull was a painful business that took eight or ten minutes.

Changing the whole body shape took an hour of painful concentration, and was complicated if the body had significantly more or less mass than Jimmy. For less mass, it could remove an arm or a leg, and redistribute mass accordingly. The extra part would die unless there was a reason to keep it alive, but that was immaterial; it still provided the right raw materials to reconstruct Jimmy.

Making a larger body required taking on flesh; not easy to do. The changeling assimilated Ronnie, the family's old German shepherd, in order to take the form of Jimmy's overweight father. Of course Ronnie was dead when he was reconstituted; the changeling left the body outside Jimmy's door, and the family just assumed it had gone there to say good-bye, how sweet.

The changeling had seen Mr. Berry in a bathing suit, so about 90 percent of its simulation was accurate. The other 10 percent might have made Mrs. Berry faint.

Similarly, the changeling could, in the dark privacy of Jimmy's bedroom, discard an arm and most of a leg and make itself a piece of flesh that had a shape similar to that of the nurse Deborah, at least the form she apparently had under her uniform, severely corseted. But it had no more detail than a department store dummy. The times being what they were, it could have had free rein of the house and not found any representation of a nude female.

It was still months away from being able to simulate anything like social graces, but to satisfy this particular desire, no grace was needed. Precisely at 7:30, Deborah brought in the breakfast tray.

"Please take off your clothes," it said, "and put them on the dresser."

Deborah may or may not have recognized the doctor's voice. She managed not to drop the tray. "Jimmy! Don't be silly!"

"Please," Jimmy said, smiling, as she positioned the lap tray. "I would like that very much."

"So would I," she whispered, and glanced back to see that the door was almost shut. "How about tonight? After dark?"

"I can see in the dark," it said in her whisper, husky. She slid her hand into his pajamas, and when she touched the penis an unused circuit closed, and it enlarged and rose with literally inhuman speed.

"Oh my God," she said. "Midnight?"

"Midnight," it repeated. "Oh my God."

Her smile was a cross between openmouthed astonishment and a leer. "You're strange, Jimmy." She backed out of the room, mouthing "midnight," and closed the door quietly.

The changeling noted this new erect state and experimented with it, and the unexpected result suddenly clarified a whole class of mammalian behavior it had witnessed with porpoise, dolphin, and killer whale.

The music teacher came for his twice-weekly visit, and was stupefied by the sudden change in Jimmy's ability. The boy had been a mystery from the start: before the accident, he had taken piano lessons from age ten to thirteen, the teacher was told, but had quit out of frustration, boredom, and puberty. Or so the parents thought. He must have been practicing secretly.

This current teacher, Jefferson Sheffield, had been hired on Dr. Grossbaum's recommendation. His specialty was music for therapy, and under his patient tutelage many mentally ill and retarded people had found a measure of peace and grace.

Jimmy's performance on the piano had been like his idiot-savant talent with language: he could repeat anything Sheffield did, note for note. Left to his own devices, he would either not play or reproduce one of Sheffield's lessons with perfect fidelity.

This morning it improvised. It sat down and started playing with what appeared to be feeling, making up things that used the lessons as raw material, but transposed and inverted them, and linked them with interesting cadenzas and inventive chord changes.

He played for exactly one hour and stopped, for the first time looking up from the keyboard. Sheffield and most of the family and staff were sitting or standing around, amazed.

"I had to understand something," it said to no one in particular. But then it gave Deborah a look that made her tremble.

Dr. Grossbaum joined Sheffield and the family for lunch. The changeling realized it had done something seriously wrong, and retreated into itself.

"You've done something wonderful, son," Sheffield said. It looked at him and nodded, usually a safe course of action. "What caused the breakthrough?" It nodded again, and shrugged, in response to the interrogative tone.

"You said that you had to understand something," he said.

"Yes," it said, and into the silence: "I had to understand something." It shook its head, as if to clear it. "I had to *learn* something."

"That's progress," Grossbaum said. "Verb substitution."

"I had to find something," it said. "I had to be something. I had to be some...one."

"Playing music let you be someone different?" Grossbaum said.

"Someone different," it repeated, studying the air over Grossbaum's head. "Make...made. Made me someone different."

"Music made you someone different," Sheffield said with excitement.

It considered this. It understood the semantic structure of the statement, and knew that it was wrong. It knew that what made it different was new knowledge about that unnamed part of its body, how it would stiffen and leak something new. But it knew that humans acted mysteriously about that part, and so decided not to demonstrate its new knowledge, even though the part was stiff again.

It saw that Grossbaum was looking at that part, and reduced blood flow, to make it less prominent. But he had noticed; his eyebrow went up a fraction of an inch. "It's not all music," he said, "is it?"

"It's all music," the changeling said.

"I don't understand."

"You don't understand," the changeling looked at its hands. "It's all music."

"*Life* is all music," Sheffield said. The changeling looked at him and nodded. Then it rose and crossed the room to the piano, and started playing, which seemed safer than talking.

It was awake at midnight, when the door eased open. Deborah closed it silently behind her and padded on bare feet to the bed. She was wearing oversized men's pajamas.

"You have clothes," it said.

"I just got up to get a glass of milk," she said, confusing it. The fluid it produced that way was not milk, and to fill a glass would take all night.

She read its expression almost correctly and smiled. "In case I get caught, silly."

A little moonlight filtered through the curtains. The changeling adjusted its irises and made it bright as day, watching her slowly unbutton the pajama top.

It noted the actual size and disposition of breasts, not the way they appeared when she was clothed. The pigmentation and placement of nipples and aureoles. (It had wondered about its own nipples, which seemed to have no function.)

She slipped into bed next to it, and it attempted to pull down the pajama bottoms.

"Naughty, naughty." She kissed it on the mouth and moved one of its hands to a breast.

The kiss was odd, but it was something it had seen, and returned with a little force.

"Oh my," she whispered. "You're hot." She reached down and stroked the part that had no name. "Aren't you the cat's pajamas."

That was pretty confusing. "No, I'm not."

"Just a saying." It moved both hands over her body, studying, measuring. Most of it was similar to the male body it inhabited, but the differences were interesting.

"Oh," she said. "More." It was studying the place that was most different. Deborah began to excrete fluid there. It went deeper. She moaned and rubbed its hand with the wet tissues there.

She closed her hand over the unnamed part, and stroked it softly. It wondered whether it was an appropriate time to leak fluid itself, and began to.

"Oh no," she said; "oh my." She shucked off her pajama bottoms and slid up his body to clasp him there, with her own wet parts, and move up and down.

It was an extraordinary sensation, similar to what he had done alone earlier, but much more intense. It allowed the body's reflexes to take over, and they pounded together perhaps a dozen times, and then its body totally concentrated on that part, galvanized, and explosively excreted — three, four, five times, the pressure decreasing.

It breathed hard into the space between her breasts. She slid down to join her mouth with its. She inserted her tongue, which was probably not an offering of food. It reciprocated.

She rolled over onto her back, breathing hard. "Glad you remember something."

EURASIA, PRE-CHRISTIAN ERA

The changeling wasn't alone on the planet. There was another creature, unrelated, who had lived on Earth longer than he could remember; who had lived thousands of lives, disappearing when he got too
old, to reappear as a young man.

He was always a man, and usually a brute.

Call him the chameleon: an alpha male who never had sons, unless an adulterer cooperated. Unlike the changeling, he did have DNA,
but it was alien; he could no more reproduce with a human than he
could with a rock or a tree.

Also unlike the changeling, he seemed to be stuck in human form.
It never occurred to him to wonder why this was so. But it didn't occur to him for tens of millennia — not until the Renaissance — that he
might have come from another world. He assumed that he was some
sort of demon or demigod, but early on realized that it was a mistake
to advertise the fact. He couldn't be killed, not even by fire, but he
did feel pain, and he felt it profoundly, in ways a human never could.
At low levels it was pleasure, and he sought out varieties of that. But
hanging and crucifixion were experiences he never wanted to do a
second time. To be burned to ashes was agony beyond belief, and re-
constructing yourself afterward was worse.

So after a few experiences that probably helped establish the myth
of the vampire, the chameleon settled into routine existence, seria-
tim lives that were fairly ordinary.

He was usually a warrior, and of course a good one. Sometimes his
career was cut short by being chopped in two or trampled or drawn
and quartered. In the chaos of battle he could usually find a few minutes of darkness, to pull himself together, and then go off in search of
another life. When his death and interment were witnessed by many,
he had to fake a grave robbery or, reluctantly, a miracle.

In ancient times, he occasionally wound up being a warlord or
even a king, by dint of superiority in battle and an instinct to advance.
But that was always more trouble than it was worth, and made it almost impossible to arrange a private death and resurrection.

Like the changeling, he was a quick study, but he was a sensualist, indifferent to knowledge. All he needed to know in order to survive, his body already knew. The rest was just for maximizing pleasure and minimizing pain that was too great to enjoy.

He picked the right side in the Peloponnesian Wars, and went through several generations as a Spartan. Then he joined Alexander's army and wound up settling in Persia. He spent a century or so as a Parthian before he eased into the Roman sphere.

It was as a Parthian that he heard the story of Jesus Christ, which interested him. Killed in public and then resurrected, he was evidently a relative. He would keep an eye out for him.

The chameleon entered the history books only once, and it was because of his interest in Christianity. In the third century, in Narbonne, he was a captain of the Praetorian Guard, and was a little too open in his curiosity about the fellow immortal. An enemy reported him, and Diocletian had him executed as a closet Christian, by archers. But his girlfriend, Irene, wouldn't leave him alone to die, and he "miraculously" recovered. Diocletian subsequently had him beaten to a pulp by soldiers with iron rods, whereupon Irene let him stay dead long enough to turn into a young soldier and escape, leaving behind the legend of Saint Sebastian.

He worked as a farmhand and soldier in Persia until 313, when the Edict of Milan made it safe to be a Christian. When he heard about that, he dropped his plow and walked to Italy, robbing people along the way, just enough to get by.

He didn't like being so close to authority, so he went back to France and shuffled between Gallia and Germania for awhile, keeping an eye out for other immortals. Things got ugly in the 542 plague, so he made his way over to England as part of the Saxon invasion.

England seemed more congenial than the Continent, as the Roman empire collapsed into chaos, and the chameleon lived many lifetimes there, first as soldier and farmer, but eventually learning a variety of trades: blacksmith, cobbler, butcher.

In 1096, he went back to soldiering, following the Crusades down to Jerusalem and beyond. He fought on both sides for a century or so, and eventually, as an Arab, went back to Egypt and started walking south along the Nile.

Making himself dark and tall, he became a Masai warrior, and it was the best life he'd yet encountered: lots of women and great food and, in exchange for a battle every now and then, sleep late in the morning and hunt for game with spears, which he enjoyed. He did that for several hundred years, still keeping an eye out for Christ or another relative, probably white.

But the first white people who showed up were bearing guns and chains. He could have resisted and conveniently "died," but he'd heard about the New World and was curious.

The ride over was about the worst thing he'd ever experienced — right up there with being boiled in oil or flayed to death. He lay in chains for weeks, stuffed in an airless hold with hundreds of others, many of whom died and lay rotting until someone got around to throwing them overboard.

It was a real chore. He thought about just bursting his chains, at night, and diving into the sea. He'd done that before, in Phoenicia, and swam dozens of leagues to shore. But Africa, after a few days under sail, would be months of swimming, so he'd just be trading one agony for another.

So he allowed himself to be carried to America, and in a way enjoyed being put up on the block — he was by far the healthiest specimen off the ship, since metabolism was irrelevant to him, other than as a source of pleasure. The Georgia man who bought him, though, was cruel. He liked to whip the new boys into submission, so at the first opportunity, the chameleon killed him, and then turned into a white man and walked away.

That was an amusing time. His version of English was almost a thousand years old, so he had to masquerade as an idiot while he learned how to communicate. He walked north, again robbing and murdering for sustenance, when he knew he wouldn't be caught.

He kept moving north until he got to Boston, and settled in there for a few hundred years.

[excerpts from]
Troll: A Love Story

Johanna Sinisalo
Translated by Herbert Lomas

I'm starting to get worried. Martes's face seems to be sort of fluctuating in the light fog induced by my four pints of Guinness. His hand's resting on the table close to mine. I can see the dark hairs on the back of his hand, his sexy, bony finger-joints and his slightly distended veins. My hand slides toward his and, as if our hands were somehow joined together under the table, his moves away in a flash. Like a crab into its hole.

I look him in the eyes. His face wears a friendly, open, and understanding smile. He seems at once infinitely lovable and completely unknown. His eyes are computer icons, expressionless diagrams, with infinite wonders behind them, but only for the elect, those able to log on.

"So why did you ask me out for a drink? What did you have in mind?"

Martes leans back in his chair. So relaxed. So carefree. "Some good conversation."

"Nothing more?"

He looks at me as if I've exposed something new about myself, something disturbing but paltry: a bit compromising, but not something that will inexorably affect a good working relationship.

It's more as if my deodorant were inadequate.

"I have to tell you honestly that I'm not up for it."

My heart starts pounding and my tongue responds on reflex, acting faster than my brain.

"It was you who began it."

When we were little and there was a schoolyard fight, the most important thing was whose fault it was. Who began it.

And as I go on Martes looks at me as if I weren't responsible for my behavior.

"I'd never have let myself in for this…if you hadn't shown me, so clearly, you were up for it. As I've told you, I'm hot shit at avoiding emotional hangups. If I've really no good reason to think the other person's interested I don't let anything happen. Not a thing. Hell, I don't even think it."

Memories are crowding through my mind while I'm sounding off — too angrily, I know. I'm recalling the feel of Martes in my arms, his erection through the cloth of his pants as we leaned on the Tammerkoski River bridge railings that dark night. I can still feel his mouth on mine, tasting of cigarettes and Guinness, his mustache scratching my upper lip, and it makes my head start to reel.

Martes reaches for his cigarettes, takes one, flicks it into his mouth, lights his Zippo and inhales deeply, with deep enjoyment.

"I can't help it if I'm the sort of person people project their own dreams and wishes onto."

In his opinion nothing has happened.

In his opinion it's all in my imagination.

I crawl home at midnight, staggering and limping — it's both the beer and the wound deep inside me. Tipsily, I'm licking my wound like a cat: my thought probes it like a loose tooth, inviting the dull sweet pain over and over again — dreams and wishes that won't stand the light of day.

The street lamps sway in the wind. As I turn in through the gateway from Pyynikki Square, sleet and crushed lime leaves blow in with me. There's loud talk in the corner of the yard.

A loathsome bunch of kids are up to something in the corner by the trash cans — young oafs, jeans hanging off their asses and their tattered windbreakers have lifted to show bare skin. They've got their backs to me, and one of them's goading another, using that tone they have when they're challenging someone to perform some deed of daring. This time it's to do with something I can't see, at their feet. Normally I'd give thugs like these a wide berth — they make my flesh crawl. They're just the sort that make me hunch up my shoulders if I pass them in the street, knowing I can expect some foul-mouthed insult — but just now, because of Martes, because I don't give a damn about anything and with my blood-alcohol count up, I go up to them.

"This is private property, it belongs to the apartment building. Trespassers will be prosecuted."

A few heads turn — they sneer — and then their attention goes back to whatever's at their feet.

"Afraid it'll bite?" one asks another. "Give it a kick."

"Didn't you hear? This is private property. Get the fuck out of here." My voice rises, my eyes sting with fury. An image from my childhood is flashing through my brain: a gang of bullies from an older class are towering above me, sneering at me, and goading me in that same tone — "Afraid it'll bite?" — and then they stuff my mouth with gravelly snow.

"Shove it up your ass, sweetie," one of these juvenile delinquent coos tenderly. He knows I've no more power over them than a fly.

"I'll call the police."

"I've called them already," says a voice behind me. The ornery old woman who lives on the floor below me and covers her rent by acting as some kind of caretaker has materialized behind me. The thugs shrug their shoulders, twitch their jackets, blow their noses onto the ground with a swagger and dawdle away, as if it was their choice. They shamble off through the gateway, manfully swearing, and the last one flicks his burning cigarette butt at us like a jet-propelled missile. They've hardly reached the street before we hear anxious running feet.

The lady snorts. "Well, they did do what they were told."

"Are the police coming?"

"'Course not. Why bother the police with scum like that? I was off to the Grill House myself."

The adrenaline's cleared my head for a moment, but now, as I struggle to dig out my keys, my fingers feel like a bunch of sausages. The woman's on her way to the gate, and that's fine, because my pissed brain's buzzing with a rigid, obsessive curiosity. I wait until she's off and start peering among the garbage cans.

And there, tucked among the cans, some young person is sleeping on the asphalt. In the dark I can only make out a black shape among the shadows.

I creep closer and reach out my hand. The figure clearly hears me coming. He weakly raises his head from the crouching position for a moment, opens his eyes, and I can finally make out what's there. It's the most beautiful thing I've ever seen. I know straight away that I want it.

It's small, slender and it's curled up in a strange position, as if it were completely without joints. Its head is between its knees, and its full black mane of hair is brushing the muddy pavement.

It can't be more than a year old. A year and a half at the most. A mere cub. By no means the huge bulk you see in illustrations of the full-grown specimens.

It's hurt or been abandoned, or else it's strayed away from the others. How did it get to the courtyard of an apartment building in the middle of the town? Suddenly my heart starts thumping and I swing around, half expecting to see a large black hunched shadow slipping from the garbage cans to the gate and then off into the shelter of the park.

I react instinctively. I crouch down by it and carefully bend one of its forearms behind its back. It stirs but doesn't struggle. Just in case, I twist the strap of my bag all around the troll so that its paws are fastened tightly to its side. I glance behind me and lift it up in my arms. It's light, bird-boned, weighing far less than a child the same size. I glance quickly at the windows. There's nothing but a reddish light glowing in the downstairs neighbor's bedroom. The glamorous head of a young woman pops up in the window, her hand drawing the curtain. Now.

In a moment we're in my apartment.

It's very weak. When I lower it onto the bed it doesn't struggle at all, just contemplates me with its reddish-orange feline eyes with vertical pupils. The ridge of its nose protrudes rather more than a cat's, and its nostrils are large and expressive. The mouth is in no way like the split muzzle of a cat or a dog: it's a narrow, horizontal slit. The whole face is so human-looking — like the face of the American woolly monkey or some other flat-faced primate. It's easy to understand why these black creatures have always been regarded as some sort of forest people who live in caves and holes, chance mutations of nature, parodies of mankind.

In the light, its cubbishness is even more obvious. Its face and body are soft and round, and it has the endearing ungainliness of all young animals. I examine its front paws: they're like a rat's or raccoon's, with flexible, jointed fingers and long nails. I untie it, and the cub makes no move to scratch or bite. It just turns on its side and curls up, drawing its tufted tail between its thighs and folding its front paws against its chest. Its tangled black mane falls over its nose, and it lets out that half-moan/half-sigh of a dog falling asleep.

I stand at the bedside, looking at the troll-cub and taking in a strong smell — not unpleasant, though. It's like crushed juniper berries with a hint of something else — musk, patchouli? The troll hasn't moved an inch. Its bony side heaves to the fast pace of its breathing.

Hesitantly I take a woolen blanket from the sofa, stand by the bed a while, and then spread it over the troll. One of its hind legs gives a kick, like a reflex, swift and strong as lightning, and the blanket flies straight over my face. I struggle with it, my heart pumping wildly, for I'm convinced the frightened beast will go for me, scratching and biting. But no. The troll lies there curled up and breathing peacefully. It's only now that I face the fact that I've brought a wild beast into my home.

My head and neck are aching. I've been sleeping on the sofa. It's ridiculously early; still dark. And there's nothing on the bed. So that's what it's all been: a fantasy that won't survive the first light of day.

Except that the blanket lies crumpled on the floor by the bed, and there's a faint little sound coming from the bathroom.

I get up and walk slowly, in the light of the streetlamps filtering through the window, creeping as quietly as I can to the bathroom door. In the dusk I can see a small black bony bottom, hind legs, a tufted twitching tail, and I realize what's happening. It's drinking from the toilet bowl. The juniper-berry smell is pungent. Then I spot a yellow puddle on my mint-green tiled floor. Naturally.

It has stopped lapping up water and has sensed that I'm there. Its torso is up from the bowl so fast I can't see the movement. Its face is dripping with water. I'm trying to convince myself that the water is perfectly clean, drinkable. I'm trying to remember when I last scrubbed the bowl. Its eyes are still dull, it doesn't look healthy, and its pitch-black coat is sadly short of gloss. I move aside from the bathroom door, and it slides past me into the living room, exactly as an animal does when it's got another route to take — pretending to be unconcerned but vividly alert. It walks on two legs, with a soft and supple lope: not like a human being, slightly bent forwards, its front paws stretched away from its sides — ah, on tiptoe, like a ballet dancer. I follow it and watch it bounce on to my bed, effortlessly, like a cat, as though gravity didn't exist — then curl up and go back to sleep again.

I go back to the kitchen for a cereal bowl, fill it with water and put it by the bed. Then I start mopping up the bathroom floor, though I've got a splitting headache. What the hell do trolls eat?

Back in my study, I leave the door open, boot up my computer, connect to the Internet and type TROLL.

http://www.finnishnature.fi

Troll (older forms: hobgoblin, bugbear, ogre), *Felipithecus trollius*. Family: Cat-apes (Felipithecidae)

A pan-Scandinavian carnivore, found only north of the Baltic and in western Russia. Disappeared completely from Central Europe along with deforestation but, according to folklore and historical sources, still fairly common in medieval times.

Not officially discovered, and scientifically classified as a mammal, until 1907. Before then assumed to be a mythical creature of folklore and fairy tale.

Weight of a full-grown male: 50–75 kg. Height standing upright: 170–190 cm. A long-limbed plantigrade, whose movements nevertheless show digitigrade features. Walk: upright on two legs. Four long-nailed toes on the hindlimbs, five on the forelimbs, both including a thumb-like gripping toe. The tail long, with a tuft. The tongue rough. The overall color a deep black, the coat dense, sleek. A thick black mane on the head of the males. Movement only at night. Main nourishment: small game, carrion, birds' nests, and chicks. Hibernates. Cubs probably conceived in the autumn before hibernation, the female giving birth to one or two cubs in spring or early summer. About the behavior of this animal, however, so extremely shy of human contact, there is very little scientific knowledge. Extremely rare. Supposedly there are about four hundred specimens in Finland. Classified as an endangered species.

This is making me no wiser. I click on SEARCH and come up with the following:

http://www.netzoo.fi/mammals/carnivores

Because of their great outward resemblance to humans or apes, trolls were originally mistaken for close relatives of the hominids; but further study has demonstrated that the case is one of convergent evolution. Misclassified a primate, the species was first erroneously designated "the Northern Troglodyte Ape" (Latin: *Troglodytas borealis*). Later it was observed that the troll belonged to a completely independent family of carnivores, the Felipithecidae, but the apelike attributions survived for a time in the nomenclature, *Felipithecus troglodytas*. At present, the established, scientifically accepted nomenclature of the species still bows to popular tradition as *Felipithecus trollius*. An interesting episode in the naming of the troll was a suggestion from the prestigious Societas pro Fauna et Flora: relying on the mythical and demonic connotations, they proposed the name *Felipithecus satanus.*

Only one other species of the Felipithecidae is known, the almost extinct yellow cat-ape (*Felipithecus flavus*), a roughly lynx-sized creature whose habitat is the heart of the Indonesian rain forest. The common ancestor of the species is believed, on fossil evidence, to have inhabited Southeast Asia.

Though, on the evidence of its mode of life and dentition, the troll is clearly a carnivore, many scientists consider that the species does not properly belong to the order of Carnivora. Theories exist that the troll is more closely related to the insectivores and primates than to the true feline predators, and this is supported by certain anatomical features.

It has been suggested that several other species whose existence has not been scientifically established beyond doubt (such as the legendary Tibetan "Abominable Snowman," or Yeti, of hearsay, and the mythical North American Sasquatch, or "Bigfoot") may also be humanity-shunning representatives of the Felipithecidae family.

Firm proof of the existence of *Felipithecus trollius* was not obtained until 1907, when the Biological and Botanical Department of the Tsar Alexander University of Helsinki received the carcass of a full-grown troll that had been discovered dead. There had been previous reports of firsthand sightings of trolls, but this legendary creature, oft-mentioned in folk tradition and in the *Kalevala*, was considered a purely mythical beast in scientific circles. Clearly, the occasional troll-cub encountered in the wilderness served to maintain myths of gnomes and goblins, especially in light of the theory that the trolls regulate any great increase in their population by abandoning newborn offspring.

The troll's ability to merge with the terrain, the inaccessibility of its habitat, its aversion to human contact, its silent night-habits and its hibernation in cave-dens, causing them rarely to leave snow tracks, may partially explain the late discovery of the species. The troll's zoological history is thus very similar to those of, for example, the okapi, not identified until 1900, the Komodo dragon (1912), and the giant panda (1937). In spite of abundant oral tradition and many sightings by the aboriginal population, accounts of these animals were long classified by scientists as myth and folklore. It is worth remembering that an estimated 14 million subspecies of animals live on the planet, of which only about 1.7 million are recognized and classified, less than 15% of all species. The relatively large cloven-footed animals, *Meganuntiacus vuquangensis* and *Pseudoryx nghetinhensis*, for example, were only discovered in 1994...

As I sit at my computer I glance from time to time at the bedroom. When I was drunk it seemed a hell of a good idea to bring this touching, rejected wild-animal cub into my pad. An animal that may grow as much as two meters tall.

But even now, when I'm totally sober, the animal has something absolutely captivating about it. Is it just a professional's appreciation of its visual grace?

Or is it that as soon as I see something beautiful I have to possess it? With my camera or with my eye or with my hand? Through the shutter or by shutting the door?

Even though I won't know what to do with it?

But nothing changes the fact that the creature's still small. And sick. And weak. And totally abandoned.

I print off a whole load of Internet material, without feeling it's any help. I return to netzoo and click on EVOLUTION.

I learn that "convergent evolution" refers to species that develop in ways resembling each other without there being any close zoological relationship. Good examples are the shark, the ichthyosaur, and the dolphin, which have developed from completely different vertebrate forms: the shark from fish, the ichthyosaur from land-dwelling reptiles, and the dolphin from land mammals. Nevertheless, they've all developed into streamlined, finned and tailed animals in the same ecological group: swift piscivorous marine predators. There are many other examples: grassland-dwelling flightless birds, such as the emu, the ostrich, and the extinct moa; or such semi-aquatic marine creatures as seals, sea lions, and herbivorous sirenians, notably the dugong and the endangered manatee.

I'm getting more informed than I ever wanted to be. According to the entry, convergent evolution means that, in widely separated terrains, the same atmospheric and environmental conditions can, through their physical properties, produce similar kinds of living organisms from totally different prototypes. Cases of convergent evolution are, on the one hand, the trolls and the Southeast Asian cat-apes, derived from a small arboreal animal slightly resembling the mustelid or raccoon, and, on the other, the apes and hominids derived from proto-primate mammals. Both occupied the same ecological niche, where bipedalism and prehensile forefingers were survival factors for the species...

Nothing to help me, though.

I look at my computer. It's just a machine.

I'll have to try elsewhere.

I can only speculate about the effect of the telephone ringing at Dr. Spiderman's — at my old flame Jori Hamalainen's, that is — "Hama-hama-hamalâinen," because getting worked up always makes him stammer. Hamahakki being Finnish for spider, he's naturally been dubbed "Spiderman." Eight rings before he replies, and his voice reveals he's ready to flip his lid.

First I fumble for the customary "How are things?", etc., but I know that this road will soon be blocked.

"Sweet Angel, golden-haired cherub," comes Spider's slightly nasal, taunting voice. "It's not very long ago you gave me a very nasty kick in the gluteus — after scarcely a couple of months of your angelic blessings. So what, I wonder, makes you call me now? And especially at this early hour."

I splutter something about how I thought we'd agreed to be friends.

"I was beginning to think your mother had talked some sense into you — she always did dream you'd be partners with a real doctor, didn't she?" Spider lashes out, making me blush. Then his tone changes, sounding almost interested. "You didn't manage to net that guy, did you?"

It's already coming home to me that this call is a terrible mistake, but Spiderman goes on relentlessly.

"There you were, your great blue eyes moist with tears, trying to stammer out that I'm not your type, that I'm not the right one, and how you'd be wounding me if you went on with a relationship where you yourself couldn't be a hundred percent committed. And meanwhile you were going on about that other guy the whole time."

Was I really? Hell, it was possible. As if I could have possessed him by talking about him, throwing his name about, would be casually.

"You really relished his name on your tongue. Martti, Martti — Martti this and Martti that. Guess how flagrant and repellent it sounded. And it was crystal clear that all your would-be serious, pretty little speech meant was this: you wanted me out of the way, so you could be free to step on the gas when this object of distant adoration — obviously your right — and — proper future commitment — gave the green light. Or what?"

I'm speechless. Incapable of saying anything.

"So then. What do you want?"

I clear my throat. This isn't going to be easy.

"What do you know about trolls?"

There's a howl of demonic laughter in my ear. "Angel, darling, now I must have your permission to be inquisitive. Are you writing an essay for school?"

I mumble something stupid about having a bet on it. "You know," I wind up helplessly, "about the sorts of things they eat." I can feel the receiver radiating embarrassed silence into Spiderman's ear.

He finally bursts out, "You ring an expensive veterinary surgeon at eight-thirty on a Sunday morning to ask what trolls eat?"

I know Spider can be a prick and always is, given the chance, but then he's never been able to resist an opportunity to show off his knowledge either. I'm right. A familiar lecturing tone creeps into his voice.

He starts ticking items off. "Frogs, small mammals. They rob birds' nests. Sometimes they've been reported to prey on lambs in outlying fields, but that's probably just rumor. There's a theory that they fish with their paws, like bears, which I've no reason to doubt. Hares. Game birds. Now and then a reindeer-calf caught by the leg can end up as a troll's dinner. Sometimes they harass white-tailed deer, too. They eat carrion when they come across it. A full-grown individual requires a kilo or two of animal protein a day. Any more questions?"

I nod at the receiver and let out assenting noises.

"Definitely carnivores, but not omnivorous like, for instance, bears. Similar digestive system to cats. So if you're betting that trolls gnaw at spruce shoots by moonlight, your money's down the drain. And if you want more information, Angel, my fairy queen, go to the library and consult Pulliainen's *The Large Predators of Finland*."

And then, cuttingly, he hangs up.

On the bed a lusterless black flank is heaving feverishly. Wild-cat digestion.

I dash to the fridge and poke about frantically. Orange marmalade, kalamata olives, fresh but already somewhat wilted arugula, imported blue cheese.

A cat. A cat. What do cats eat?

Cat food.

And in a flash I recollect something: what's the guy's name downstairs? Kaikkonen? Korhonen? Koistinen? The man with the young foreign wife. They've got some sort of a pet. Once I saw the man opening the front door, about to go in, and he was carrying a red-leather harness.

So they've got a cat, for I've seen neither of them walking a dog.

PALOMITA:

Sleep's a well — I float up from it like a bubble. The water's black honey. My arms and legs are trying to stir in the syrupy night. I drag my lids open, so my eyes smart.

I'm damp with sweat and my heart's starting to race. For a moment I think the sound I hear is the bell on the bar counter back at Ermita. The bell that orders me out of the back room. But luckily my hand touches something, my eyes open, and I'm surrounded by the gray-blue of the room's make-believe night.

I've been in a very deep sleep, as I always am when Pentti's away. When I'm alone, as soon as I drop off I feel I'm spinning downward. I don't need to tense every bit of my body, like when Pentti's beside me. No need to wake up at every sound. Pentti, when he's asleep, sounds like someone suffocating.

The ringing isn't at all like the horrible silvery bar-bell at Ermita. It's tinnier and rougher and makes you jump. Ring-ring-ring it goes in the empty hall that Pentti's removed all the coats from and locked them up in the closet for the time he's off on his trip. I slip my slippers on and get my bathrobe off the chair. The bell rings again and again, as if someone's in a terrible state. I get the footstool out of the cupboard and climb on it to peep through the peephole.

It's the man from upstairs who's ringing the bell. He's fair and tall and curly-haired. I've seen him once before on the staircase outside.

I've learned always to look through the peephole. Pentti doesn't want me to open the door to anyone except those he's told me to. The peephole's a well, where little crooked people live. Many times a day I get on to the stool and look out at the staircase. There aren't often people there, but whenever I see one it's a reward. The man rings the bell once more, and then he tosses his head. He's giving up.

I've no idea why I do. But cautiously I open the door.

He's speaking Finnish fast, and I can only pick up a word here and there. The words are twisty and misty, and they've long bits that ought to be said with your mouth open right to the back. Lucky for me I don't have to depend much on Finnish, as Pentti hardly says anything and I don't go anywhere.

The man says, "Excuse me." He says his name, which I can't hear properly, but it sounds like Miguel. He says he's from the floor above, and he keeps on asking for some sort of food and repeating some word I simply don't know.

It seems to be dawning on him that I don't understand. Up to now he's only been able to see his own problem, but now he's beginning to see me. He begins speaking English, which I understand better, though not very well either, because at home we spoke Chabacano and Tagalog in the village, and they had to cut school short for me.

"Cat food?" he asks. "Do you have any cat food you could lend me?"

In spite of myself, a smile crosses my face. We haven't got a cat. Pentti wouldn't put up with anything like that. Once, when he was drunk again, he took a lucky doll I'd been given by Conchita at the bar and flushed it down the toilet. He'd noticed I used to nurse it in my arms sometimes, before going to bed. The doll clogged the drain, and Pentti had to pump away with a plunger for ages before it flushed clear again.

I shake my head and say no, no cat food. I ask if he speaks Spanish, but he signals no, with troubled eyes. I grope for some English words, trying to help. Just around the corner there's a small store that sells almost everything. One evening Pentti sent me to get some beer there, gave me some money and a piece of paper with the order scribbled on. I handed them over to the shopkeeper, and he handed me back six cold brown bottles. I didn't know I was supposed to get a receipt, and when I got back Pentti said I'd kept some of the change. Myself, I did think they were a bit expensive. I haven't been back to the little shop since, but I do remember it was stocked with almost as much stuff as the market.

Miguel wrinkles his forehead. I feel sorry for him. I can't understand why he can't run those two blocks to the deli/newsstand, which is almost a little department store, but I'm eager to think of some way to help him. I think about cats, I think about what they eat. Cats swarm in the harbor. They love fish.

I leave the door open and rush into the kitchen. I open the freezer and take out a packet from a big bag of frozen fish Pentti bought on sale. The packets rattle like firewood. I go back to the door and push a frosty packet into Miguel's hand.

"The microwave. Put it in the microwave," I say, clearly. Those are words I've often heard, and I know them well. Miguel stares at the packet of fish and shifts it from hand to hand because it's so cold.

He squeezes the packet. Thanks flow from his lips in a mixture of English and Finnish. And then he's off, hopping up the stairs, a man with an angelically beautiful face and hair like a wheatfield in sunshine. I hear the door slam shut on the floor above.

I must try to pay this back in some way, I reflect, as I push the fish into the microwave. She must be a Filipina, for she speaks a little English and Spanish; she looks Asian. Is she more than sixteen years old? A bought bride, she must be, purchased for the old geezer down below at some marriage market.

And they have no cat. My face glows: I ought to have been quicker on the uptake about that pretty, soft, red-leather harness.

I set the microwave on "defrost" and start it. When the humming begins, the troll's ears perk up. It gives a jerk but, as nothing's threatening it, it calms down again. The smell of fish spreads through the room. I take the dish out of the microwave and test the fish with my finger. It's warm around the edges and has begun to turn pale; it's frozen in the middle, but most of it is at room temperature and a gelatinous gray. I slice some pieces off the defrosted bits, put them on aluminum foil, and take them into the living room. The troll's nostrils tremble, but it shows no interest in what it smells. I take some fish in my hand and sit on the edge of the bed. The troll opens its eyes slightly and regards me with its vertical pupils. I hold a piece of fish close to its nostrils, its mouth. It sniffs at the fish faintly, wearily, then closes its eyes again and turns its head away almost humanly. It curls its black slender bony back towards me, and its belly gives out a very, very small but recognizable sound: the rumble of hunger.

It looks at me like a puppy dog, but there are live coals in its orange eyes.

It's lying curled up into a ball. I go to the bedside gingerly and hold my breath as I sit down on the edge of the bed beside it and observe its slender, heaving black sides, its helpless but sinewy being. Suddenly its paw straightens out. Its long supple fingers and fierce nails come toward me, and I almost snatch my hand away but don't, I don't, and its fingers wrap around my wrist for a moment; its hot slender paw touches me: for a fleeting moment, and my eyes fill with tears.

Three days have gone by, and it simply isn't eating.

Dr. Spiderman had mentioned birds' nests. I tried a raw egg first, cracked into a bowl, then an unshelled one, but it wouldn't have either of them. I went to the supermarket for some quails' eggs, and it did show a little interest in these, but perhaps it was just their color, spottedness, and small size reminding it of something. Anyway it didn't eat those either.

I look at the black figure on the bed, at once restless, exhausted, and — it's obvious — painfully hungry. I can't let it outside. Out there are the thugs in their steel-toe-capped boots, getting their thrills by drenching drunks with gasoline, throwing cats from the roofs of multi-story blocks, and mugging gays. And if I tell anyone I'll just as certainly lose the creature.

Its juniper-berry smell plays in my nostrils. Its own species didn't want it. It was too much ballast, a burden. They abandoned this light, slender, supple being, worthy of being immortalized in black marble.

Back to the cursed highway of knowledge, to the electronic asphalt, stretching in all directions, with no path leading where it should: to the forest.

For the hell of it, I put the cursor on to the *Kalevala* link of netzoo and click there. The net *Kalevala* has its own index. I wait briefly while the machine scrolls up references to trolls and demons. There's no end of them. The biggest group is in the poem called "The Demon Skis," where Lemminkdinen, skiing along, is chasing a demon that's scampering away from him, and the demon, as it dashes off, sends the stewpots flying in a Lapland village. I log on to the bride's guide poem, "Instructions and a Warning." Here the bride complains about her bridegroom, and this makes me think of the Filipino girl downstairs:

> *I'd be better off*
> *in better places,*
> *with larger lands,*
> *and roomier rooms,*
> *a fuller-blooded man,*
> *better built;*
> *I'm given to this no-good,*
> *left with this loafer:*
> *took his carcass from a crow,*
> *robbed his nose from a raven,*
> *mouthed like a famished wolf,*
> *haired like hell's troll,*
> *bellied like a bear.*

That's the complete demon reference. I wasn't expecting to find instructions for feeding trolls in the *Kalevala*, but, surprisingly, the falling meter sweeps you along. The following troll fragment is, very aptly, Vainambinen's, which he sings to the accompaniment of a *kantele*.

> *None in the forest*
> *that loped on four legs,*
> *that bounded and bobbed,*
> *but lingered to listen,*
> *suck in some ecstasy:*
> *squirrels came switching*
> *from leaf-spray to leaf-spray,*
> *stoats came and stopped there,*
> *settled on fences.*
> *Elks hopped on the heath,*
> *lynxes leaped about laughing.*

A wolf woke in the swamp,
a troll rose on the rocks,
a bear reared on the heath
from its pen in the pines,
its den in the spruce thicket.

I've had my fill of the *Kalevala*. The SEARCH function locates links here and there — to biology, mythology, various fairy tales, and old stories in their hundreds if not thousands. But nothing concrete. I'll have to look elsewhere.

I've already been out of the apartment several times, and every time I come back to find my troll in the same place on the bed, heart-rendingly in almost the same position, scarcely able to raise its head.

It stands in a museum display-cabinet on the ground floor of the library, looking like a streamlined thundercloud. Its coat has lost much of its shiny black during the years spent in the glass case. To suggest the beast's environment, it's been surrounded by a miscellany of foliage, lichen, and musty-looking plastic stones. The taxidermist has stuffed it in a slightly crouching position, and the long and supple fingers on the forelimbs stretch towards the glass, so that as you approach the cabinet you're startled and take an instinctive step backward. Its muzzle is creased into a sneer, and the strikingly large teeth are dark yellow — perhaps from being conserved so long. I observe that the taxidermist was incorrectly informed about trolls' eyes. To catch the fury and danger of the animal it has been given brown glass-button eyes, which give it a sad, lost look. These might be suitable for a bear, say, but are totally unlike the troll's actual eyes, which are large, fiery slants with pupils that are vertical stripes. I press my hands and nose and lips to the glass. It mists over by my mouth as I whisper, "Help me."

Looking For Clues

Nalo Hopkinson

In 2002, Nalo Hopkinson was guest of honor at WisCon, the annual gathering of the feminist science fiction community. In her guest of honor speech, reproduced here, she describes her experience as a reader, searching for people like her in "the images of appropriate personhood" presented to her by popular media. Her discussion touches on issues of race and gender.

I've been thinking a lot about comic books recently. I had an interesting discussion a little while ago with the owner of a comics store in another city. He tried to convince me that comics were a color-blind medium, so I wouldn't be able to tell which comics were by artists of color. He said this with the air of someone who's thought long and hard about the issue.

So have I, though I admit not with the expertise in the field that he has. I can't say that I was an avid comics reader as a child, but I certainly did like comics a lot, and read them whenever I could get my hands on them. Don't remember how I got my hands on them. I know that when I was living in Guyana when I was sixteen with my Aunt Barbara (my father's half brother's ex-wife), her son handsome Mark (my cousin) had boxes full of *Mad* magazines and *Eerie* and *Barbarella* and *Plop!* Anyone remember *Plop!*? It was kind of like a two-bit *Twilight Zone* on newsprint. It was horror comics, an anthology of them with each issue, and the punch line of each story was "plop!" as something nasty went plop in a nasty way. I loved those comics that my handsome cousin Mark had; all of them. For years, *Vampirella* was my gold standard of what a woman's breasts should do if you slapped a strip of leather four inches wide over each of them and had her run and leap and tumble. But I'm getting over the body dysphoria now.

Yet long before I got to handsome Cousin Mark's house and *Mad* and *Eerie* and *Plop!* and *Vampirella*; long before Cousin Mark let me play his Bowie's *Diamond Dogs* album — which sounded mighty strange in the suburbs of Georgetown, Guyana, let me tell you — long before I would lie on his bed when he wasn't around and stare up at the Kiss poster he had taped to the ceiling, and try to imagine what in the world would induce those four white guys to get kitted out like that, and why in the world I found it so compelling; long before I was sixteen, I was a comics reader. As I said, I started when I was a kid.

And in retrospect, it's very clear why a little middle-class black Caribbean girl living in the tropical countries of Jamaica, Trinidad, and Guyana would be drawn to the Marvel and DC universes, isn't it? I mean, just look at the Sub-Mariner, for instance: wears swim trunks, comes from a warm place surrounded by water, speaks with an accent different from those of the other superheroes, has different features from them, and darker skin. Obviously, this man comes from the Caribbean. I knew how to spot my people.

It got more complicated with Daredevil. I knew that when he took his red tights off, he was a white American. But while he was in Daredevil drag, I was subconsciously reading him as a black man, and for reasons I now find very troubling: when he was Daredevil, the skin of his suit was colored; he was all about physique and physical action; and he was a mischief-maker, caused trouble wherever he went. Had to be a black man, right? It was decades before I was able to identify my child's absorbed and unspoken internalized racism on the topic, and could understand that the "blackness" I was reading as codified into Daredevil was a mythical conception of black maleness imposed from outside black realities. In many ways, comic books, comic books that hadn't been and still largely aren't written with people like me in mind, began my education into the politics of difference.

There were other differences, too. Remember the Fantastic Four? Reed Richards, the stretchy, clever scientist guy; his brother-in-law Johnny, the Human Torch; Ben, the powerful, wise-cracking Thing, made out of what appeared to be orange brick; and Mrs. Sue Richards, Reed's wife. Yeah, the Fantastic Four; three cool guys who could do neat stuff, and a woman. And what was her superpower? Why, she could disappear. What else would you expect a good fifties wife and mother to do? While the guys were flying around beating up and immobilizing the bad guys, she'd have literally disappeared. The guys would be going *thwack!* and *pow!*, and she'd be invisible, whimpering, "Oh, my. Oh, Reed, oh, oh."

I was a muscular, big child with a decided lack of aptitude for invisibility. I didn't have perfectly upturned blonde hair, and I wasn't anybody's Mrs. I may have been ten years old. That unimaginably daunting future that I was told awaited me — the inevitable one of becoming wife and mother — was one I knew I could put off thinking about for a very long time. I wanted fantasies of personal power, not of disappearing. So naturally, I identified with the Thing. Many women and girls did and do this as we search the received wisdom of popular culture, looking to find ourselves. We fixate on Spider-Man, not Mary Jane. On Superman, not Lois Lane. Hell, even the Swamp Thing held more fantasy appeal than his girlfriend whose name I can't remember. Sure, he had green algae dangling from his nose and looked like the kind of thing you pull up out of a clogged drain, but boy, could he kick some bad guy butt!

At some point, Marvel got smart and created Ororo — Storm, the beautiful African woman who could command the weather. She does straighten her hair, as every good black woman is supposed to, and her eyes are blue for some reason, but she is *there*. Then there was She-Hulk, who delighted me because she was the first strong, muscular woman I'd seen depicted; but what was with those high heels? She perched on them like a giraffe on a cork. The message was clear; if you were unfortunate enough to be a big, strong woman, you'd better have masses of curly hair, gobs of makeup, and an Imelda-sized wardrobe of pumps to distract the eye from all that unsightly, unladylike muscle.

I suspect we've all done this, in one way or another; gone digging through the images of appropriate personhood with which we're presented — images which often exclude us completely — and looked for the clues that yes, people like us do in fact exist, and can in fact be seen as valuable, strong, sexy, beautiful. For me, I've often been doing it in complete isolation as a matter of faith. If one of me exists, then, unlikely as my experience of the world tells me it is, there *must* be others, musn't there? There must be people who find chunky women's bodies beautiful, mustn't there? After all, chunky women keep having kids, so someone must be joining us in that endeavor. There must be more bookaholic, tomboy girls who climb trees with books clenched in their teeth so that they'll have something to do when they got up there? There must be more freaky people who find blue lipstick more interesting than the ubiquitous shades of red, who find sexy Annie Lennox even sexier when she's in Elvis drag, and the cave troll more appealing than the exiled prince. I can't be the only person in the world who finds Marilyn Manson hot, can I? And if people like me exist, our lives must be just as worth telling stories about, right? Perhaps the stories just get buried and don't make it into the mainstream, for all the reasons that I probably don't need to break down to this crowd of people. But you eventually figure out that those stories don't get hidden entirely. You learn that people like you are out there; you just have to look. You learn to apply a different filter to the messages that the world gives you. You learn to look for clues. It's kind of like figuring out a bunch of hanky codes.

And your friends sometimes hand you clues, too. Writer Ashok Mathur put me on to this one; take a look at the television show *Bewitched*; Samantha the witch wants to marry Darrin the mortal, but he's embarrassed at her witch roots. So she agrees to give up her witch heritage and live as a mortal woman in a no-name American suburb. Good thing she was pallid enough to pass, huh?

When the mainstream doesn't address the issues overtly, those issues still seem to sneak out in coded, often unconscious ways. They are our world's guilty secrets, and they get blurted out. As a child, I recognized pop culture images for what they are; the stamp of approval from the powers that be, from the official storytellers of my world. I wanted that recognition. I wanted to be told that I could exist. Not understanding what I was doing, I collected and treasured those few, unconscious, accidental hints that I could. I was drawn to those covert, coded representations, even though I didn't recognize what was going on, or even really what I needed from them. I read whatever comics came my way, and I preferred the fantastical ones to the realistic ones. On television, I was hooked on *The Lone Ranger* (I waited impatiently for the moments when Tonto would get in on the action), on *Batman* — the unmasking of Catwoman as Eartha Kitt was kind of a juvenile conversion experience for me — there was someone who could be an auntie of mine, right there in the fantasy world on the screen! I had never seen anything like it. If she could finesse and finagle her way into the magic box, well, I didn't know quite what, not then, but it made me feel very good. I devoured *Star Trek* old school with its mixed-race magic man, Mr. Spock, and I devoured *The Time Tunnel*, and of course *Bewitched* and *I Dream of Jeannie* (that hot-blooded harem girl who was acceptably blonde), and when *The Brady Bunch* came along, I sucked that up too — I knew a fantasy world when I saw it. I don't say that everything I took in was good for the psyche of a developing mind, but me, I was looking for clues.

It was probably pretty inevitable that I would find the science fiction and fantasy shelves in the adult section of public library where my mother worked. At home, I'd been reading the copies of *Gulliver's Travels* and Homer's *Iliad* which my father taught to senior high school, and I'd been reading folktales collected and retold by Jamaicans Philip Sherlock and Louise Bennet-Coverly. I no longer read comics so much, but I was still fascinated by tales of the unreal and the impossible. Mostly it was that they were so different from the life I was leading, and with which I was way too familiar. So yes, it was escapism, that damning word. I'd bet that most of us here have been accused at some time of reading escapist literature. I thought I could kiss writer Walter Mosley when he published his comments on science fiction, first in the *New York Times*, and then republished in *Dark Matter: A Century of Speculative Fiction from the African Diaspora*, edited by Sheree R. Thomas. Mosley said that escapism was the wrong way to look at it; that in order to make change, humans first had to imagine the directions in which we want to go. At last; vindication. I love that man.

So there I was, using my mother's adult library card to borrow science fiction. I made a beeline first for Michael Crichton's *The Andromeda Strain*, because when the movie had appeared, I'd been too young to see it. This was well before video, so there was no hunting down the video and watching that. Reading the actual book was my only option. Then I discovered a collection of short stories, and read Harlan Ellison's "Shattered Like a Green Glass Goblin." If I had thought that the American suburbs of the Brady Bunch were alien, Harlan's version of Haight-Ashbury raised "alien" to a whole new level for a middle-class black girl living in Kingston, Jamaica. Clearly, there were worlds I had never imagined. Pretty soon, I was reading only science fiction and fantasy. The stories introduced me to concepts that had never occurred to me before, and that sure as hell weren't being taught in school. I hoovered it all in, even when I hadn't the first clue what was going on in the stories; I'd learned that kind of forbearance while reading my father's classical European literature, full of people who didn't look like me doing things I couldn't imagine for reasons I couldn't understand. All of sf was new to me. Even the hackneyed plot of the man and woman who crash on the desert planet and become the new Adam and Eve was fresh to me. A science-fiction reader was born.

And it pretty much stayed that way from my teens through my twenties, when I was working as a clerk in a public library; heaven for a bookaholic. I had by then found the work of a brilliant writer named Samuel R. Delany. Chip Delany's *Dhalgren* broke my brain apart and remade it. That book hacked my mind, rewrote its programming. I was a different person when I was finished reading it. I managed to inveigle the library to purchase more of Chip's books, and read those, too. Each one unfurled something new in my head. One day, leafing through a hardcover copy of *Stars in My Pocket Like Grains of Sand* that I'd borrowed and brought home, I turned to the inside back cover. There was a photograph of Chip; the first I'd ever seen. For me, it was like that moment when Catwoman took off her mask to reveal the black woman underneath. With Chip, I had missed all the clues. Samuel R. Delany was a black man; the first black man I'd ever been aware of in this field. I stared and stared at the picture, incredulously, and then I began to cry. I wept for about half an hour. It felt as though my universe had just doubled in size. I kept asking myself, but why is it so important that he's black? It doesn't make any difference, does it? Race doesn't matter, does it? I'd been taught that it didn't, no more than class, gender, physical ability, age, or sexuality did. I'd been taught that no-one was worth more than anyone else, that I should ignore arbitrary differences. And yet, I looked at that photograph of Chip, and I bawled like a baby. It was a clue that I couldn't ignore, even if at the time I couldn't quite figure out the answer to why differences amongst people both did and didn't matter. Years later, I was at a con with Chip when a young man asked him a question. That young man, gay and black, as Chip is, had just attended a writing workshop where he'd found it very difficult to get understanding of why the things he was writing about were important. He asked Chip how a black gay man could find his voice in science fiction. Almost before the words were out of his mouth, a white woman overrode him with, "Well, I just don't see race in my life. I don't make it a problem. I don't see race. It just doesn't exist as an issue."

Very gently, Chip replied, "If you can't see something that threatens my life daily, then you can't help me fight it. You can't be my ally."

I love the genres of science fiction and fantasy. They have given me many of the answers to dilemmas that were making my life very difficult to live. Don't get me wrong, though; often, just as much as the messages coming from the rest of the world, science fiction, fantasy and horror avoid talking about the troublesome — in other words, you know something is there *because* people are doing such weird contortions to avoid talking about it. Ian Hagemann, a regular at WisCon, once said on a panel that when he reads science fiction futures that are full of white people and no one else, he wonders when the race war happened that wiped out the majority of the human race, and why the writer hasn't mentioned it. That comment may stay with me for life. Years later I read Élisabeth Vonarburg's astounding novel *The Maerlande Chronicles* (the American title is *In the Mothers' Land*), and when the character of Kelys walked on stage and was described as a black woman, I all but wriggled with joy; in Élisabeth's novel, the world had ended twice, yet we were still there.

Like so much in our lives, reading in these genres is a matter of looking for clues. I treasure the writers who do talk about the elephants in the room that no-one's supposed to mention: the stories about the women men don't see; the writing that dares to imagine third and fourth and fifth genders; the Xenogeneses and the Wraeththus. I treasure the writers who dare to imagine that black people will have a future: there is a special place on my bookshelves for Élisabeth Vonarburg's *The Maerlande Chronicles* and Harlan Ellison's "Paladin of the Lost Hour," and umpteen stories by Ursula Le Guin as well as for all the Delany, Butler, Due, and Barnes books. I treasure the works by writers who make me dare to think beyond straight and gay, male and female, and to see that the spectra are much broader than that.

And I treasure more than I can say spaces like this, that make it possible for us to gather, to talk and argue about this literature that we all love, and to challenge ourselves to push its boundaries.

I've recently finished working on a new novel — *The Salt Roads* — where I tried to take it all on: sex and history and race and colonization and gender and power and religion. Damned thing near killed me. It took almost three years, during which time I was also taking a Master's degree, holding down up to three part-time gigs at any one time, giving appearances, editing an anthology, and starting and ending relationships of my own. I am beyond exhausted, and often close to incoherent as a result. But I hope that some of what I've had to say has dropped some clues, some hints to spark your own thinking. We — all of us — are real. The clues are out there.

Nirvana High

Eileen Gunn and Leslie What

Eileen Gunn won the Nebula Award this year for "Coming to Terms," from her collection, *Stable Strategies and Others*, published by Tachyon Publications. The Tiptree judges short-listed the entire volume, specifically mentioning the title story ("Stable Strategies for Middle Management") and this collaboration with Leslie What. We chose "Nirvana High" because "Stable Strategies" has been anthologized *almost* as many times as it deserves, and we really like Gunn and What's all-too-contemporary story about growing up different.

Sunday morning. Barbara awoke from a Technicolor dream in which she was holding hands with the sexiest person in the universe (though the person's head was blank and fuzzy, and she was afraid it might be a girl instead of a boy), and dove straight into a vision predicting her chemistry teacher's death. Barbara watched the accident unfold as it would happen that night: Mrs. Rathbone, dressed in her scarlet microfiber inflatable-bra-and-bustle outfit with spangles and silver fringe, was going to teleport from the Microsoft Park marina to Microsoft Stadium on the other side of the lake. It would be a fundraiser for the basketball team at Cobain High, which meant that nobody Barbara knew would attend. Special-ed students didn't do team sports.

The textile-arts class had added the fringe and spangles on Friday to get extra credit. Everyone was nervous, especially Mrs. R. She had never tried to teleport so far in public before.

Barbara never knew the why of things that she foresaw, so she wasn't sure if it was the distance or maybe some kind of interference from the spangles and fringe that would cause Mrs. Rathbone to rematerialize surrounded by a hundred cubic meters of frigid lake water, flooding the stadium.

Not that it mattered: she couldn't change the outcome anyway. She lay in bed, in the room she shared with her younger sister, holding the dread inside and ignoring the details of what she had just seen. Mrs. R was the only person she liked in the entire school.

Eventually her alarm clock went off, its tiny voice soft and insinuating: "B.J., this is the beginning of a wonderful new day! It's truly lovely weather outside, and today's Sunday, a great day to develop the extrovert in your personality!" It sounded like her mother, and its voice got louder and more insistently cheery if she ignored it. "Barbara! If you get up right now, you can — " She whacked it with the heel of her hand and it shut up. Her sister was already downstairs watching cartoons. She had begun before dawn and would continue until bedtime, pausing only for commercials. Sometimes the whole cartoon was a commercial.

Barbara washed her face and carefully shaved designs in her scalp with a tiny electric razor. She hoped it looked okay: she couldn't really see what she was doing in the back. She put more glue on the dreads, just in case. Then she got dressed and went down to the kitchen for breakfast.

"Well, good morning, B.J.," said her mother. "You're up early for Sunday. That new alarm clock must be *working*, hey?" Her mother looked at her hair, started to say something, then reconsidered. Instead, she grabbed Barbara's wrists, turned them over, and inspected them in the sunlight. "You can hardly see the scars now." She nodded in satisfaction. "I'm so glad we went ahead with the plastic surgery. Your father was wrong — it's certainly worth the extra money."

"Waste of dough, Mom," said Barbara. "Scars rule."

Her mother let go of her. "This bacon your father got for breakfast — I worry about the sodium content. On the *Today Show* they were talking about sodium and nitrous in packaged meats. It causes cancer."

"Nitrates, Mom. Nitrous is what you inhale." But her mother was already off on another subject, spouting some completely incomprehensible psychobabble she'd heard on TV that morning. "Mom, was I adopted?" Her mother didn't answer.

Throughout the day, Barbara did her best to keep her mind off her premonition, so her parents wouldn't notice anything unusual. They were worried enough about her self-esteem, without her troubling them with something real. Mostly she stayed in her room, listening to Airhead real loud on the phones and trying to figure out the words.

At dinner, she picked at her food: soggy ramen noodles with overcooked peapods and undercooked carrots. For dessert, a kiwi-fruit-flavored Jello with embedded banana slices. The Jell-O had achieved a colloidal state, and the banana slices hung suspended in light-green goo. It reminded her of chemistry class. She pushed it away and excused herself from the table.

"You didn't take very much to eat," said her mother. "You've been awfully quiet."

Barbara groaned and pulled on her jacket. "I'm going to the basketball fundraiser," she said. She didn't really want to go, but she had to be there. She had to see what happened.

"Dressed like that?" asked her father. "What the hell did you do to your hair?"

"That's nice," said her mother quickly. "You make some friends who like basketball. That's a *good* idea."

She figured she'd go to the marina, where Mrs. R was starting from. The crowds would be at the stadium, waiting for her to reappear.

Barbara knew there was nothing she could do. When she was a kid, when she first started promoting, she tried to change things. She told her father not to eat at the JellyBelly Deli, but her remark whetted his appetite for knishes; he got salmonella. She told her sister not to get up on the high slide, but Tina didn't like being ordered around; she broke her arm. The incident with her mother's car was especially unfortunate.

Barbara caught on, and now kept her mouth shut — it didn't make any difference in the results, but at least she didn't get blamed for it. She had never promoted anything this serious before, but she knew what she had to do: stay out of the way of the inevitable.

At the marina, a platform had been set up overlooking Lake Washington, with a field of folding chairs in front of it. Most of the chairs were empty, except way up near the stage. Barbara sat on the side in the back and tried to look invisible.

Klieg lights were waving through the sky, and cameras from the school TV station were trained on Mrs. R's presumed trajectory, although no one had ever been observed in the act of teleportation. Huge screens from the Microsoft-Sony Educational Channel had been set up to make the experience of being there as real as watching it on TV. The Cobain Marching Band was on the platform playing the school song, "Live Through This." The drum majors, dressed as Courtney Love, screamed out the lyrics. The norms really made a big deal of all this fascist school-spirit stuff. Barbara wondered how they faked it.

She moved quickly into a seat at the back, leaving a space between herself and a skinny geek with a scramble of hair at the top. He looked like a spesh — funny she didn't know him.

And then, there she was on the screen, bigger than life: Mrs. R, spangles twinkling, silver fringe fluttering. She'd obviously been given a heavy dusting of glitter just before taking the stage, and she left a shimmery trail behind her, like a slug.

Cobain's principal, Mr. Madonna, an XXY with extra-high intuitive qualities and an inclination to hold pep rallies, introduced her, though he said she needed no introduction, then led the band in a medley of sentimental grunge. Barbara loathed grunge.

And then Mrs. R stepped forward very quietly and started to, well, ripple. She wavered, like hot air on the highway in August.

In her dream, Barbara had seen all the details: the water, the noise, the rush of people to the exits, Mrs. R's cold, white, limp body lying alone on the stage afterward.

The reality was worse. The audience at the stadium was really spooked, not to mention they got wet. The CPR team entered the hall cautiously, and way too late. At Microsoft Park, the audience couldn't figure out what was going on. The guy next to her couldn't seem to believe it. He kept saying, "This is incredible!" over and over again. Finally he turned to Barbara and asked, "Why did she do herself like that in front of everybody?" Barbara got up out of her seat and walked away.

He followed her, still babbling. "She's the oldest spesh I've ever seen. She must have been one of the first. If she held out that long, what made her crack?"

"She didn't do it to herself," Barbara said finally. Mrs. R wouldn't have. She was sane. She was happy. She couldn't have done it to herself.

"My God, I hope you're right." He grabbed her elbow. Barbara almost pulled away, but he didn't seem dangerous. "Come on," he said.

She felt the ground beneath her feet fall away, then return. Wooden flooring. It was dark. The guy let go of her elbow. What kind of a nut was he? Where had he taken her? What the fuck was going on? He hit a light switch, and she realized where she was: Mrs. R's chem lab.

"Jesus!"

"Don't be scared: watch." He grabbed a beaker and some flasks from a cabinet. "You take a little of this, a pinch of that. Use your bunsen burner like a blowtorch, and — "

"No! I'm outta here!"

The air in the room grew thick with noxious clouds that fizzled and popped and made her nose burn. He grabbed her and pulled her tightly to him, forcing his mouth onto hers. The clouds in the room turned black and heavy, and she couldn't breathe — she couldn't even take a breath. She started to pass out, his mouth on hers, his tongue down her throat. My mother was right, she thought. I shouldn't talk to strange guys.

The next thing she knew, they were back outside the marina. He was still kissing her, and he'd pressed up against her real close. He had a hard-on, and she was kissing him back.

She broke away.

"Did that help?" he said.

"What the fuck is the matter with you?"

"I thought you could use a rush. Like in her honor, you know?"

"You are seriously fucked," said Barbara. "Stay away from me." She ran for the bus.

At the school door on Monday morning, Barbara pushed her right hand against the security switch that verified her ID, scanned her person for possible weapons, and then evaluated her emotional state to determine whether or not she would use them. The twitch switch, they called it. Since they could no longer ban guns, the schools tried to keep out students who would use them irresponsibly.

The solenoid seemed to hesitate. She forced herself to take a deep calm breath and slowly traced the raised lettering with the fingers of her free hand. "Donated by Microsoft-ADT Intrusion Insurance." I am not an intruder, she thought, without feeling. It worked; the switch beeped its discreet little signal, and the door opened to admit her to school.

A norm, by his looks one of the CAs — the criminally active students — was standing by the lockers. He turned to stare at Barbie as she walked down the hall. The CAs weren't too friendly to the special-skills students. None of the norms were, but the CAs, who sometimes tipped toward the sociopathic end of the scale, worried Barbara more than the other norms. Supposedly every student at Cobain was a suicide risk, but you kind of got the feeling that the CAs might just take you with them.

"Hey, spesh," said the norm, fiddling with a bone-handled folding knife. "Guess what I'm thinking."

Her class was through the first door, and she had to pass him to get there. She put an edge on her voice that was sharper than his knife. "*I'm* thinking you'd look pretty funny with half a dick.... And now *you're* thinking 'I wonder if she can see into the future,' because that wasn't what you were thinking at all."

The norm looked confused. "Psycho bitch," he muttered, but he turned back to his locker and didn't pursue her as she walked by.

———

In class, she took her seat at the back of the lab, in the Microsoft-Dow section, still fuming at what jerks norms were. Pretty much everyone had heard about the drowning at Lake Washington; Barbara didn't bother to block it from her mind, even though she usually guarded her thoughts around the telepaths.

Minerva, seated next to her, looked up. "Entertain us!" she called out. "Barbie was *there* when Mrs. Rathbone made like a salmon and went extinct."

Before Barbara could brace herself, almost everyone in the classroom was pushing for a place inside her brain, probing her consciousness with questions like icy fingers. Telepaths froze her nose, the way they plugged in at will.

"Did she die all at once, or was it slow and lingering?"

"Did our test scores die with her?"

"Did her bra fill up with water?"

"Entertain us!"

"Entertain us!"

"Entertain us!"

That was a Cobain thing. It meant one thing to the teachers, another to the students. To the teachers it meant "pay attention." To the students it meant "stop whatever you're doing that's interesting and do what we want you to do." To Kurt Cobain, of course, it had meant "stick a shotgun in your mouth."

All she needed to do was answer. Tell them all the grim details. Make it sound funny, make it sound like she didn't care. If she gave them what they wanted, she'd be one of the gang. So why couldn't she do it?

"Nevermind," Barbie said.

"Did she leave a note?" Minerva asked. She gave a nervous laugh.

"That's not funny," Barbie said. "It was an accident."

The ITV buzzed on and Mr. Madonna spoke to the class.

"Special-skills students," he said, "As most of you know, Mrs. Rathbone met with a tragic accident last night, in the service of Cobain High. I am sure she would want you to quietly resume your studies and to welcome Mr. Collins, who will be will be with you shortly. We can all be proud of Mrs. Rathbone, because Microsoft-Boeing will be presenting the basketball team with new uniforms in her memory. Grief counseling will be provided in the cafeteria at lunchtime, courtesy of Microsoft-Taco Bell, and there will be a celebration of life sponsored by Microsoft–Coca-Cola on Friday at noon."

"Yeah?" shouted Carl. "What's in it for me?"

Grief counseling probably wasn't going to be necessary for most of the students, because Mrs. R was one of the few special-ed teachers who had the power to control her class, and most of the kids hadn't liked her very much. The other teachers had the psychic strength of Fig Newtons, but when you gave Mrs. R a hard time, she teleported you straight to detention.

And Barbara had been her pet. There was no denying that: Barbara could have said anything in that class and gotten away with it. This had put her in an awkward predicament. When you can say anything you want, and the teacher takes your questions absolutely seriously and understands what you were really asking and answers *that* question, it's not so much fun to be smartass all the time. It's more interesting to think up really good questions. Especially when you're actually getting interested in the subject. This is what had earned her the nickname "Barbie" in the first place.

"Mrs. Rathbone's Teen-Talk Barbie," Carl had called her when she asked too many questions about chemistry. Just like the Barbie doll that said "Trigonometry is fun! Want some help with it?" and "I find chemistry very stimulating!"

Carl's names for people stuck like birdshit because of the leadership thing: some people had it, most people didn't. Minerva once told her straight out: "I don't trust anybody except for Carl. And I wouldn't trust him, except he makes me."

Why don't you just stay out of my head, Barbara thought, but the TPs fought to get in, just because it bugged her. Barbara shut an imaginary door and locked her thoughts away in an imaginary room, then sat back in her chair and flashed what she hoped was a smug and knowing look. Why give these shitheads the details?

"Aaaaaugh! Too late," Minerva groaned. "She's closed us out, the bitch." There was a slight note of respect in the way she said "bitch."

Barbara smiled. She brought up an image of the three little pigs inside the imaginary room, with the big bad wolf and her classmates outside. She made the wolf piss on Carl.

"Up yours," said Carl. "I'm ditchin' you, bitch." There wasn't any respect in his tone. With that, he left her head. The others followed, even Minerva. Barbara bricked up the outside of the door and settled back in her imaginary room. She stopped thinking about the pigs, but kept the door and the bricks fixed firmly in her mind.

Then, for the first time since Saturday morning, Barbara began to think about Mrs. Rathbone. She'd known about a lot of dank things, not just chemistry. Though chemistry was dank enough.

She had never told Mrs. R how much she liked her. She'd actually liked this teacher as if she was a person. Well, as much as she could like somebody that old. And now Mrs. R was dead.

Entertain us, Barbie thought. She forgot the brick wall. A vision washed over her: a stocky, bearded man in a cheap green suit walking down a corridor, accompanied by a too-thin, too-tall boy in just-pressed clothes. Oh, fuck: the horny chemist from last night.

Minerva caught on and screamed to the others. "Hey! She sees the sub! It's a beard! And he's with some toothpick dweezle wannabe." The other TPs tuned in to Barbara's premonition.

"Wannabe," said Carl. "That's his name now. Juan-na-be. Juan for short." All the dumb toadies laughed. It was too late, but Barbara put up a block anyway. She brought the picture of the boy to a place no one could find. He wasn't a telepath, that much she was sure.

The sub, Mr. Collins, was totally weird. The minute he walked in, everybody could tell he was paranormal, though they couldn't figure out what he did. The telepaths went for broke on it, but couldn't crack him. He sent two of them down to the assistant principal's office. And they went, which was pretty strange in itself. Maybe that's what he did, thought Barbara. Maybe he bent people to his will, in spite of themselves. Maybe that's how he got girlfriends, since he was such a fat old dork.

"Barbara! Earth to Barbara!" said Mr. Collins in a commanding voice.

"Um. Yes, Mr. Collins?" Oops. Keep the brick wall up. Maybe this guy was a TP.

"You gotta stay tuned in, Barbie! Entertain us!" He thought for a moment. "Here's something easy! Separate the leaders from the sheep! Yes or No! Give me an answer: Do the inner electrons of an atom participate in chemical bonding?"

Barbara felt the class waiting for her to respond to the teacher's challenge. Minerva probed her mind just a little, just a poke to get her attention. Carl glared. Barbara knew she could side with the new teacher or side with the class. She looked Mr. Collins right in the eye and said, "They get a little horny now and then, but that's about it."

Mr. Collins called on the new kid, T'Shawn, who answered, "No."

"Lucky guess, Juan," said Carl in a singsong voice.

That's not his name, thought Barbara. I should call him by his real name. Fuck it, she thought, I might as well call myself Barbie and give up. Why fight it? If it sticks, it sticks. That was leadership ability. Good thing everybody didn't have it.

Anyway, it wasn't a guess, everyone knew the answer. Maybe that's what Mr. C. meant about separating the leaders from the crowd. She was curious about Juan, but every time she let down the brick wall to glance his way, she saw a fuzzy cloud form around his head, then start to disintegrate. If she continued to look, she would see something she didn't want to know.

"Who wants to tell us about today's reading assignment? Barbara?" He'd already picked up on the fact that she was interested in chemistry. This was not going to do her rep any good.

"I have no idea, Mr. Collins, but Minerva could probably tell you."

Mr. Collins looked at Minerva. "Maureen?" he said.

Minerva recited in a bored voice. "Valence electrons are those electrons farthest from the nucleus, which are responsible for chemical bonding within the atom. I could go on, but I don't really give a fuck."

The rest of the class snickered. Mr. Collins looked confused. Barbie felt a little sorry for him, but then she thought of Mrs. R, dead and everything, and hardened her heart to this grotesque nerd. He didn't even know most of the class could read his mind.

Juan — T'Shawn — spoke out of turn, but politely. "Mr. C, is this your first day of substitute teaching?"

"Nevermind," Mr. Collins answered, smiling broadly. His cheeks puffed up and took on a ruddy tone. His beard somehow looked softer and whiter.

"Hey, it's Santa," said Carl. "Santa C." The suckups snickered again.

Mr. C opened his mouth to speak, then seemed to change his mind. He shook his head and a wave of laughter shook its way up from his gut and burst out of him like the explosion in the sink. "Ho, ho, ho!" boomed Mr. C. "Ho! Ho! Ho!" Mr. C was starting to look scary rather than jolly, though he kept on laughing. Even the telepaths seemed a bit subdued. His beard looked scruffy now, and Barbie noticed that his ears were kind of pointy. Had they been that way before?

"What's so funny?" she asked. Her voice quavered a little. It had been doing that a lot lately.

Mr. C's laughter trailed off; he coughed a little and seemed more like a teacher than he had all morning. "Some of us need to get a handle on the real drama of chemistry," he said. "It's life and death stuff, guys. You've got to take it more seriously. Quiz tomorrow. I strongly recommend that you study sections twelve-nine through twelve-twelve: 'Predicting Redox Reactions.'"

The bell rang, signaling second lunch. Second lunch was noisier than first lunch, and chances of getting physically damaged were somewhat higher than they were in the halls between classes, though certainly not as great as at the bus stop after school. Barbie usually brought a sandwich and ate it on the bench in front of the secretarial station, the safest place on campus.

"Macaroni and cheese, or beans and rice with a choice of condiments," said Minerva, wrinkling her nose. "That's all that's left. They're laughing at us right now in the cafeteria." She eyed Barbie's backpack. "Wish *I* could see into the future. I would have known to bring my lunch."

Carl rushed to hold the door, watching to make sure no one told Mr. C that the telepaths would know the answers to any test. They'd probe Mr. C's brain like fruit-salad Jell-O, pulling out plump little facts and formulas. The telepaths would, anyway. Barbie and Juan and a few of the others would have to study. She tried to predict her grade, but she just couldn't see it. If he graded on a curve, Barbie knew she'd be in trouble.

"Ace it," whispered Minerva, reading her thoughts. "Look ahead and predict what I'm gonna write on my paper. I bet I'll get an A."

Barbie nodded. "Yeah, you will, but I can't see the test. I can't control when I premote." That's why the government wouldn't give her a scholarship: no military applications, they said. You couldn't count on it, but it thrust itself on you at the worst times.

"So why don't you just copy off my test when I do it? Sit close, and I'll let you see it. It's retro, but it works."

Barbie sighed. She hated having to explain this. "I can't cheat," she said. "I can see the consequences, or something."

"Well, nevermind then," said Minerva, with a toss of her shiny bald head. She stomped away to join Carl and the other telepaths. They walked down the hallway in a group, heading toward the cafeteria.

Barbie walked slowly down the hall in the other direction, toward her locker.

Here's a formula for creating a teenager: take a negative charge, constrain it in time and space, add a catalyst, and get away. Get away, Barbara thought, and she started running down the empty hallway. Faster, she thought. Why not? Even the monitors had gone to lunch.

Then she heard footsteps following her, light as raindrops on a window. Startled, she stopped and turned, twisting her stun ring. She was ready to fight if she had to. It was Juan behind her. He braked to a halt about seven feet away, grinned, and shrugged his shoulders apologetically.

She kept her finger on the stun ring's safety, but she wasn't really afraid of this guy. At least he didn't have pointy ears.

A vision flashed before her — of the principal, Mr. Madonna, nibbling Mr. C's ears. She blinked and it went away. They do that? she thought. Jeeze. The things she didn't want to know about.

"I heard what you said to Maureen," Juan said. He licked the corner of his mouth. "I want you to know I don't cheat either. At least not in any conventional sense of the term."

Barbie started walking down the hall towards him, and towards the cafeteria. She could tell he wasn't going to jack her or anything. He fell in step beside her.

"I'm sorry if what I did last night, like, made it worse for you," he said. "I heard she was a spesh. I wanted to be in her class. When I thought she killed herself, I was really mad at her."

Barbara didn't want to talk about it. "So, who'd *you* kill, to end up at Cobain?" she asked.

"That's rude," said T'Shawn with a slight smile. He shrugged. "The principal at Dick Silly thought I'd be better off with a bunch of other young people who were troubled like myself. For my social development, of course."

Dixie Lee Ray was the academic magnet school sponsored by Microsoft-IBM. There were hardly any speshes there, and certainly no telepaths, who usually developed "behavior problems" by the age of fourteen.

They stopped by Barbara's locker, and she fumbled with the lock and opened it. As she put her chem book inside, T'Shawn held the door and leaned in to give her a kiss. She thought for a second — but only a second. She kissed him back.

When school ended, Barbie walked as slow as she could, trying to look natural, like she wasn't in a hurry. Minerva spotted her and waited.

"Are you okay?" Minerva said. "Don't forget what I told you.

About the test? My answers are yours," she said. She seemed hesitant to leave, and the niggling worry that she was about to be busted caught Barbie off guard. Before she could stop herself, she was thinking of Juan.

"Oh," said Minerva. "That's what your problem is."

Barbie shrugged.

"Hey, entertain us," said Minerva. "You've got it bad, don'cha?" She smoothed her bald head and closed her eyes, concentrating. Barbie expected to feel the icy probe, but didn't. "Your pathetic secret is safe with me," Minerva said.

Barbie was embarrassed to face her.

"I'm not gonna tell, don't you get it?" She reached out as if to pat Barbie on the shoulder, but must have thought better of it. "Nevermind," she said with a salute. "See you tomorrow."

The next day, when Mr. C passed out the quiz sheets, Barbara felt ready. Nervous, but ready. "Don't turn them over until I say it's time," he said.

Carl looked at the wall clock. He closed his eyes in mock sleep and murmured smugly, "Wake me five minutes before the bell rings." Barbie wanted to kick him.

Mr. C stood behind the low counter, surrounded by buckets and burners and flasks of labeled chemicals. "Okay now, everyone turn over your sheets. Entertain us!"

Papers rustled like leaves. Minerva giggled. "Prank! A blank!"

"They're all fucking blank," said Carl. He sat up.

Mr. C's face went slack and his eyes rolled back to show the whites. He swayed from side to side and a low rumbling noise came from the area near his mouth.

"Oh gross," said Minerva. "Here it comes — his claim to fame. God, I hope he isn't a contortionist."

"I thought they killed them at birth," said Carl.

"That's abortionists," said Minerva.

"He's not a contortionist," said Juan. "It's something else."

Mr. C opened his eyes, but the expression was glazed and unfocused. His lips moved as if he were chewing something. A low voice came out between them, but the words didn't match the way his lips moved. It was like he was being used as a megaphone by someone inside his head.

"Ticonderogas sharpened and ready?" asked a gentle voice. "It's so good to be back here in the Northwest. Born in Portland, you know. This is a test I always wanted to give my students at Caltech, but unfortunately not a one of them was expendable. Geniuses every one, the little bastards." He cleared his throat. "The test takes the form of a real-life chemistry experiment. I hope you studied hard, because you'll need to stop the reaction before it kills you."

Mr. C seemed to be growing taller and thinner. His neck got longer, his skin grew looser, hanging in wrinkled wattles, like a turkey's.

"Oh my God! He's so incredibly old! Ooh! I can't look," said Minerva, covering her eyes.

"What happening to Mr. C?" Barbie asked. "Is he gonna die too?"

Carl got that look, like he was probing the teacher. His jaw dropped. All the telepaths listened in.

Minerva whispered to Barbie. "It's not Mr. C," she said. "It's some scientist dude.... Huh! I know who it is! Mr. C is channeling Linus Pauling! Mr. C. can talk to the dead!"

"Whet," said Barbie. "Who's Linus Pauling?"

"I dunno, he's sort of blank inside, because he's not really here — he's dead. I think he invented vitamin C or something."

Pauling scooped a yellow lump from an unlabeled cannister and transferred it to a burette. "I love this!" he said, clapping his hands. He opened the valve on the bottom of the burette, just enough to let an anorexic stream of powder drip onto the counter. He fiddled with his keys and walked slowly to the door. "Locks from the inside," he said, putting the key in the lock and turning it. "Just in case we want you whippersnappers to stay put." From his pocket he brought out a small bottle and added an eyedropper full of clear liquid to the burette. "Whoa, baby," said Pauling. His eyes glistened.

White gas roiled up and wafted toward them as the students watched in disbelief. By the time the visible cloud reached the front row, the entire class was coughing and rubbing their eyes.

"Augggh!" cried Carl, in tears. "It's concentrated dog fart!"

The odor was pungent and extremely unpleasant. Barbie choked. Carl was wrong: dog farts smelled better.

"Anybody study the material?" Pauling asked. "Hope so, for your sake."

"Hydrogen sulfide?" Barbie asked tentatively. Juan nodded.

"This substance is, of course, extremely unpleasant to breathe," said Pauling with a chuckle. "And oh yes, it could in fact kill you." He reached into a cardboard box on the floor and pulled out two containers and a rubber gas mask. "We have here two chemicals with which I'm sure you are all quite familiar, as you have just read Chapter Twelve. Each chemical will react in a different way with the element I've just liberated into the air. One should neutralize its effects; one may create a substance even more noxious than the one you're breathing right now." He chuckled.

"Hey-hey. If you're guessing, your odds of staying alive are fifty-fifty. If you studied last night, your chances improve."

His face disappeared beneath the gas mask. Then he jumped up on top of the counter, pulled his shirt-tails out of his pants, and shook his hair down over his face. He bent his knees and played an invisible guitar. A familiar voice echoed from the gas mask, singing. "No one is ever too young to die...."

"This is no time to entertain us," yelled Carl, tossing a half-full can of Pepsi at the Cobain impersonator.

"Mr. C! Don't do this!" screamed Minerva. "It's not fair!"

"Life isn't fair," said the man who looked like Linus Pauling. "You twerps have the attention span of fruit flies. Solve the problem, or you'll have their life expectancy too." He adjusted his gas mask. "This is it. Give me the answer or die trying."

The fumes from the spilled chemical were becoming unbearable. Barbie felt as though her nose was on fire, and her eyes stung. It was the second time in two days that a guy had tried to suffocate her, which kind of pissed her off. Then she noticed that she couldn't actually smell the stuff anymore, though her nose still burned. Maybe it shorted out, she thought. Did noses do that? She was starting to feel sick.

Suddenly, T'Shawn grabbed her wrist, and they both rose to the ceiling. She sucked in a deep lungful of untainted air. The chemistry test, heavier than air, was roiling below. Some of the students were trying to get out, but the door was locked and the windows were barred. "Are they all going to die?" she asked.

"Don't worry," said T'Shawn. He leaned in close to kiss her. "We'll take care of it."

It was exciting to be near him like that, unnoticed and apart from the pandemonium below. She slid her hands around his waist and drew him closer. He put his mouth on her earlobe, and she suddenly understood about ear nibbling: your ears were hotwired to your twat. Electricity spread throughout her body.

They were both breathing hard. He reached up under her shirt.

"Don't," said Barbara. "I mean, there's all these people."

"I don't think they're paying any attention," said T'Shawn. He reached between her legs, and for a moment all she could think about was getting him inside her. His hand, his cock, whatever.

She fumbled with his belt buckle, trying to get it undone.

"We've got time," he said. "We can do it and get out. We've got time."

"I never flunked a chemistry test in my life."

He laughed. The sounds of coughing below grew louder.

"What the fuck," yelled Carl, from the floor. "Anything's better than just standing around with our thumbs up our asses." He reached for a cannister, without even bothering to read the label.

"All right!" said T'Shawn. "Acetic acid." He laughed.

"No," said Barbara. "We really have to help them."

"Not yet," he said. "We've got a couple of minutes."

Minerva was choking and sobbing.

"I'm sorry," she said, and let go of him. She took a deep breath, and dropped to the floor. She made her way to the front of the classroom, eyes watering, and found the canisters that Mr. C. had set out. Hydrogen peroxide — that would do it. Oxidize the hydrogen sulfide and stop the reaction. She grabbed the H_2O_2 and baptized the burette.

The production of caustic gas stopped, and Mr. C gave her a thumbs up, then unlocked the door and opened the windows. He smiled genially. "Barbara, you did very well, though it took you a bit longer than I expected. A+ for you. Carl, you were about to toss acetic acid into the burette, which would have liberated the hydrogen sulfide more quickly, raising it to lethal levels. I'm afraid you flunked. The rest of you will be graded on the curve. Take five megs of vitamin C and get a good night's sleep away from nuclear fallout. Next time I tell you to study for a quiz, I'll expect better results."

"Way to go, Carl," said Minerva hoarsely.

"Asshole," said Angela. "Class president. Hah. Class turd."

Carl was studying his shoes. He didn't look up.

Friday was the day of the Celebration of Life for Mrs. R. The bus from Cobain Magnet High lumbered through the gates of the cemetery. Inside, Barbara looked at a hillside marked with uneven rows of oddly shaped tombstones. Grey granite plinths, long red chaise-lounges like swimming-pool furniture, low cement scrolls with lambs lying on top, Japanese garden lanterns. It wasn't a nice tidy cemetery where all the headstones were set flush with the ground so they didn't get in the way of the lawnmowers. It was a little wild-looking, with weird bits — kind of like Barbara's hair, actually. There were weeds.

A row of huge cement boxes blocked the road beyond the sign. They were maybe eight feet long, four feet square. Not recyclable. These boxes were built to last, and to keep whatever was inside from getting free. Barbara wondered what they were. Then the bus stopped abruptly and the rude truth about cemeteries hit home. Duh.

"He-e-ere we are!" said Mr. Simmons, the death sciences instructor. He got up from his seat and stood in the aisle, facing the special-skills students. Nobody paid any attention to him, except for Barbara, who wished she'd gotten a seat further back with her friends, not that she had any.

Mr. Simmons jangled his keyring against a bronze plaque that was bolted to the back of the driver's seat. At one time it had read "Sponsored by Microsoft-Boeing," but someone had lasered it to say "Sponsored by Microsoft-Boring."

The class quieted down. "Everybody out for Eternity," said Mr. Simmons cheerfully.

The students dragged themselves out of their seats and fought for standing room in the aisle. Carl was first off the bus, of course. He leaped into the grey November chill and scoped out the terrain.

"Note the cement bunkers to your left as you exit the bus," said Carl. "If anybody starts shooting, get those bunkers between you and the guns as fast as you can."

Barbara wondered if she could project her thoughts to bounce off the sides of the boxes, like billiard balls. Risky, but she thought she could do it. She rounded her thoughts into a ball, smoothed off the clues to who she was, and flung them at an angle between two cement boxes. "They're tombs, not bunkers, you sphincter!" She blanked her mind and tried to look nonchalant.

" — sphincter! — sphincter! — sphincter!" Huh. There *was* such a thing as a psychic echo.

Carl whipped his head around, and all the other telepaths snickered. He looked suspiciously at Barbara, but she was doing logarithms in her head. "Buttmunch," he muttered.

Hah. Leadership suck. Nobody was going to shoot at them in the cemetery. Jeez.

Mr. Simmons was talking about some guy who was buried in the cemetery. "Interesting man, Bruce Lee," he said in a musing tone. "He was an actor and a martial arts expert. Bit of a philosopher, too. Started his own martial arts school...."

"There was a TV show called *Kung Fu*," he continued. "Supposed to be about the spiritual side of Asian martial arts. But Bruce Lee found that there were no acting parts for a Chinese martial artist and philosopher on a show about Chinese martial arts and philosophy. They gave his part to a hippie white guy."

"That guy's buried next to Brandon Lee, that goth actor," said Minerva. "Wonder if they're related."

———

Mrs. R's grave was towards the back of the cemetery, near the chain-link fence that separated it from the playground at Volunteer Park. It was dark there even in the middle of the day, and it didn't have the great view of the mountains that Brandon Lee had. Kind of where you'd expect to find someone who made a teacher's salary.

There were a lot of people all milling about in the cold. All the science classes from Cobain were there, of course, plus some college types who had probably gone to Cobain years before. There were old people she didn't know, and even older people she was sure she'd never even heard of. Mrs. R's family, probably.

A plumpish bearded guy in a dark suit sat on a folding chair near the grave, his head in his hands. He was trembling a little bit; he was crying, Barbie realized. She looked around, feeling helpless. She didn't know guys would cry.

She held her body in a polite position that looked as if she was listening to the service, and set up a double-thick brick wall inside herself. She counted the bricks and got up to two thousand. She looked at the sky, which was astir with dark, bulbous clouds. She glanced around the crowd, and slipped away to its farthest edge. She didn't want to listen to what people were saying about Mrs. R.

The road she was standing on was old, and had sunk a bit into the earth. There was a high curb containing the hillside, and Barbara sat down on its edge. The speakers' voices droned on, trying to make sense of stuff that didn't have to make sense.

At the back of the crowd, Carl stood on a gravestone to get a better view. Other kids followed his lead, of course, and soon there was a whole cluster of them standing there, a meter taller than anyone else.

Barbara cringed. She looked at the tombstones next to her, an odd arrangement of bed-like slabs of polished red granite with cylindrical pillows at their heads. There were two long ones, side by side, and a short one set at a right angle, like camp cots in a small tent.

She read the inscription on the short one's pillow. Regina Mary Dugan. Born 1896, died 1901. A five-year-old child. The others would be her parents, Barbara thought. She read their pillows, to give the family all its names. Mary Frances Dugan, 1845–1883. T. Constantine Dugan, 1874–1901.

So Mary Frances died 13 years before Regina Mary was born. Her grandmother? Poor little kid. Buried next to some grandmother she'd never even met. With her father, probably. He died the same year, so maybe it was an accident that killed them both. Or a fire, and he tried to rescue her. Where was Regina's mother? Remarried? Dead somewhere else, no doubt.

All these tombstones, Barbara thought, and though she tried to push it away, a vision came to her — in flashes, like a slide show. Pictures, click-click-click, each one a different gravesite, with different mourners. Each one a ceremony for someone who had died. Thousands of them. Dead now, dead then, dead to come. All those people left behind, weeping, alone. Their time would come, too. Buried with strangers.

She didn't want to think about it. Box it up, she thought, in one of those cement vaults. Put your feelings aside, keep them in a box where no one can get to them. Even you. Even *you* can't get to them — that's how it works. That's what Minerva does, and Carl. That's the secret of high school. Box yourself in, bottle yourself up. Explode at leisure.

She heard shouts from her classmates. Each student had been given a 1.5-liter bottle of Coke. They shook the bottles, and now they were uncapping them in unison. She was missing her chance to show respect. Shaking her bottle of Coke, she ran to join the others.

Brown foam surged from the crowd of students into the open grave. Kids cheered. A few cried. Barbara was one of them.

She tossed a handful of dirt in after the Coke. "Goodbye," she whispered.

Then it was over.

"Okay, kids, back to the bus," said Mr. Simmons. "Pick up those bottles before you go."

Carl shook his head and dropped cross-legged on the grass. He gestured toward row upon row of graves. "Forget it. What's the point of going to school if you're gonna die?"

"Hey, Carl's flipping!" said Minerva, delighted. "Entertain us!"

"Just tell me why I should bother," said Carl.

"Get a grip or be a slave," said Minerva.

"Please," said Carl. "Shove the motivational crap. Entertain us."

"Okay," said T'Shawn. He waved his Coke bottle and leaped up a good five feet in the air, scissor-kicking his legs at the same time. When he landed, everyone was staring at him. He started screaming, "Here we are now, entertain us, here we are now, entertain us...."

Carl started leaping too, though Barbara could tell that at first he was astonished to find himself in the air. "Here we are now, entertain us, here we are now, entertain us...."

The whole class found themselves bouncing all over the Lakeview Cemetery, most of them singing, some of them simply yelping in surprise. The other classes, teachers, and funeral attendees stared at first, then began to twitch and bounce a little bit as T'Shawn found the limit of his strength. Slowly he lowered his classmates to earth. He and Carl came down last.

T'Shawn looked at Carl and shrugged. "I don't know what gets into me, but sometimes I feel like I want to teach the world to sing."

"Then it's a good thing this gig wasn't sponsored by Microsoft–Ex-Lax," said Minerva.

"Entertain us," said T'Shawn.

"Nevermind," said Barbara.

The group headed back to the bus.

Five Fucks

Jonathan Lethem

In this story by MacArthur Fellowship ("genius grant") winner Jonathan Lethem, sexual desire undoes the very fabric of time and space. Men and women are aliens locked into combat until the end of time. Literally. It's the *reductio ad absurdum* of "can't live with 'em, can't live without 'em."

[1]

"I feel different from other people. Really different. Yet whenever I have a conversation with a new person it turns into a discussion of things we have in common. Work, places, feelings. Whatever. It's the way people talk, I know, I share the blame, I do it too. But I want to stop and shout no, it's not like that, it's not the same for me. I feel different."

"I understand what you mean."

"That's not the right response."

"I mean what the fuck are you talking about."

"Right." Laughter.

She lit a cigarette while E. went on.

"The notion is like a linguistic virus. It makes any conversation go all pallid and reassuring. 'Oh, I know, it's like that for me too.' But the virus isn't content just to eat conversations, it wants to destroy lives. It wants you to fall in love."

"There are worse things."

"Not for me."

"Famine, war, floods."

"Those never happened to me. Love did. Love is the worst thing that ever happened to me."

"That's fatuous."

"What's the worst thing that ever happened to you?"

She was silent for a full minute.

"But there, *that's* the first fatuous thing I've said. Asking you to consider *my* situation by consulting *your* experience. You see? The virus is loose again. I don't want you to agree that our lives are the same. They aren't. I just want you to listen to what I say seriously, to believe me."

"I believe you."

"Don't say it in that tone of voice. All breathy."

"Fuck you." She laughed again.

"Do you want another drink?"

"In a minute." She slurped at what was left in her glass, then said, "You know what's funny?"

"What?"

"Other people do feel the way you do, that they're apart from everyone else. It's the same as the way every time you fall in love it feels like something new, even though you do the exact same things over again. Feeling unique is what we all have in common, it's the thing that's always the same."

"No, I'm different. And falling in love is different for me each time, different things happen. Bad things."

"But you're still the same as you were before the first time. You just feel different."

"No, I've changed. I'm much worse."

"You're not bad."

"You should have seen me before. Do you want another drink?"

The laminated place mat on the table between them showed pictures of exotic drinks. "This one," she said. "A zombie." It was purple.

"You don't want that."

"Yes I do. I love zombies."

"No you don't. You've never had one. Anyway, this place makes a terrible zombie." He ordered two more margaritas.

"You're such an expert."

"Only on zombies."

"On zombies and love is bad."

"You're making fun of me. I thought you promised to take me seriously, believe me."

"I was lying. People always lie when they flirt."

"We're not flirting."

"Then what are we doing?"

"We're just drinking, drinking and talking. And I'm trying to warn you."

"And you're staring."

"You're beautiful. Oh God."

"That reminds me of one. What's the worst thing about being an atheist?"

"I give up."

"No one to talk to when you come."

[2]

Morning light seeped through the macrame curtain and freckled the rug. Motes seemed to boil from its surface. For a moment she thought the rug was somehow on the ceiling, then his cat ran across it, yowling at her. The cat looked starved. She was lying on her stomach in his loft bed, head over the side. He was gone. She lay tangled in the humid sheets, feeling her own body.

Lover — she thought.

She could barely remember.

She found her clothes, then went and rinsed her face in the kitchen sink. A film of shaved hairs lined the porcelain bowl. She swirled it out with hot water, watched as the slow drain gulped it away. The drain sighed.

The table was covered with unopened mail. On the back of an envelope was a note: *I don't want to see you again. Sorry. The door locks.* She read it twice, considering each word, working it out like another language. The cat crept into the kitchen. She dropped the envelope.

She put her hand down and the cat rubbed against it. Why was it so thin? It didn't look old. The fact of the note was still sinking in. She remembered the night only in flashes, visceral strobe. With her fingers she combed the tangles out of her hair. She stood up and the cat dashed away. She went out into the hall, undecided, but the weighted door latched behind her.

Fuck him.

The problem was of course that she wanted to.

It was raining. She treated herself to a cab on Eighth Avenue. In the backseat she closed her eyes. The potholes felt like mines, and the cab squeaked like rusty bedsprings. It was Sunday. Coffee, corn muffin, newspaper; she'd insulate herself with them, make a buffer between the night and the new day.

But there was something wrong with the doorman at her building.

"You're back!" he said.

She was led incredulous to her apartment full of dead houseplants and unopened mail, her answering machine full of calls from friends, clients, the police. There was a layer of dust on the answering machine. Her address book and laptop disks were gone; clues, the doorman explained.

"Clues to what?"

"Clues to your case. To what happened to you. Everyone was worried."

"Well, there's nothing to worry about. I'm fine."

"Everyone had theories. The whole building."

"I understand."

"The man in charge is a good man, Miss Rush. The building feels a great confidence in him."

"Good."

"I'm supposed to call him if something happens, like someone trying to get into your place, or you coming back. Do you want me to call?"

"Let me call."

The card he handed her was bent and worn from traveling in his pocket. CORNELL PUPKISS, MISSING PERSONS. And a phone number. She reached out her hand; there was dust on the telephone too. "Please go," she said.

"Is there anything you need?"

"No." She thought of E.'s cat, for some reason.

"You can't tell me at least what happened?"

"No."

She remembered E.'s hands and mouth on her — a week ago? An hour?

Cornell Pupkiss was tall and drab and stolid, like a man built on the model of a tower of suitcases. He wore a hat and a trench coat, and shoes which were filigreed with a thousand tiny scratches, as though they'd been beset by phonograph needles. He seemed to absorb and deaden light.

On the telephone he had insisted on seeing her. He'd handed her the disks and the address book at the door. Now he stood just inside the door and smiled gently at her.

"I wanted to see you in the flesh," he said. "I've come to know you from photographs and people's descriptions. When I come to know a person in that manner I like to see them in the flesh if I can. It makes me feel I've completed my job, a rare enough illusion in my line."

There was nothing bright or animated in the way he spoke. His voice was like furniture with the varnish carefully sanded off. "But I haven't really completed my job until I understand what happened," he went on. "Whether a crime was committed. Whether you're in some sort of trouble with which I can help."

She shook her head.

"Where were you?" he said.

"I was with a man."

"I see. For almost two weeks?"

"Yes."

She was still holding the address book. He raised his large hand in its direction, without uncurling a finger to point. "We called every man you know."

"This — this was someone I just met. Are these questions necessary, Mr. Pupkiss?"

"If the time was spent voluntarily, no." His lips tensed, his whole expression deepened, like gravy jelling. "I'm sorry, Miss Rush."

Pupkiss in his solidity touched her somehow. Reassured her. If he went away, she saw now, she'd be alone with the questions. She wanted him to stay a little longer and voice the questions for her.

But now he was gently sarcastic. "You're answerable to no one, of course. I only suggest that in the future you might spare the concern of your neighbors, and the effort of my department — a single phone call would be sufficient."

"I didn't realize how much time had passed," she said. He couldn't know how truthful that was.

"I've heard it can be like that," he said, surprisingly bitter. "But it's not criminal to neglect the feelings of others; just adolescent."

You don't understand, she nearly cried out. But she saw that he would view it as one or the other, a menace or self-indulgence. If she convinced him of her distress, he'd want to protect her.

She couldn't let harm come to E. She wanted to comprehend what had happened, but Pupkiss was too blunt to be her investigatory tool.

Reflecting in this way, she said, "The things that happen to people don't always fit into such easy categories as that."

"I agree," he said, surprising her again. "But in my job it's best to keep from bogging down in ontology. Missing Persons is an extremely large and various category. Many people are lost in relatively simple ways, and those are generally the ones I can help. Good day, Miss Rush."

"Good day." She didn't object as he moved to the door. Suddenly she was eager to be free of this ponderous man, his leaden integrity. She wanted to be left alone to remember the night before, to think of the one who'd devoured her and left her reeling. That was what mattered.

E. had somehow caused two weeks to pass in one feverish night, but Pupkiss threatened to make the following morning feel like two weeks.

He shut the door behind him so carefully that there was only a little huff of displaced air and a tiny click as the bolt engaged.

"It's me," she said into the intercom.

There was only static. She pressed the button again. "Let me come up."

He didn't answer, but the buzzer at the door sounded. She went into the hall and upstairs to his door.

"It's open," he said.

E. was seated at the table, holding a drink. The cat was curled up on the pile of envelopes. The apartment was dark. Still, she saw what she hadn't before: he lived terribly, in rooms that were wrecked and provisional. The plaster was cracked everywhere. Cigarette stubs were bunched in the baseboard corners where, having still smoldered, they'd tanned the linoleum. The place smelled sour, in a way that made her think of the sourness she'd washed from her body in her own bath an hour before.

He tilted his head up, but didn't meet her gaze. "Why are you here?"

"I wanted to see you."

"You shouldn't."

His voice was ragged, his expression had a crushed quality. His hand on the glass was tensed like a claw. But even diminished and bitter he seemed to her effervescent, made of light.

"We — something happened when we made love," she said. The words came tenderly. "We lost time."

"I warned you. Now leave."

"My life," she said, uncertain what she meant.

"Yes, it's yours," he shot back. "Take it and go."

"If I gave you two weeks, it seems the least you can do is look me in the eye," she said.

He did it, but his mouth trembled as though he were guilty or afraid. His face was beautiful to her.

"I want to know you," she said.

"I can't let that happen," he said. "You see why." He tipped his glass back and emptied it, grimacing.

"This is what always happens to you?"

"I can't answer your questions."

"If that happens, I don't care." She moved to him and put her hands in his hair.

He reached up and held them there.

[3]

A woman has come into my life. I hardly know how to speak of it.

I was in the station, enduring the hectoring of Dell Armickle, the commander of the Vice Squad. He is insufferable, a toad from Hell. He follows the donut cart through the offices each afternoon, pinching the buttocks of the Jamaican woman who peddles the donuts and that concentrated urine others call coffee. This day he stopped at my desk to gibe at the headlines in my morning paper. "Union Boss Stung In Fat Farm Sex Ring — ha! Made you look, didn't I?"

"What?"

"Pupkiss, you're only pretending to be thick. How much you got hidden away in that Swedish bank account by now?"

"Sorry?" His gambits were incomprehensible.

"Whatsis?" he said, poking at my donut, ignoring his own blather better than I could ever hope to. "Cinnamon?"

"Whole wheat," I said.

Then she appeared. She somehow floated in without causing any fuss, and stood at the head of my desk. She was pale and hollow-eyed and beautiful, like Renée Falconetti in Dreyer's *Jeanne d'Arc*.

"Officer Pupkiss," she said. Is it only in the light of what followed that I recall her speaking my name as though she knew me? At least she spoke it with certainty, not questioning whether she'd found her goal.

I'd never seen her before, though I can only prove it by tautology: I knew at that moment I was seeing a face I would never forget.

Armickle bugged his eyes and nostrils at me, imitating both clown and beast. "Speak to the lady, Cornell," he said, managing to impart to the syllables of my given name a childish ribaldry.

"I'm Pupkiss," I said awkwardly.

"I'd like to talk to you," she said. She looked only at me, as though Armickle didn't exist.

"I can take a hint," said Armickle. "Have fun, you two." He hurried after the donut cart.

"You work in Missing Persons," she said.

"No," I said. "Petty Violations."

"Before, you used to work in Missing Persons —"

"Never. They're a floor above us. I'll walk you to the elevator if you'd like."

"No." She shook her head curtly, impatiently. "Forget it. I want to talk to you. What are Petty Violations?"

"It's an umbrella term. But I'd sooner address your concerns than try your patience with my job description."

"Yes. Could we go somewhere?"

I led her to a booth in the coffee shop downstairs. I ordered a donut, to replace the one I'd left behind on my desk. She drank coffee, holding the cup with both hands to warm them. I found myself wanting to feed her, build her a nest.

"Cops really do like donuts," she said, smiling weakly.

"Or toruses," I said.

"Sorry? You mean the astrological symbol?"

"No, the geometric shape. A torus. A donut is in the shape of one. Like a life preserver, or a tire, or certain space stations. It's a little joke of mine: cops don't like donuts, they like toruses."

She looked at me oddly. I cursed myself for bringing it up. "Shouldn't the plural be *tori*?" she said.

I winced. "I'm sure you're right. Never mind. I don't mean to take up your time with my little japes."

"I've got plenty of time," she said, poignant again.

"Nevertheless. You wished to speak to me."

"You knew me once," she said.

I did my best to appear sympathetic, but I was baffled.

"Something happened to the world. Everything changed. Everyone that I know has disappeared."

"As an evocation of subjective truth — " I began.

"No. I'm talking about something real. I used to have friends."

"I've had few, myself."

"Listen to me. All the people I know have disappeared. My family, my friends, everyone I used to work with. They've all been replaced by strangers who don't know me. I have nowhere to go. I've been awake for two days looking for my life. I'm exhausted. You're the only person that looks the same as before, and has the same name. The Missing Persons man, ironically."

"I'm not the Missing Persons man," I said.

"Cornell Pupkiss. I could never forget a name like that."

"It's been a burden."

"You don't remember coming to my apartment? You said you'd been looking for me. I was gone for two weeks."

I struggled against temptation. I could extend my time in her company by playing along, indulging the misunderstanding. In other words, by betraying what I knew to be the truth: that I had nothing at all to do with her unusual situation.

"No," I said. "I don't remember."

Her expression hardened. "Why should you?" she said bitterly.

"Your question's rhetorical," I said. "Permit me a rhetorical reply. That I don't know you from some earlier encounter we can both regret. However, I know you now. And I'd be pleased to have you consider me an ally."

"Thank you."

"How did you find me?"

"I called the station and asked if you still worked there."

"And there's no one else from your previous life?"

"No one — except him."

Ah.

"Tell me," I said.

She'd met the man she called E. in a bar, how long ago she couldn't explain. She described him as irresistible. I formed an impression of a skunk, a rat. She said he worked no deliberate charm on her, on the contrary seemed panicked when the mood between them grew intimate and full of promise. I envisioned a scoundrel with an act, a crafted diffidence that allured, a backpedaling attack.

He'd taken her home, of course.

"And?" I said.

"We fucked," she said. "It was good, I think. But I have trouble remembering."

The words stung. The one in particular. I tried not to be a child, swallowed my discomfort away. "You were drunk," I suggested.

"No. I mean, *yes*, but it was more than that. We weren't clumsy like drunks. We went into some kind of trance."

"He drugged you."

"No."

"How do you know?"

"What happened — it wasn't something he wanted."

"And what did happen?"

"Two weeks disappeared from my life overnight. When I got home I found I'd been considered missing. My friends and family had been searching for me. You'd been called in."

"I thought your friends and family had vanished themselves. That no one knew you."

"No. That was the *second* time."

"Second time?"

"The second time we fucked." Then she seemed to remember something, and dug in her pocket. "Here." She handed me a scuffed business card: CORNELL PUPKISS, MISSING PERSONS.

———

"I can't believe you live this way. It's like a prison." She referred to the seamless rows of book spines that faced her in each of my few rooms, including the bedroom where we now stood. "Is it all criminology?"

"I'm not a policeman in some cellular sense," I said, and then realized the pun. "I mean, not intrinsically. They're novels, first editions."

"Let me guess; mysteries."

"I detest mysteries. I would never bring one into my home."

"Well, you have, in me."

I blushed, I think, from head to toe. "That's different," I stammered. "Human lives exist to be experienced, or possibly endured, but not solved. They resemble any other novel more than they do mysteries. Westerns, even. It's that lie the mystery tells that I detest."

"Your reading is an antidote to the simplifications of your profession, then."

"I suppose. Let me show you where the clean towels are kept."

I handed her fresh towels and linen, and took for myself a set of sheets to cover the living room sofa.

She saw that I was preparing the sofa and said, "The bed's big enough."

I didn't turn, but I felt the blood rush to the back of my neck as though specifically to meet her gaze. "It's four in the afternoon," I said. "I won't be going to bed for hours. Besides, I snore."

"Whatever," she said. "Looks uncomfortable, though. What's Barbara Pym? She sounds like a mystery writer, one of those stuffy English ones."

The moment passed, the blush faded from my scalp. I wondered later, though, whether this had been some crucial missed opportunity. A chance at the deeper intervention that was called for.

"Read it," I said, relieved at the change of subject. "Just be careful of the dust jacket."

"I may learn something, huh?" She took the book and climbed in between the covers.

"I hope you'll be entertained."

"And she doesn't snore, I guess. That was a joke, Mr. Pupkiss."

"So recorded. Sleep well. I have to return to the station. I'll lock the door."

"Back to Little Offenses?"

"Petty Violations."

"Oh, right." I could hear her voice fading. As I stood and watched, she fell soundly asleep. I took the Pym from her hands and replaced it on the shelf.

I wasn't going to the station. Using the information she'd given me, I went to find the tavern E. supposedly frequented.

I found him there, asleep in a booth, head resting on his folded arms. He looked terrible, his hair a thatch, drool leaking into his sweater arm, his eyes swollen like a fevered child's, just the picture of raffish haplessness a woman would find magnetic. Unmistakably the seedy vermin I'd projected and the idol of Miss Rush's nightmare.

I went to the bar and ordered an Irish coffee, and considered. Briefly indulging a fantasy of personal power, I rebuked myself for coming here and making him real, when he had only before been an absurd story, a neurotic symptom. Then I took out the card she'd given me and laid it on the bar top. Cornell Pupkiss, Missing Persons. No, I myself was the symptom. It is seldom as easy in practice as in principle to acknowledge one's own bystander status in incomprehensible matters.

I took my coffee to his booth and sat across from him. He roused and looked up at me.

"Rise and shine, buddy boy," I said, a little stiffly. I've never thrilled to the role of Bad Cop.

"What's the matter?"

"Your unshaven chin is scratching the table surface."

"Sorry." He rubbed his eyes.

"Got nowhere to go?"

"What are you, the house dick?"

"I'm in the employ of any taxpayer," I said. "The bartender happens to be one."

"He's never complained to me."

"Things change."

"You can say that again."

We stared at each other. I supposed he was nearly my age, though he was more boyishly pretty than I'd been even as an actual boy. I hated him for that, but I pitied him for the part I saw that was precociously old and bitter.

I thought of Miss Rush asleep in my bed. She'd been worn and disarrayed by their two encounters, but she didn't yet look this way. I wanted to keep her from it.

"Let me give you some advice," I said, as gruffly as I could manage. "Solve your problems."

"I hadn't thought of that."

"Don't get stuck in a rut." I was aware of the lameness of my words only as they emerged, too late to stop.

"Don't worry, I never do."

"Very well then," I said, somehow unnerved. "This interview is concluded." If he'd shown any sign of budging I might have leaned back in the booth, crossed my arms authoritatively, and stared him out the door. Since he remained planted in his seat, I stood up, feeling that my last spoken words needed reinforcement.

He laid his head back into the cradle of his arms, first sliding the laminated place mat underneath. "This will protect the table surface," he said.

"That's good, practical thinking," I heard myself say as I left the booth.

It wasn't the confrontation I'd been seeking.

On the way home I shopped for breakfast, bought orange juice, milk, bagels, fresh coffee beans. I took it upstairs and unpacked it as quietly as I could in the kitchen, then removed my shoes and crept in to have a look at Miss Rush. She was peaceably asleep. I closed the door and prepared my bed on the sofa. I read a few pages of the Penguin softcover edition of Muriel Spark's *The Bachelors* before dropping off.

Before dawn, the sky like blued steel, the city silent, I was woken by a sound in the apartment, at the front door. I put on my robe and went into the kitchen. The front door was unlocked, my key in the deadbolt. I went back through the apartment; Miss Rush was gone.

I write this at dawn. I am very frightened.

[4]

In an alley which ran behind a lively commercial street there sat a pair of the large trash receptacles commonly known as Dumpsters. In them accumulated the waste produced by the shops whose rear entrances shared the alley; a framer's, a soup kitchen, an antique clothing store, a donut bakery, and a photocopyist's establishment, and by the offices above those storefronts. On this street and in this alley, each day had its seasons: Spring, when complaining morning shifts opened the shops, students and workers rushed to destinations, coffee sloshing in paper cups, and in the alley, the sanitation contractors emptied containers, sorted recyclables and waste like bees pollinating garbage truck flowers; Summer, the ripened afternoons, when the workday slackened, shoppers stole long lunches from their employers, the cafes filled with students with highlighter pens, and the indigent beckoned for the change that jingled in incautious pockets, while in the alley new riches piled up; Autumn, the cooling evening, when half the shops closed, and the street was given over to prowlers and pacers, those who lingered in bookstores and dined alone in Chinese restaurants, and the indigent plundered the fatted Dumpsters for half-eaten paper bag lunches, batches of botched donuts, wearable cardboard matting and unmatched socks, and burnable wood scraps; Winter, the selfish night, when even the cafes battened down iron gates through which night-watchmen fluorescents palely flickered, the indigent built their overnight camps in doorways and under sidestreet hedges, or in wrecked cars, and the street itself was an abandoned stage.

On the morning in question the sun shone brightly, yet the air was bitingly cold. Birds twittered resentfully. When the sanitation crew arrived to wheel the two Dumpsters out to be hydraulically lifted into their screeching, whining truck, they were met with cries of protest from within.

The men lifted the metal tops of the Dumpsters and discovered that an indigent person had lodged in each of them, a lady in one, a gentleman in the other.

"Geddoudadare," snarled the eldest sanitation engineer, a man with features like a spilled plate of stew.

The indigent lady rose from within the heap of refuse and stood blinking in the bright morning sun. She was an astonishing sight, a ruin. The colors of her skin and hair and clothes had all surrendered to gray; an archaeologist might have ventured an opinion as to their previous hue. She could have been anywhere between thirty and fifty years old, but speculation was absurd; her age had been taken from her and replaced with a timeless condition, a state. Her eyes were pitiable; horrified and horrifying; witnesses, victims, accusers.

"Where am I?" she said softly.

"Isedgeddoudadare," barked the garbage operative.

The indigent gentleman then raised himself from the other Dumpster. He was in every sense her match; to describe him would be to tax the reader's patience for things worn, drab, desolate, crestfallen, unfortunate, etc. He turned his head at the trashman's exhortation and saw his mate.

"What's the — " he began, then stopped.

"You," said the indigent lady, lifting an accusing finger at him from amidst her rags. "You did this to me."

"No," he said. "No."

"Yes!" she screamed.

"C'mon," said the burly sanitateur. He and his second began pushing the nearer container, which bore the lady, towards his truck.

She cursed at them and climbed out, with some difficulty. They only laughed at her and pushed the cart out to the street. The indigent man scrambled out of his Dumpster and brushed at his clothes, as though they could thereby be distinguished from the material in which he'd lain.

The lady flew at him, furious. "Look at us! Look what you did to me!" She whirled her limbs at him, trailing banners of rag.

He backed from her, and bumped into one of the garbagemen, who said, "Hey!"

"It's not my fault," said the indigent man.

"Yugoddagedoudahere!" said the stew-faced worker.

"What do you mean it's not your fault?" she shrieked.

Windows were sliding open in the offices above them. "Quiet down there," came a voice.

"It wouldn't happen without you," he said.

At that moment a policeman rounded the corner. He was a large man named Officer McPupkiss who even in the morning sun conveyed an aspect of night. His policeman's uniform was impeccably fitted, his brass polished, but his shoetops were exceptionally scuffed and dull. His presence stilled the combatants.

"What's the trouble?" he said.

They began talking all at once; the pair of indigents, the refuse handlers, and the disgruntled office worker leaning out of his window.

"Please," said McPupkiss, in a quiet voice which was nonetheless heard by all.

"He ruined my life!" said the indigent lady raggedly.

"Ah, yes. Shall we discuss it elsewhere?" He'd already grasped the situation. He held out his arms, almost as if he wanted to embrace the two tatterdemalions, and nodded at the disposal experts, who silently resumed their labors. The indigents followed McPupkiss out of the alley.

"He ruined my life," she said again when they were on the sidewalk.

"She ruined mine," answered the gentleman.

"I wish I could believe it was all so neat," said McPupkiss. "A life is simply *ruined*; credit for the destruction goes *here* or *here*. In my own experience things are more ambiguous."

"This is one of the exceptions," said the lady. "It's strange but not ambiguous. He fucked me over."

"She was warned," he said. "She made it happen."

"The two of you form a pretty picture," said McPupkiss. "You ought to be working together to improve your situation; instead you're obsessed with blame."

"We can't work together," she said. "Anytime we come together we create a disaster."

"Fine, go your separate ways," said the officer. "I've always thought 'We got ourselves into this mess and we can get ourselves out of it' was a laughable attitude. Many things are irreversible, and what matters is moving on. For example, a car can't reverse its progress over a cliff; it has to be abandoned by those who survive the fall, if any do."

But by the end of this speech the gray figures had fallen to blows and were no longer listening. They clutched one another like exhausted boxers, hissing and slapping, each trying to topple the other. McPupkiss chided himself for wasting his breath, grabbed them both by the back of their scruffy collars, and began smiting their hindquarters with his dingy shoes until they ran down the block and out of sight together, united again, McPupkiss thought, as they were so clearly meant to be.

[5]

The village of Pupkinstein was nestled in a valley surrounded by steep woods. The villagers were a contented people except for the fear of the two monsters that lived in the woods and came into the village to fight their battles. Everyone knew that the village had been rebuilt many times after being half destroyed by the fighting of the monsters. No one living could remember the last of these battles, but that only intensified the suspicion that the next time would surely be soon.

Finally the citizens of Pupkinstein gathered in the town square to discuss the threat of the two monsters, and debate proposals for the prevention of their battles. A group of builders said, "Let us build a wall around the perimeter of the village, with a single gate which could be fortified by volunteer soldiers."

A group of priests began laughing, and one of them said, "Don't you know that the monsters have wings? They'll flap twice and be over your wall in no time."

Since none of the builders had ever seen the monsters, they had no reply.

Then the priests spoke up and said, "We should set up temples which can be filled with offerings: food, wine, burning candles, knitted scarves, and the like. The monsters will be appeased."

Now the builders laughed, saying, "These are monsters, not jealous gods. They don't care for our appeasements. They only want to crush each other, and we're in the way."

The priests had no answer, since their holy scriptures contained no accounts of the monsters' habits.

Then the Mayor of Pupkinstein, a large, somber man, said, "We should build our own monster here in the middle of the square, a scarecrow so huge and threatening that the monsters will see it and at once be frightened back into hiding."

This plan satisfied the builders, with their love of construction, and the priests, with their fondness for symbols. So the very next morning the citizens of Pupkinstein set about constructing a gigantic figure in the square. They began by demolishing their fountain. In its place they marked out the soles of two gigantic shoes, and the builders sank foundations for the towering legs that would extend from them. Then the carpenters built frames, and the seamstresses sewed canvases, and in less than a week the two shoes were complete, and the beginnings of ankles besides. Without being aware of it, the citizens had begun to model their monster on the Mayor, who was always present as a model, whereas no one had ever seen the two monsters.

The following night it rained. Tarpaulins were thrown over the half-constructed ankles that rose from the shoes. The Mayor and the villagers retired to an alehouse to toast their labors and be sheltered from the rain. But just as the proprietor was pouring their ale, someone said, "Listen!"

Between the crash of thunder and the crackle of lightning there came a hideous bellowing from the woods at either end of the valley.

"They're coming!" the citizens said. "Too soon — our monster's not finished!"

"How bitter," said one man. "We've had a generation of peace in which to build, and yet we only started a few days ago."

"We'll always know that we tried," said the Mayor philosophically.

"Perhaps the shoes will be enough to frighten them," said the proprietor, who had always been regarded as a fool.

No one answered him. Fearing for their lives, the villagers ran to their homes and barricaded themselves behind shutters and doors, hid their children in attics and potato cellars, and snuffed out candles and lanterns that might lead an attacker to their doors. No one dared even look at the naked, miserable things that came out of the woods and into the square; no one, that is, except the Mayor. He stood in the shadow of one of the enormous shoes, rain beating on his umbrella, only dimly sensing that he was watching another world being fucked away.

[6]

I live in a shadowless pale blue sea.

I am a bright pink crablike thing, some child artist's idea of an invertebrate, so badly drawn as to be laughable.

Nevertheless, I have feelings.

More than feelings. I have a mission, an obsession.

I am building a wall.

Every day I move a grain of sand. The watercolor sea washes over my back, but I protect my accumulation. I fasten each grain to the wall with my comic-book feces. (Stink lines hover above my shit, also flies which look like bow ties, though I am supposed to be underwater.)

He is on the other side. My nemesis. Someday my wall will divide the ocean, someday it will reach the surface, or the top of the page, and be called a reef. He will be on the other side. He will not be able to get to me.

My ridiculous body moves only sideways, but it is enough.

I will divide the watercolor ocean, I will make it two. We must have a world for each of us.

I move a grain. When I come to my wall, paradoxically, I am nearest him. His little pink body, practically glowing. He is watching me, watching me build.

There was a time when he tried to help, when every day for a week he added a grain to my wall. I spent every day that week removing his grain, expelling it from the Wall, and no progress was made until he stopped. He understands now. My wall must be my own. We can be together in nothing. Let him build his own wall. So he watches.

My wall will take me ten thousand years to complete. I live only for the day that it is complete.

The Pupfish floats by.

The Pupfish is a fish with the features of a mournful hound dog and a policeman's cap. The Pupfish is the only creature in the sea apart from me and my pink enemy.

The Pupfish, I know, would like to scoop me up in its oversized jaws and take me away. The Pupfish thinks it can solve my problem.

But no matter how far the Pupfish took me, I would still be in the same ocean with *him*. That cannot be. There must be two oceans. So I am building a wall.

I move a grain.

I rest.

I will be free.

All of Us Can Almost...

Carol Emshwiller

This is a story about the confluence of gender roles, power plays, sex, pride, and desperation.

So of course it is very funny.

...fly, that is. Of course lots of creatures can *almost* fly. But all of us are able to match any others of us, wingspan to wingspan. Also to any other fliers. But though we match each other wing to wing, we can't get more than inches off the ground. If that. But we're impressive. Our beaks look vicious. We could pose for statues for the birds representing an empire. We could represent an army or a president. And actually, we are the empire. We may not be able to fly, but we rule the skies. And most everything else too.

Creatures come to us for advice on flying. They see us kick up dust and flap and stretch and are awed.

We croak out what we have to say in quacks. We tell them, "The sky is a highway. The sky is of our time and recent. The sky is flat. It's blue because it's happy." They thank us with donations. That's how we live.

The sound of our clacking beaks carries across the valley. It adds to our reputation as powerful — though what good is it really? It's just noise.

Nothing said of us is true, but must we live by truths? Why not keep on living by our lies?

Soaring! Think of it! The stillness of it. Not even the sound of flapping. They say we once did that. Perhaps we still can and just forgot how to begin. How make that first jump? How get the lift? But we grew too large. We began to eat the things that fell, and lots of things fall.

I could leap off a cliff. Test myself. But I might become one of those things tumbling down. Even my own kind would tear me apart.

Loosely...very loosely speaking, I do fly. My sleep is full of nothing but that. The joy of it.

But where's the joy in *almost* doing it? Flapping in circles. Making a great wind for nothing but a jump or two. We don't even look good to ourselves.

I don't know what we're made for. It's neither sky nor water nor... especially not...the waddle of the land. We can't sing. Actually, we can't do anything. Except look fierce.

Pigeons circle overhead. Meadowlarks sing. Geese and ducks, in Vs, do their seasonal things. We stay. We *have* to. Winter storms come and we're still here. We puff up as much as we can and wrap our wings around ourselves. Perhaps that's what our wings were for in the first place. We're designed merely to shelter ourselves. Even our dreams of flying are yet more lies.

But none of the others are as strong as we are...at least none *seem* to be. We win with looks alone and a big voice. We stand, assured and sure.

When creatures ask me for a ride, I say, "I'd take you up anytime you want — hop and skip and up we go — except you're too heavy. Next time measure wings, mine against some other of us. You'll need a few inches more on each side. Tell a bigger one I said to take you up."

"Take to the air along with us," I say. "Follow me up and up." I'm shameless. But I suspect it's only the young that really believe. The older ones pretend to because of our beaks, because of the wind we can stir up — our clouds of dust.

Still, I go on, "Check out my wingspan. Check out my evil eye. Listen. *My* voice."

They jump at my squawk.

They bring me food just to watch me tear at it. At least I'm good at that. I put on a good show. Every creature backs away.

One of the young ones keeps wanting me to take him up. He won't stop asking. I say, "A sparrow could do better." That's true, but he takes it as a joke. I say, "Why not at least ask a male?"

"Males scare me."

Finally, just to shut him up, I say, "Yes, but not until the next section of time."

He runs off yelling, "Whee! Whee! Whee! She's taking me up!"

Now how will I get out of it? I only have from one moon to the other. But who knows? One of the big males may have eaten him by that time. They don't care where their food comes from. He was right to be scared.

Who knows how we lost our ability to fly? Maybe we're just lazy. Maybe we just don't exercise our flying muscles. How could we fly, sitting around eating dead things all the time? If anyone can fly, it seems to me more likely one of us smaller females could than a big male.

That little one keeps coming back and saying, "*Really? Are you really* going to take me up?"

And I keep saying, "I said I would, didn't I? When have any of us ever lied?" (Actually, when have we ever told the truth?)

He keeps yelling back and forth to all who'll listen. The way he keeps on with it, I could eat him myself.

But we have to be careful. Sometimes those ground dwellers get together and decide not to feed us. Whoever they don't feed always dies. They waddle around trying to get someone of us to share, but we don't. We're not a sharing kind.

I *should* like these ground dwellers because of the food they bring, but I don't. I pretend to, just like they pretend to believe us. They call us Emperor, Leader, Master, but why are they doing this? It could be a conspiracy to keep us fat and lazy so we won't be lords of the sky anymore. So we're tamed and docile. Maybe they started this whole thing, stuffing us with their leftovers. Maybe they're the real emperors of the sky. Master of the sky though never in it any more than we are. At least they can climb trees.

I wonder what they want us for? Or maybe it's the best way to know where we are and what we're doing.

Feed your enemies. Tame them.

I ask some of us, "Where is that cliff they say we used to soar out from?"

"Was there a cliff? Did there used to be a cliff?"

I'm sure there must have been one. How could birds the size of us get started without one — a high one? Maybe that's our problem: we've lost our cliff. We forgot where it is.

Evenings, when all are in their burrows, and my own kind, wrapped in their wings, are clustered under the lean-tos set out for us by lesser beings, I stretch and flap. Reach. Jump. Only the nightingale sees me flop. It's a joy to be up to hear her and to be flipping and flopping.

I'll take that pesky little one all the way to wherever that cliff of ours is. Wouldn't that be something? See the sights? Be up in what we always call "our element."

But there's a male, has his eye on me. Has had for quite some time. That's another good reason to take off. I'd like to get out of here before the time is ripe.

Or perhaps he's heard the little one yelling, "Whee, Whee," and likes the idea of me with one of those little ones on my back. Easy pickin's, *both* of us. Little one for one purpose and me for another. I can just see it, me distracted, defending the little, and the big taking care of both things while I struggle, front *and* back.

He may be the biggest, but I don't want him. Maybe that's how we got too big to fly: we kept mating with the biggest. It's our own fault we got so big. I'm not going to do that. Well, also the big ones are the strongest. This biggest could slap down all the other males.

If not for the fact that we hardly speak to each other, we females could get together and stop it. Go for the small and the nice. If there are any nice. Not a single one of us is noted for being nice.

I hate to think what mating will be like with one so huge. I'd ask other females if we were the kind who asked things of each other.

He keeps following me around. I don't know how I'm going to avoid him if he's determined. I won't get any help from any of the others. They'll just come and watch. Probably even squawk him onward. I've done it myself.

I'm thinking of ways to avoid that male, so when that little one comes to ask, yet again, "Why wait for next moon?" I say, "You're right. We'll do it now, but I have to find our platform."

"Why?"

"Have you ever seen any of us take off from down here? Of course you haven't. I need a place to soar from."

"Can't we start flying from right here so everybody can see me?"

"No. I have to have a place to take off from. Get on my back. I'll take you there."

"I can walk faster than this all by myself."

"I know, but bear with me."

"My name is Hobie. What's yours?"

"We don't have names. We don't need them."

The big one comes waddling after us. A few of us follow him, wanting to see what's going to happen. I don't think the big realizes how far I'm going. Nobody does.

When we get to the end of the nesting places, Hobie says, "I've never been this far. Is this all right to do?"

"It's all right."

"Your waddling is making me sick."

"We'll rest in a few minutes."

I don't dare stop now, so near the nests. Everybody will waddle out to us. We have to get out of sight. Out there I could eat Hobie myself if need be. I don't suppose anybody will be feeding us way out here.

I don't stop soon enough. Hobie throws up on my back. It smells of dirt-dwellers' food. And we're still not out of sight.

"Hang on. I'll stop at that green patch just ahead."

I waddle a little faster, but that just makes him fall off. I'm thinking, Oh well, go on back and let the big male do what he wants to do. It can't last more than a couple of minutes. If he breaks my legs it might be better than what I'm going through now.

But I wait for Hobie to get back on. I say, "Not much farther." He climbs on slowly. I wonder if he suspects I might eat him.

That big is coming along behind us, but he's slower even that I am. Who'd have thought I was worth so much trouble.

In the green patch there's water — a stream. We both drink, and I start washing my back. Hobie keeps saying, "I couldn't help it."

"I know that. Now stop talking so I can think."

I leave footprints. Maybe best if I go along the stream for a while. Then we can drink anytime we want. I turn toward the high side, where the stream comes down from. If there really is a takeoff platform, it's got to be high.

"Where are we going?"

"There's a place in the sky that'll give me a good lift."

"What kind of a place?"

"A cliff."

"How far is it?"

"Oh, for the sky's sake, keep quiet."

"Why does your kind always say 'for the sky's sake'?"

"Because we're sky creatures. Not like you. Now let me think about walking."

Even in this little stream there's fish. Wouldn't it be nice if I could catch one by myself?

"Hang on!"

I dive. But I forgot about the water changing the angle of view. I miss. I say, "Next time."

Hobie says, "I can."

I let him off to stand on the bank and dive, and he does it. Gives the fish to me even though I'll bet he's getting hungry too.

"Thank you, Hobie. Now get one for yourself."

At dusk we find a nice place to nest in among the trees along the stream — soft with leaves. Hobie curls up right beside my beak. Practically under it. I'm more afraid of my bite than he is. I hope I don't snap him up in my sleep.

Toward morning we hear something coming...lumbering along. Sounding tired for sure. We both know who. Hobie doesn't like big males any more than I do. He scrambles up on my back and says, "Shouldn't we go?"

Because I'm so much smaller than any male, I waddle a lot faster. It gets steeper, but I'm still doing pretty well. It's so steep I have hopes of finding our cliff. I turn around and look back down and here comes the big, but a long ways off. Staggering, stumbling. Am I really worth all this effort?

"Are we far enough ahead? Are we getting someplace? How long now?"

"Do you ever say anything that isn't a question?"

"You do it. That's a question."

I'm not used to waddling all day long, especially not uphill. It's the hardest thing I've ever done. But the big.... He's still coming. It's getting steeper. I hope one as large as he is can't get up here. This is just what I wanted. The launching platform has got to be here. How did it ever come to be that we got stuck down in the flat places?

And finally, here it is, *the* flat place at the top of the cliff. I look over the edge. I'm so scared just looking I start to feel sick. I'm not sure I can even pretend to jump.

"Why are you shaking so much? It's going to make me sick again."

Should I eat Hobie now before he tells everybody I not only can't fly, I can't even get close to the edge without trembling and feeling sick?

But it's been nice having company. I've gotten used to his paws tangled in my feathers, making a mess of them. I'd miss his questions.

I move back and look over the other side. It's steep on that side too, though not so much. This platform is a promontory going off into nothing on all sides but one. It must have been perfect for fliers.

I look around to see if I can see any signs that it was used as a launching place, but there's nothing. I suppose, up here so high, the weather would have worn away any signs of that. I wonder if that big male knows anything more about it than I do.

It's breezy up here. I flap my wings to test myself, but I do it well away from the edges.

Hobie says, "Go, go, go."

Maybe I should just get closer and closer to the edge...get used to it little by little...until I don't feel quite so scared.

I look over the side again, though from a few feet away. I see the big male is still coming. I see him turn around and look down at exactly the same spot where we did. Then he looks up. Right at us. He spreads his wings at us so I'll see his wingspan. Then he turns side view. That's so I'll get a good look at his profile...the big hooked beak, the white ruff... Then he starts up again.

I look over the more sloping side again. I think I might be able to slide down there, though it's a steep slide. At the bottom there's a lot of trees and brush. That would break our fall.

That big one is getting so close I can hear him shuffling and sliding just like I did. I sit over by the less steep side and wait.

Pretty soon I see the fierce head looking up at us, the beady eye, and then the whole body. He has an even harder time than I had lifting himself on to the launching platform.

Hobie says, "I'm scared of males," and I say, "I am too."

As soon as the big catches his breath, he says, "You're beautiful."

I say, "That's neither here nor there."

He says, "I love you." As if any of us knew what that word meant.

I say, "Love is what you feel for a nice piece of carrion."

He looks a mess. I must too. Dusty, feathers every which way. Hobie and I filled up on fish back at the stream, but I don't think he did. He looks at Hobie like the next meal. I back up a little closer to the slide. I say, "This one's mine." *That*, he'll understand.

He's inching closer. He thinks I don't notice. If he grabs me, there's no way I can escape. I back up even more.

And then... I didn't mean to. Off we go. Skidding, sliding, but like flying. Almost! Almost!

Hobie is yelling, "Whee. Whee. Whee." At least he's happy.

When we get down as far as the trees and bushes, I grab at them with my beak to slow us. And then I hear the big coming behind us. I never thought he...such a big one...would dare follow.

There's a great swish of gravel sliding with us. Even more as the big comes down behind us. Here he is, landed beside us, but, thank goodness, not exactly on.

Hobie and I are more or less fine. Scratched and bruised and dusty, but the big is moaning.

We're in a sort of ditch full of lots of brush and trees. It looks to be uphill on all sides. I wonder if either of us...the big and I...could waddle out of it. Hobie could.

Hobie and I dust off.

Hobie says. "That was great. I wish the others could have seen me."

He can't, can he? Can't *possibly* think that was flying?

Then I see that the big one's legs slant out at odd angles. His weight was his undoing. My relative lightness saved me.

The big says, "Help me." But why should I? I say, "It's all your fault in the first place."

He's in pain. I brush him off. I even dare to preen him a bit. I don't think he'll hurt me or try to mate. He couldn't with those broken legs, anyway. He needs me. He has to be nice. That'll be a change.

These big males are definitely bigger than they need to be. He's twice my size. Where will all this bigness lead? Just to less and less, ever again, the possibility of flight, that's where.

Hobie doesn't even need to be asked. "I'm hungry. Can I go get us some food?"

"Of course you can."

"After you flew me, I owe you lots."

Off he goes into the brush. I take a look at the big one's legs and wonder what to do. Can I make splints? And what to use to bind them with? Though there's always lots of stringy things in our carrion if Hobie finds us food.

"You're not only never going to fly, you may never waddle either."

He just groans again.

"I'll try to straighten these out." I give him a stick to bite on. And then I do it. After, I look for sticks as splints.

In no time Hobie brings three creatures. I think one for each of us, but he says he ate already. He's says this place is all meals. Nothing has been hunting here in a long time, maybe never. He says, "You could even hunt for yourself."

Now there's a thought. I think I will.

I leave the three creatures for the big male and start out, but the big says, "Don't leave me." Just like a chick.

I say, "If you eat Hobie, that's the last you'll ever see of me." And I go.

Hobie is right, all the little meals are easy to catch. I eat four and keep all the stringy things. I also look around at where we are and if we could ever get out. There's that little stream from below, cool and clear, bubbling along not far from where we fell. Beside it there's a nice place for a nest. I think about chicks. How I'd try to get them flapping right from the start. Even the baby males. And maybe, if we all were thinner and had to scramble for our food like I just had to do, and if all the food would get to know the danger and make us scramble harder and we'd get even thinner and stronger, and first thing you know we wouldn't have to climb out of here, we'd fly. All of us. Could that really come to be?

I throw away the stringy things I was going to make splints with. I have everything under control. I'll tell Hobie he can go on home if he wants to, though I'll tell him I do wish he'd stay, just for the company. And just in case we never do learn to fly again, we'd need his help when the food gets smarter and scarcer.

The Brains of Female Hyena Twins: On the Future of Gender

Gwyneth Jones

As Debbie Notkin pointed out in the introduction to this book, there is no social consensus on what gender is — or how it relates to feminism. The following essay by Gwyneth Jones explores gender from a scientific perspective, a discussion that suggests reasons for the confusion that swirls around sex and gender. This paper was originally presented at the conference of the Academic Fantastic Fiction Network held at Reading University in October 1994.

Female hyenas have high levels of androstenedione (a male hormone) throughout life, which possibly contributes to their aggressive nature. Interestingly...they behave normally in reproduction and are excellent mothers, showing that the "female" parts of the brain are protected from the androgens that masculinize their aggressive behavior....

> — Laurence Frank, behavioral research associate, in *New Scientist*, 5 March 1994

Carey points out that we already have a wonderful genetic marker for violence: "It's detectable at birth and in many cases before birth," he says. "The high-risk genotype is probably about nine-fold more likely to engage in violent acts...for some crimes the ratio is even more dramatic." Carey's marker is being male.

> — Rosie Mostel, in *New Scientist*, 26 February 1994, quoting behavioral geneticist Gregory Carey.

Two out of three women around the world presently suffer from the most debilitating disease known to humanity. Common symptoms of this fast-spreading ailment include chronic anemia, malnutrition, severe fatigue…. Premature death is a frequent outcome…. The disease is often communicated from mother to child, with markedly higher transmission rates among females. No, this disease is not HIV. It is poverty.

— *The Health Of Women: A Global Perspective*, edited by Marge Koblonsky, Judith Timyan, Gill Gay

The battle of the sexes heats up and cools down, waves of "feminism" rise and fall: but received wisdom regards human gender as a given: one of the pillars of the universe. Men and women are two sides of the same coin. No matter how they bicker, in the end and by and large they have to accept the complementary nature of their relationship, and get along the same old way…. But increasingly this "business as usual" worldview is maintained in the teeth of the evidence. In the course of the last century worldwide creation of wealth has been making insidious attacks, finally far more damaging than anything sexual-politicians can achieve, on the concept of gender. The lowering of the death rate, high infant survival, improved standards of living, improved quality of life itself, all go to create a situation in which, inexorably, the human male's propensity for violence; and the human female's capacity for childbearing, come to be regarded not as natural facts of life but as *problems*, that threaten the prosperity and comfort of human society. And human history suggests that once we have perceived some factor in our world as a problem (whether it's the nature of the fixed stars, or the scourge of infectious disease) sooner or later, someone will come up with a technological fix.

For the last ten years, as a writer of feminist science fiction, I have been conducting a strictly amateur investigation into the nature and function of human sexual behavior. I have approached the subject in different ways in novels, stories and critical essays; I've done a fair amount of reading around the area, and, like all good science fiction writers, I've taken note of developments in the real world. In the course of the decade, I've seen "feminism" as a broadly-based political movement discredited, and I've seen it re-established as literary and academic forum with its own private squabbles, media stars and market-niche; an accepted cultural sub-group. I've seen women *en masse* rejecting radical political solutions, yet at the same time becoming more vocal, more visible, more conscious and more openly resentful of their disadvantages. I've seen the New Man defrocked, and the return of the unrepentant male supremacist. Yet at the same time I've seen emerging a global acknowledgement of endemic crimes against women — rape as a weapon of war, bride burning, domestic violence — that have been tacitly condoned, if not openly approved, for millennia upon millennia. As I try to grapple, in my fiction, with complexity and the tensions I see in the real world, I've found myself returning, in the exasperated way one tries to recur to the starting point of a quarrel, *ad fontes*. (That means "to the springs." It's Latin for let's get back to where this all started.) Just what exactly is this thing called sex? What is it for, what is it supposed to do? This paper is a report on my investigation, and at the same time a description of how I, as an SF writer, go about the work of extracting ideas for my fiction from real world science.

There are quite a few popular science texts on sex around at the moment. It seems I'm not alone in my interest. Most of them (Richard Dawkins's *The Selfish Gene*; Matt Ridley's *The Red Queen*; Gail Vines's *Raging Hormones*) are extended essays from popularizers with their own agendas: determined to challenge, rouse, or excite their audience one way or another. These are "sexy" books, as we say nowadays. I preferred *The Differences Between the Sexes*, the published proceedings of the Eleventh International Conference on Comparative Physiology, held three years ago in Switzerland. *The Differences Between the Sexes* (edited by R.V. Short and E. Balaban; published by Cambridge University Press, 1994) is a collection of original scientific papers, described as "the first overview of this subject ever attempted." This text does not set out to provoke anybody. The attentive reader can discern a whole spectrum of political opinion, faintly inscribed between the lines in these pages. But any special pleading is buried deep in persnickety scattergraphs, and unlikely to stir the emotions unduly. Broadly, this is a book about sex as physiology, on every scale. There is no discussion of the symptoms or sensations of sexual arousal, only of chemical reactions. The organisms or body parts involved — lizards, ants, elephants, fishes, possibly parasitical mitochondria, Mullerian ducts and avian w chromosomes, are not perceived as doing sex for pleasure. They do it for exclusively economic reasons. But don't imagine that this makes for a dry and dull textbook. The sex-for-money story here is possibly even more fascinating than the one you find in the more familiar tabloid context.

So, exactly what do we — represented by the international science community — know about sex, at this stage in the game? Let me refresh your memories on modern sex-science lore. We know that eutherian mammals — that's animals like us — with the xx or xy sex chromosome pair, are default females. Hence the expression mammals, animals with milk-producing breasts. So, if you castrate a male rabbit embryo at an early stage in its development it doesn't grow up sexless, it develops as a normal female. (This is charmingly called Ohno's law, after Susumu Ohno, who first proved it.) Whereas birds, with a zz or zw pair, the W being the female chromosome, are default males. Thus, if you feed a peahen male hormones, she gets a bit pushy and irritable but physically nothing much happens. If you suppress her female hormones, she grows a flamboyant peacock's tail. The "cryptic" or dowdy plumage of the female in bird species is not a deficiency, then, as we have intuitively assumed. It is a positive interference in the natural course of things. Marsupials, or non-eutherian mammals, don't fit into this scheme of the chromosome pair sexing. They're a peculiar lot.

We know that gonadal sex, the development of testes or ovaries, is normally determined in eutherian mammals at conception. All other features of sexual dimorphism — external and internal organs, differences in brain structure and body size, all sexual behaviors, are produced subsequently by the action of the gonadal steroids, (progestins, androgens, and estrogens), powerful chemical concoctions that are carried in the circulation to act throughout the body, including the brain. It's as you long suspected, you're not responsible for anything you do under the influence of sex, it's just a drug experience. Marsupials, however, don't work quite the same way... (But I can't begin to tell you about the marsupials, it's just too bizarre. You wouldn't believe me. You'll have to read it for yourselves).

What else could I mention? There are the parthenogenetic species, animals that consist naturally of female individuals only. (It's not suggested that they evolved out of the pre-Cambrian stew like so: they have separated off from gonochoric, that is sexual species, somewhere along the line.) Some of them mate with males of related-sexual-species, and have various means of using or discarding the sperm DNA after conceptions. Some produce eggs without any genetic recombination at all: they're obligate separatists. I think the most famous of these species, the Texan parthenogenetic whiptail lizards studied by David Crews of the University of Texas, Austin, have passed into popular-science folklore, so you'll probably know that all-female lizard species exist. But did you know that individuals of these species have a habit of copulating with each other, taking turns at adopting male or female roles — a behavior which has a measurable impact on sex-hormone expression and on breeding success? The act itself has only been observed in captivity (there are some delightful photos), but the butch partner's role includes inflicting neck-bites, severe enough to produce a lasting bruise. Wild animals picked up for examination have been found with exactly similar hickeys on their throats, so it looks like it's not just the decadent lab-cage trollops, they're playing butch and femme out on the range too.

You may have heard of the SRY gene (sometimes written Sry). That stands for sex-determining region, Y gene. The definitive, universal marker that makes males male achieved national news status when the discovery was announced a year or so ago. The detective story of the hunt for SRY is in here: a paper by Jennifer Graves of La Trobe University, Victoria, Australia. It's truly fascinating. But there's also, hot from the press, research that has unearthed some "bizarre rodents" — the Iberian mole vole, the Kamchatka wood lemming, the Amami spinous country rat — where maleness is not determined by the SRY, and maybe even not by the XY pair. The hunt for the actual, holy essence of la différence isn't over yet.

What else? There's a paper on sexual dimorphism in primates, presenting evidence from skeletal analysis that female proto-gorillas, humans, chimps, may have been hunky as the males. Rather than males being selected out for larger size and strength, the females may have been selected down to a smaller body-size on the grounds of reproductive success. This is one of the papers where a quite provocative point is hidden in the scattergraphs. It is a basic tenet of male supremacist thought that humanity is naturally unequal, because men have always been the big strong owners of harems of docile little females... It gives them legitimacy. (I do not see it myself. If someone knocks me down because he's bigger than me, and then explains it's okay, because he's been bigger than me for two million years, I don't feel any better about it at all.) But it's quietly done: no excitement, no politics, just a modest suggestion that you take a look at the figures.

There are the female to male and male to female transsexual fishes. You'll have heard of them, maybe. They've passed into popular science folklore along with the Texan lizards. It appears that in many species of fishes if you remove the dominant male from a social group, the largest female then becomes male. In other circumstances, fish that are born "male" become female. Douglas Shapiro and others, of Michigan, have been investigating this phenomenon. They've discovered that sex-change is not destiny. The female-to-male or male-to-female change isn't inevitable in a simple set of circumstances like "remove the male." It is triggered by a particular and complex interaction of social and environmental factors: broadly, only when it's going to be profitable. You've heard of Sexual Darwinism. Here you get a classic, beautifully explained study of the precise economic factors that lead an individual fish to "decide" — speaking anthropomorphically — to change that mumsy apron for the go-getter's posing pouch.

There's sexually differentiated liver-function in rats; featuring mind-boggling lists of steroid metabolizing enzyme activity. There's a paper on song-control brain area dimorphism in the nucleus hyperstriatalis ventrale in male canaries; as opposed to male and female zebra finches, a duetting species; reassessing the significance of sexually dimorphic brain structure, and the relationship of brain-area volume to efficient function. There's a paper on *Drosophila melanogaster* pheromones (you can't leave out the fruit flies). And much more.

It's no surprise that the picture isn't much altered from Aristotle's view of the sexes. (The relevant quotation is provided in translation in the front of the book. I thought that was a stylish touch — *ad fontes* indeed.)[1] Cosmologists can add or subtract a few billion years from the age of the universe at will, without colliding with common sense. Sexual dimorphism belongs to a different order. Male sexual behavior, generally, is aggressive and dominant. Female sexual behavior, generally, is submissive and compliant. This is what we know, this is what we see. The advent of electron tunneling microscopy is not going to reveal, suddenly, that it's female red deer that grow the big antlers, and start beating the shit out of each other every September; or that male elephant seals are the helpless victims of institutionalized rape on the beaches. There are some popular sex-science writers who take violent exception to Aristotle. But they are no use to me. I'm never interested in imaginative interpretation with my science. I only have to pick it out and leave it on the side of my plate. I provide that element for myself.

The editors of *The Differences Between the Sexes* are less radical than some of their contributors (to the extent that R.V. Short, in his afterword, declares that "nobody questions the significant differences in average weight, height, and strength between men and women, testimony no doubt to our polygynous past..." apparently unaware that Robert Martin and others, the primate body-size snatchers from Zurich, have done exactly that). In many of the papers one can discern a fashionable shift in concept from simplicity to complexity, from clear results to fuzziness. Thus, in the primate-size paper, Robert Martin and his team do not claim that the theory of the big, polygynous male ape and human ancestor is wrong, they present evidence for a more complex situation. Science becomes a palimpsest, not a single text: it becomes, in some ways, a kind of fiction. But though trends in modern science have a discernible influence there is an old-fashioned anti-radical consensus in these papers, a commitment to pure description — as far as humanly possible — above interpretation, that gives me confidence. I can work with these results, without much hassly filtering out of contaminates.

I don't think I have to apologize for reading *The Differences Between the Sexes* politically. I am, sincerely, in awe at the quality of some of the papers (so far as an amateur can appreciate them). But I'm a science fiction writer, not a scientist. I approach these essays as I would an article on the curious plight of Hubble's Constant. I'm looking for hooks and riffs; material I can use.

The scientific version of the sexual politics debate can be summed up roughly thus: Are animals individuals, whose behavior is affected, marginally and circumstantially, by sexual function? Or is sexual/reproductive function the essential, defining core of the organism? You'll find one or the other view expounded, with more or less of tub-thumping self interest, by writers like Richard Dawkins, Matt Ridley, Elaine Morgan, Gail Vines. The editors of *Differences*, in their separate afterwords, neatly represent the opposing camps. The papers tend, if anything, towards the former position. What I find in *The Differences Between the Sexes* is a general chipping away at the area that can be labeled male or female in physiology and in behavior; and a shift in concept from sex-specific to sex typic. "Sex-specific behaviors are numerically a minority. Most sexual behaviors are 'sex typic' meaning they can be produced by either...but are shown more frequently in one sex" (Manfred Gahr, "Brain Structure: causes and consequences of brain sex"). But the sex-is-destiny argument is also supported. Sex difference is largely malleable, but it is unambiguous. There is no sliding scale in behavior, function, or identity: it seems we are dealing with a switch, not a dial. There is male, and there is female. The identities may be confused by a genetic copying error, or successive in a single lifetime, or (in terms of behavior) learned, unlearned, alternated, adopted, or simulated at will: but they are always distinct.

The investigation is fascinating. I'm equally interested in the fact that it exists at all. There was a time, quite recently, when popular science books about sex were how-to manuals with soft focus covers; or collections of prurient statistics about the sexual habits of people who like talking dirty to market researchers. In the last few decades, technology has made the secrets of reproductive function accessible as never before. The mystery of sex can be examined, it can be taken apart. There are signs of a development that is familiar in the history of science. A set of phenomena that was a puzzling given: not even a locked box but apparently a solid block, has changed its nature. Jupiter has moons, the atom has internal structure.... As we know from previous experience, this is a precarious situation. Once we start taking something of this order apart, we never manage to fit the pieces together again quite the way they were before.

I'm not sure how far the general public participates in scientific revolutions. There's a theory that thought gets into the air and worries people — so that the individual human animal in the street eventually starts to feel uncertain about Heisenberg's uncertainty principle, or kind of stretched by the implications of general relativity. There has been a wave of female emancipation recently, it's true, and over these same decades. But there've been waves of female emancipation before, and nothing much happened. As I remarked in my opening paragraph, the evidence is that most people actively enjoy the battle of the sexes. They do not want a sexual reconciliation. However, in this context it's interesting to note the recent career of the term gender. Does gender, which means difference, mean the same as sex? Increasingly, and to the irritation of pedants, people are using the terms as if they're interchangeable. (I called this paper "on the future of gender." On disk it's called s e x, because it's shorter.) We talk about gender roles, gender studies, gender politics, gender-related issues. Irate terminology-watchers (for instance Richard Dawkins) demand indignantly, "If you mean sex, why don't you say so? What is this decadent newspeak!" I suspect that people may be becoming increasingly aware that they don't mean sex, when they say gender. When you are asked to check the box on the form, the question's not about physiology, it is about social role: about difference. You are not being asked, "Do you have ovaries?" You're being asked, "Are you going to stay at home and look after the children?" Or, to put it another way: "If we give you this job, are you going to work for three weeks and then take an extended career break at our expense, to indulge your sociopathic addiction to childbearing?"

Sexual behavior is malleable. Sex hormones are mind-altering drugs that can be used by anyone, female or male. If I dose myself with testosterone, I will become aggressive, non-altruistic (and hairy) as any genetic male. We know this can be done, and we can be sure it will be done. Because if there is one thing we know about animals, whether they're whiptail lizards, nematodes, or humans, it's that if an animal once finds it can do something, and profit ensues, then it will do that something, though the heavens fall. (This is called evolution.) We can adjust our sexual behavior, and thereby our social roles. We can't — not yet — alter reproductive function. The option of having no children is now available to sexually active women as never before: but no hormone treatment will turn a man into a fertile woman. However, reproduction, as instanced by that job application dilemma, is not strictly the issue. It can be argued that since human females don't experience estrus, sex has always been primarily a social activity for our species, engaged in for social benefit, from the point of view of the selfish individual human animal. (Leaving the selfish gene a helpless hitchhiker on life's journey.) Most certainly now, more than ever, it's social function that matters.

Animals do sex for money: for strictly economic reasons. "They choose" the sexual behaviors, weaponry, body-size, and where feasible the sexual identity that "they believe" — to personify a complex of highly impersonal factors — will ensure greatest reproductive success. That's Sexual Darwinism, and as scientific theories go, it seems to work. Without reproductive success — on a mega scale — humans wouldn't be where they are today. But more and more, for selfish individual human animals both male and female, reproduction is not money. Money is money: is status, territory, resources. According to the science in *The Differences Between the Sexes*, we will all adjust our sexual behavior accordingly.

The world is overpopulated, we should all be having fewer children. But women who have more economic rights than ever before — in this country for instance, and in other rich countries of the white

North — see childbearing as another kind of access to resources: which they have a right to enjoy at any price, and even when they are way past biological childbearing age. Meanwhile nationalists in China, in Africa, and in the Balkans (to name but a few locales) are controlling women's fertility for the ancient, animal reasons and on a genocidal scale. Femaleness is in trouble. But Maleness is no better off. All over the world, men are having to compete directly with women in dominance ranking contests: in parliaments, in the job market, in the media — a situation that they find very disturbing indeed. In the world at war, ordinary, natural male-competitive behavior — killing the defeated rival's offspring and impregnating his females — is suddenly stigmatized as criminal, just when the competition's getting really fierce. It's enough to drive a species crazy.... I do not say that "sex" is suddenly a problem. The conflicts between male and female interests are the same as always. The problem, perhaps, is that there is now a solution, of sorts, available.

If sexual behavior and function are malleable, and yet sexual identity, difference, remains obstinately intact — which is what the science predicts and what we see happening around us — then we don't have two complementary sexes any more, each safe in its own niche. All there is left is gender: an us-and-them situation. Two tribes, separated by millennia upon millennia of grievances and bitterness, occupying the same territory, and scrabbling over the same diminished supply of resources. This is the situation, the riff that I've found and used, and which you'll find explored in my novels *White Queen*, *North Wind*, and *Phoenix Café*. I'm a writer of fiction, a composer of metaphors and myths. But like the writers of *The Differences Between the Sexes*, I try to take a scientific view of things. My ideas are always open to further investigation, reassessment, the development of new and more searching experiments. I certainly hope I'm wrong about the way the battle of the sexes is shaping (though I admit I'd almost prefer open war to the alternative, where women return *en masse* to their traditional imprisonment). But for the moment, that's what I see, so that's what I turn into story.

I'd like to say more about the future of gender.... There are philosophical considerations, suppose we manage not to tear each other apart. Animals do sex for money. Humans also think, and this concept of difference — either/or, same/not same — is immeasurably important to our thought. How deeply is our sense of the other bound to our sexuality? This is another aspect of the gender question that has been tackled in various ways in feminist science fiction, but it has plenty of potential for further exploration. What happens to that crucial image of the other — the face opposite, the self that is not-self — if the importance of sex begins to be eroded? But that's a whole new question, and beyond my scope at present.

You may be wondering what happened to the brains of female hyenas. It's another strange but true sex-science story, not actually featured in *Differences*, but recently in the pop-science news, about testosterone use and abuse in the animal world: but I had so many, that I forgot to use it. Anyway, it's a great book. Highly recommended.

---

1 The fact is that animals, if they are subjected to a modification in minute organs, are liable to immense modifications in their general configuration. The phenomenon may be observed in the case of gelded animals; only a minute organ of the animal is mutilated, and the animal passes from the male to the female form. We may infer, then, that if in the primary conformation of the embryo an infinitesimally minute but essential organ sustains a change of magnitude, the animal will in one case turn to male and in the other to female; and also that if the said organ be obliterated altogether, the animal will be of neither one sex nor the other...

The female is softer in disposition, is more mischievous, less simple, more impulsive, and more attentive to the nurture of the young; the male, on the other hand, is more spirited, more savage, more simple and less cunning. The traces of these characteristics are more or less visible everywhere, but they are especially visible where character is the more developed, and most of all in man.

The fact is, the nature of man is the most rounded off and complete, and consequently in man the qualities above referred to are found most clearly. Hence woman is more compassionate than man, more easily moved to tears, at the same time is more jealous, more querulous, more apt to scold and strike. She is, furthermore, more prone to despondency and less hopeful than man, more void of shame, more of false speech, more deceptive, and of more retentive memory. She is also more wakeful, more shrinking, more difficult to rouse to action, and requires a smaller quantity of nutriment.

—Aristotle, *Historia Animalium*

Another Story
or A Fisherman of the Inland Sea

Ursula K. Le Guin

Writers like Charles Dickens used to compose novels as if they were biographies (or autobiographies) of fictional characters, with the story spanning their entire lives. While the novel has evolved into a tighter focus, some (like John Irving) still do that today. Ursula Le Guin plays with that form in this long story. We follow Hideo through his childhood on a farm on the planet O, to his young adulthood in higher education offworld, to his scientific research in teleportation, and then through much of the rest of his life. And always in the background, there is the family unit as defined on O: two men, two women, their children, all in the specific roles of Morning, Evening, Day, and Night.

This story was originally published in 1994, and the jury placed it on the short list. That same year, Le Guin published two other notable stories: "Forgiveness Day," which was also short-listed, and "The Matter of Seggri," which shared the award with Nancy Springer's novel *Larque on the Wing*. Two years later Le Guin returned to O and examined the residents' marital customs more deeply in "Mountain Ways," which earned her another Tiptree Award.

To the Stabiles of the Ekumen on Hain, and to Gvonesh, Director of the Churten Field Laboratories at Ve Port: from Tiokunan'n Hideo, Farmholder of the Second Sedoretu of Udan, Derdan'nad, Oket, on O.

I shall make my report as if I told a story, this having been the tradition for some time now. You may, however, wonder why a farmer on the planet O is reporting to you as if he were a Mobile of the Ekumen. My story will explain that. But it does not explain itself. Story is our only boat for sailing on the river of time, but in the great rapids and the winding shallows, no boat is safe.

So: once upon a time when I was twenty-one years old I left my home and came on the NAFAL ship *Terraces of Darranda* to study at the Ekumenical Schools on Hain.

The distance between Hain and my home world is just over four light-years, and there has been traffic between O and the Hainish system for twenty centuries. Even before the Nearly As Fast As Light drive, when ships spent a hundred years of planetary time instead of four to make the crossing, there were people who would give up their old life to come to a new world. Sometimes they returned; not often. There were tales of such sad returns to a world that had forgotten the voyager. I knew also from my mother a very old story called "The Fisherman of the Inland Sea," which came from her home world, Terra. The life of a ki'O child is full of stories, but of all I heard told by her and my othermother and my fathers and grandparents and uncles and aunts and teachers, that one was my favorite. Perhaps I liked it so well because my mother told it with deep feeling, though very plainly, and always in the same words (and I would not let her change the words if she ever tried to).

The story tells of a poor fisherman, Urashima, who went out daily in his boat alone on the quiet sea that lay between his home island and the mainland. He was a beautiful young man with long, black hair, and the daughter of the king of the sea saw him as he leaned over the side of the boat and she gazed up to see the floating shadow cross the wide circle of the sky.

Rising from the waves, she begged him to come to her palace under the sea with him. At first he refused, saying, "My children wait for me at home." But how could he resist the sea king's daughter? "One night," he said. She drew him down with her under the water, and they spent a night of love in her green palace, served by strange undersea beings. Urashima came to love her dearly, and maybe he stayed more than one night only. But at last he said, "My dear, I must go. My children wait for me at home."

"If you go, you go forever," she said.

"I will come back," he promised.

She shook her head. She grieved, but did not plead with him. "Take this with you," she said, giving him a little box, wonderfully carved, and sealed shut. "Do not open it, Urashima."

So he went up onto the land, and ran up the shore to his village, to his house: but the garden was a wilderness, the windows were blank, the roof had fallen in. People came and went among the familiar houses of the village, but he did not know a single face. "Where are my children?" he cried. An old woman stopped and spoke to him: "What is your trouble, young stranger?"

"I am Urashima, of this village, but I see no one here I know!"

"Urashima!" the woman said — and my mother would look far away, and her voice as she said the name made me shiver, tears starting to my eyes — "Urashima! My grandfather told me a fisherman named Urashima was lost at sea, in the time of his grandfather's grandfather. There has been no one of that family alive for a hundred years."

So Urashima went back down to the shore; and there he opened the box, the gift of the sea king's daughter. A little white smoke came out of it and drifted away on the sea wind. In that moment Urashima's black hair turned white, and he grew old, old, old; and he lay down on the sand and died.

Once, I remember, a traveling teacher asked my mother about the fable, as he called it. She smiled and said, "In the Annals of the Emperors of my nation of Terra it is recorded that a young man named Urashima, of the Yosa district, went away in the year 477, and came back to his village in the year 825, but soon departed again. And I have heard that the box was kept in a shrine for many centuries." Then they talked about something else.

My mother, Isako, would not tell the story as often as I demanded it. "That one is so sad," she would say, and tell instead about Grandmother and the rice dumpling that rolled away, or the painted cat who came alive and killed the demon rats, or the peach boy who floated down the river. My sister and my germanes, and older people, too, listened to her tales as closely as I did. They were new stories on O, and a new story is always a treasure. The painted cat story was the general favorite, especially when my mother would take out her brush and the block of strange, black, dry ink from Terra, and sketch the animals — cat, rat — that none of us had ever seen: the wonderful cat with arched back and brave round eyes, the fanged and skulking rats, "pointed at both ends" as my sister said. But I waited always, through all other stories, for her to catch my eye, look away, smile a little and sigh, and begin, "Long, long ago, on the shore of the Inland Sea there lived a fisherman…"

Did I know then what that story meant to her? that it was her story? that if she were to return to her village, her world, all the people she had known would have been dead for centuries?

Certainly I knew that she "came from another world," but what that meant to me as a five-, or seven-, or ten-year-old, is hard for me now to imagine, impossible to remember. I knew that she was a Terran and had lived on Hain; that was something to be proud of. I knew that she had come to O as a Mobile of the Ekumen (more pride, vague and grandiose) and that "your father and I fell in love at the Festival of Plays in Sudiran." I knew also that arranging the marriage had been a tricky business. Getting permission to resign her duties had not been difficult — the Ekumen is used to Mobiles going native. But as a foreigner, Isako did not belong to a ki'O moiety, and that was only the first problem. I heard all about it from my othermother, Tubdu, an endless source of family history, anecdote, and scandal. "You know," Tubdu told me when I was eleven or twelve, her eyes shining and her irrepressible, slightly wheezing, almost silent laugh beginning to shake her from the inside out — "you know, she didn't even know women got married? Where she came from, she said, women don't marry."

I could and did correct Tubdu: "Only in her part of it. She told me there's lots of parts of it where they do." I felt obscurely defensive of my mother, though Tubdu spoke without a shadow of malice or contempt; she adored Isako. She had fallen in love with her "the moment I saw her — that black hair! that mouth!" — and simply found it endearingly funny that such a woman could have expected to marry only a man.

"I understand," Tubdu hastened to assure me. "I know — on Terra it's different, their fertility was damaged, they have to think about marrying for children. And they marry in twos, too. Oh, poor Isako! How strange it must have seemed to her! I remember how she looked

at me — " And off she went again into what we children called The
Great Giggle, her joyous, silent, seismic laughter.

To those unfamiliar with our customs I should explain that on O,
a world with a low, stable human population and an ancient climax
technology, certain social arrangements are almost universal. The
dispersed village, an association of farms, rather than the city or state,
is the basic social unit. The population consists of two halves or moieties. A child is born into its mother's moiety, so that all ki'O (except
the mountain folk of Ennik) belong either to the Morning People,
whose time is from midnight to noon, or the Evening People, whose
time is from noon to midnight. The sacred origins and functions of
the moieties are recalled in the Discussions and the Plays and in the
services at every farm shrine. The original social function of the moiety was probably to structure exogamy into marriage and so discour-
age inbreeding in isolated farmholds, since one can have sex with or
marry only a person of the other moiety. The rule is severely rein-
forced. Transgressions, which of course occur, are met with shame,
contempt, and ostracism. One's identity as a Morning or an Evening
Person is as deeply and intimately part of oneself as one's gender, and
has quite as much to do with one's sexual life.

A ki'O marriage, called a sedoretu, consists of a Morning woman
and man and an Evening woman and man; the heterosexual pairs are
called Morning and Evening according to the woman's moiety; the
homosexual pairs are called Day — the two women — and Night — the
two men.

So rigidly structured a marriage, where each of four people must
be sexually compatible with two of the others while never having sex
with the fourth — clearly this takes some arranging. Making sedoretu
is a major occupation of my people. Experimenting is encouraged;
foursomes form and dissolve, couples "try on" other couples, mix-
ing and matching. Brokers, traditionally elderly widowers, go about
among the farmholds of the dispersed villages, arranging meetings,
setting up field dances, serving as universal confidants. Many marriages begin as a love match of one couple, either homosexual or
heterosexual, to which another pair or two separate people become

attached. Many marriages are brokered or arranged by the village elders from beginning to end. To listen to the old people under the village great tree making a sedoretu is like watching a master game of chess or tidhe. "If that Evening boy at Erdup were to meet young Tobo during the flour-processing at Gad'd..." "Isn't Hodin'n of the Oto Morning a programmer? They could use a programmer at Erdup...." The dowry a prospective bride or groom can offer is their skill, or their home farm. Otherwise undesired people may be chosen and honored for the knowledge or the property they bring to a marriage. The farmhold, in turn, wants its new members to be agreeable and useful. There is no end to the making of marriages on O. I should say that all in all they give as much satisfaction as any other arrangement to the participants, and a good deal more to the marriage-makers.

Of course many people never marry. Scholars, wandering Discussers, itinerant artists and experts, and specialists in the Centers seldom want to fit themselves into the massive permanence of a farmhold sedoretu. Many people attach themselves to a brother's or sister's marriage as aunt or uncle, a position with limited, clearly defined responsibilities; they can have sex with either or both spouses of the other moiety, thus sometimes increasing the sedoretu from four to seven or eight. Children of that relationship are called cousins. The children of one mother are brothers or sisters to one another; the children of the Morning and the children of the Evening are germanes. Brothers, sisters, and first cousins may not marry, but germanes may. In some less conservative parts of O germane marriages are looked at askance, but they are common and respected in my region.

My father was a Morning man of Udan Farmhold of Derdan'nad Village in the hill region of the Northwest Watershed of the Saduun River, on Oket, the smallest of the six continents of O. The village comprises seventy-seven farmholds, in a deeply rolling, stream-cut region of fields and forests on the watershed of the Oro, a tributary of the wide Saduun. It is fertile, pleasant country, with views west to the Coast Range and south to the great floodplains of the Saduun and the gleam of the sea beyond. The Oro is a wide, lively, noisy river full of fish and children. I spent my childhood in or on or by the Oro, which runs through Udan so near the house that you can hear its voice all night, the rush and hiss of the water and the deep drumbeats of rocks rolled in its current. It is shallow and quite dangerous. We all learned to swim very young in a quiet bay dug out as a swimming pool, and later to handle rowboats and kayaks in the swift current full of rocks and rapids. Fishing was one of the children's responsibilities. I liked to spear the fat, beady-eyed, blue ochid; I would stand heroic on a slippery boulder in midstream, the long spear poised to strike. I was good at it. But my germane Isidri, while I was prancing about with my spear, would slip into the water and catch six or seven ochid with her bare hands. She could catch eels and even the darting ei. I never could do it. "You just sort of move with the water and get transparent," she said. She could stay underwater longer than any of us, so long you were sure she had drowned. "She's too bad to drown," her mother, Tubdu, proclaimed. "You can't drown really bad people. They always bob up again."

Tubdu, the Morning wife, had two children with her husband Kap: Isidri, a year older than me, and Suudi, three years younger. Children of the Morning, they were my germanes, as was Cousin Had'd, Tubdu's son with Kap's brother Uncle Tobo. On the Evening side there were two children, myself and my younger sister. She was named Koneko, an old name in Oket, which has also a meaning in my mother's Terran language: "kitten," the young of the wonderful animal "cat" with the round back and the round eyes. Koneko, four years younger than me, was indeed round and silky like a baby animal, but her eyes were like my mother's, long, with lids that went up towards the temple, like the soft sheaths of flowers before they open. She staggered around after me, calling, "Deo! Deo! Wait!" — while I ran after fleet, fearless, ever-vanishing Isidri, calling, "Sidi! Sidi! Wait!"

When we were older, Isidri and I were inseparable companions, while Suudi, Koneko, and Cousin Had'd made a trinity, usually coated with mud, splotched with scabs, and in some kind of trouble — gates left open so the yamas got into the crops, hay spoiled by being jumped on, fruit stolen, battles with the children from Drehe Farmhold. "Bad, bad," Tubdu would say. "None of 'em will ever drown!" And she would shake with her silent laughter.

My father Dohedri was a hardworking man, handsome, silent, and aloof. I think his insistence on bringing a foreigner into the tight-woven fabric of village and farm life, conservative and suspicious and full of old knots and tangles of passions and jealousies, had added anxiety to a temperament already serious. Other ki'O had married foreigners, of course, but almost always in a "foreign marriage," a pairing; and such couples usually lived in one of the Centers, where all kinds of untraditional arrangements were common, even (so the village gossips hissed under the great tree) incestuous couplings be-tween two Morning people! two Evening people! — Or such pairs would leave O to live on Hain, or would cut all ties to all homes and become Mobiles on the NAFAL ships, only touching different worlds at different moments and then off again into an endless future with no past.

None of this would do for my father, a man rooted to the knees in the dirt of Udan Farmhold. He brought his beloved to his home, and persuaded the Evening People of Derdan'nad to take her into their moiety, in a ceremony so rare and ancient that a Caretaker had to come by ship and train from Noratan to perform it. Then he had persuaded Tubdu to join the sedoretu. As regards her Day marriage, this was no trouble at all, as soon as Tubdu met my mother; but it pre-sented some difficulty as regards her Morning marriage. Kap and my father had been lovers for years; Kap was the obvious and willing can-didate to complete the sedoretu; but Tubdu did not like him. Kap's long love for my father led him to woo Tubdu earnestly and well, and she was far too good-natured to hold out against the interlocking wishes of three people, plus her own lively desire for Isako. She always found Kap a boring husband, I think; but his younger brother, Uncle Tobo, was a bonus. And Tubdu's relation to my mother was infinitely tender, full of honor, of delicacy, of restraint. Once my mother spoke of it. "She knew how strange it all was to me," she said. "She knows how strange it all is."

"This world? our ways?" I asked.

My mother shook her head very slightly. "Not so much that," she said in her quiet voice with the faint foreign accent. "But men and women, women and women, together — love — It is always very strange. Nothing you know ever prepares you. Ever."

The saying is, "a marriage is made by Day," that is, the relationship of the two women makes or breaks it. Though my mother and father loved each other deeply, it was a love always on the edge of pain, never easy. I have no doubt that the radiant childhood we had in that household was founded on the unshakable joy and strength Isako and Tubdu found in each other.

So, then: twelve-year-old Isidri went off on the suntrain to school at Herhot, our district educational Center, and I wept aloud, standing in the morning sunlight in the dust of Derdan'nad Station. My friend, my playmate, my life was gone. I was bereft, deserted, alone forever. Seeing her mighty eleven-year-old elder brother weeping, Koneko set up a howl too, tears rolling down her cheeks in dusty balls like raindrops on a dirt road. She threw her arms about me, roaring, "Hideo! She'll come back! She'll come back!"

I have never forgotten that. I can hear her hoarse little voice, and feel her arms round me and the hot morning sunlight on my neck.

By afternoon we were all swimming in the Oro, Koneko and I and Suudi and Had'd. As their elder, I resolved on a course of duty and stern virtue, and led the troop off to help Second-Cousin Topi at the irrigation control station, until she drove us away like a swarm of flies, saying, "Go help somebody else and let me get some work done!" We went and built a mud palace.

So, then: a year later, twelve-year-old Hideo and thirteen-year-old Isidri went off on the suntrain to school, leaving Koneko on the dusty siding, not in tears, but silent, the way our mother was silent when she grieved.

I loved school. I know that the first days I was achingly homesick, but I cannot recall that misery, buried under my memories of the full, rich years at Herhot, and later at Ran'n, the Advanced Education Center, where I studied temporal physics and engineering.

Isidri finished the First Courses at Herhot, took a year of Second in literature, hydrology, and oenology, and went home to Udan Farmhold of Derdan'nad Village in the hill region of the Northwest Watershed of the Saduun.

The three younger ones all came to school, took a year or two of Second, and carried their learning home to Udan. When she was fifteen or sixteen, Koneko talked of following me to Ran'n; but she was wanted at home because of her excellence in the discipline we call "thick planning" — farm management is the usual translation, but the words have no hint of the complexity of factors involved in thick planning, ecology politics profit tradition aesthetics honor and spirit all functioning in an intensely practical and practically invisible balance of preservation and renewal, like the homeostasis of a vigorous organism. Our "kitten" had the knack for it, and the Planners of Udan and Derdan'nad took her into their councils before she was twenty. But by then, I was gone.

Every winter of my school years I came back to the farm for the long holidays. The moment I was home I dropped school like a book bag and became pure farm boy overnight — working, swimming, fishing, hiking, putting on Plays and farces in the barn, going to field dances and house dances all over the village, falling in and out of love with lovely boys and girls of the Morning from Derdan'nad and other villages.

In my last couple of years at Ran'n, my visits home changed mood. Instead of hiking off all over the country by day and going to a different dance every night, I often stayed home. Careful not to fall in love, I pulled away from my old, dear relationship with Sota of Drehe Farmhold, gradually letting it lapse, trying not to hurt him. I sat whole hours by the Oro, a fishing line in my hand, memorizing the run of the water in a certain place just outside the entrance to our old swimming bay. There, as the water rises in clear strands racing towards two mossy, almost-submerged boulders, it surges and whirls in spirals, and while some of these spin away, grow faint, and disappear, one knots itself on a deep center, becoming a little whirlpool, which spins slowly downstream until, reaching the quick, bright race between the boulders, it loosens and unties itself, released into the body of the river, as another spiral is forming and knotting itself round a deep center upstream where the water rises in clear strands above the boulders.... Sometimes that winter the river rose right over the rocks and poured smooth, swollen with rain; but always it would drop, and the whirlpools would appear again.

In the winter evenings I talked with my sister and Suudi, serious, long talks by the fire. I watched my mother's beautiful hands work on the embroidery of new curtains for the wide windows of the dining room, which my father had sewn on the four-hundred-year-old sewing machine of Udan. I worked with him on reprogramming the fertilizer systems for the east fields and the yama rotations, according to our thick-planning council's directives. Now and then he and I talked a little, never very much. In the evenings we had music; Cousin Had'd was a drummer, much in demand for dances, who could always gather a group. Or I would play Word-Thief with Tubdu, a game she adored and always lost at because she was so intent to steal my words that she forgot to protect her own. "Got you, got you!" she would cry, and melt into The Great Giggle, seizing my letterblocks with her fat, tapering, brown fingers; and next move I would take all my letters back along with most of hers. "How did you see that?" she would ask, amazed, studying the scattered words. Sometimes my otherfather Kap played with us, methodical, a bit mechanical, with a small smile for both triumph and defeat.

Then I would go up to my room under the eaves, my room of dark wood walls and dark red curtains, the smell of rain coming in the window, the sound of rain on the tiles of the roof. I would lie there in the mild darkness and luxuriate in sorrow, in great, aching, sweet, youthful sorrow for this ancient home that I was going to leave, to lose forever, to sail away from on the dark river of time. For I knew, from my eighteenth birthday on, that I would leave Udan, leave O, and go out to the other worlds. It was my ambition. It was my destiny.

I have not said anything about Isidri, as I described those winter holidays. She was there. She played in the Plays, worked on the farm, went to the dances, sang the choruses, joined the hiking parties, swam in the river in the warm rain with the rest of us. My first winter home from Ran'n, as I swung off the train at Derdan'nad Station, she greeted me with a cry of delight and a great embrace, then broke away with a strange, startled laugh and stood back, a tall, dark, thin girl with an intent, watchful face. She was quite awkward with me that evening. I felt that it was because she had always seen me as a little boy, a child, and now, eighteen and a student at Ran'n, I was a man. I was complacent with Isidri, putting her at her ease, patronizing her. In the days that followed, she remained awkward, laughing inappropriately, never opening her heart to me in the kind of long talks we used to have, and even, I thought, avoiding me. My whole last tenday at home that year, Isidri spent visiting her father's relatives in Sabtodiu Village. I was offended that she had not put off her visit till I was gone.

The next year she was not awkward, but not intimate. She had become interested in religion, attending the shrine daily, studying the Discussions with the elders. She was kind, friendly, busy. I do not remember that she and I ever touched that winter until she kissed me good-bye. Among my people a kiss is not with the mouth; we lay our cheeks together for a moment, or for longer. Her kiss was as light as the touch of a leaf, lingering yet barely perceptible.

My third and last winter home, I told them I was leaving: going to Hain, and that from Hain I wanted to go on farther and forever.

How cruel we are to our parents! All I needed to say was that I was going to Hain. After her half-anguished, half-exultant cry of "I knew it!" my mother said in her usual soft voice, suggesting not stating, "After that, you might come back, for a while." I could have said, "Yes." That was all she asked. Yes, I might come back, for a while. With the impenetrable self-centeredness of youth, which mistakes itself for honesty, I refused to give her what she asked. I took from her the modest hope of seeing me after ten years, and gave her the desolation of believing that when I left she would never see me again. "If I qualify, I want to be a Mobile," I said. I had steeled myself to speak without palliations. I prided myself on my truthfulness. And all the time, though I didn't know it, nor did they, it was not the truth at all.

The truth is rarely so simple, though not many truths are as complicated as mine turned out to be.

She took my brutality without the least complaint. She had left her
own people, after all. She said that evening, "We can talk by ansible,
sometimes, as long as you're on Hain." She said it as if reassuring me,
not herself. I think she was remembering how she had said good-bye
to her people and boarded the ship on Terra, and when she landed
a few seeming hours later on Hain, her mother had been dead for
fifty years. She could have talked to Terra on the ansible; but who was
there for her to talk to? I did not know that pain, but she did. She took
comfort in knowing I would be spared it, for a while.

Everything now was "for a while." Oh, the bitter sweetness of
those days! How I enjoyed myself — standing, again, poised on the
slick boulder amidst the roaring water, spear raised, the hero! How
ready, how willing I was to crush all that long, slow, deep, rich life of
Udan in my hand and toss it away!

Only for one moment was I told what I was doing, and then so
briefly that I could deny it.

I was down in the boathouse workshop, on the rainy, warm afternoon of a day late in the last month of winter. The constant, hissing
thunder of the swollen river was the matrix of my thoughts as I set
a new thwart in the little red rowboat we used to fish from, taking
pleasure in the task, indulging my anticipatory nostalgia to the full
by imagining myself on another planet a hundred years away remembering this hour in the boathouse, the smell of wood and water, the
river's incessant roar. A knock at the workshop door. Isidri looked in.
The thin, dark, watchful face, the long braid of dark hair, not as black
as mine, the intent, clear eyes. "Hideo," she said, "I want to talk to
you for a minute."

"Come on in!" I said, pretending ease and gladness, though half-
aware that in fact I shrank from talking with Isidri, that I was afraid
of her — why?

She perched on the vise bench and watched me work in silence for
a little while. I began to say something commonplace, but she spoke:

"Do you know why I've been staying away from you?"

Liar, self-protective liar, I said, "Staying away from me?"

At that she sighed. She had hoped I would say I understood, and spare her the rest. But I couldn't. I was lying only in pretending that I hadn't noticed that she had kept away from me. I truly had never, never until she told me, imagined why.

"I found out I was in love with you, winter before last," she said. "I wasn't going to say anything about it because — well, you know. If you'd felt anything like that for me, you'd have known I did. But it wasn't both of us. So there was no good in it. But then, when you told us you're leaving... At first I thought, all the more reason to say nothing. But then I thought, that wouldn't be fair. To me, partly. Love has a right to be spoken. And you have a right to know that somebody loves you. That somebody has loved you, could love you. We all need to know that. Maybe it's what we need most. So I wanted to tell you. And because I was afraid you thought I'd kept away from you because I didn't love you, or care about you, you know. It might have looked like that. But it wasn't that." She had slipped down off the table and was at the door.

"Sidi!" I said, her name breaking from me in a strange, hoarse cry, the name only, no words — I had no words. I had no feelings, no compassion, no more nostalgia, no more luxurious suffering. Shocked out of emotion, bewildered, blank, I stood there. Our eyes met. For four or five breaths we stood staring into each other's soul. Then Isidri looked away with a wincing, desolate smile, and slipped out.

I did not follow her. I had nothing to say to her: literally. I felt that it would take me a month, a year, years, to find the words I needed to say to her. I had been so rich, so comfortably complete in myself and my ambition and my destiny, five minutes ago; and now I stood empty, silent, poor, looking at the world I had thrown away.

That ability to look at the truth lasted an hour or so. All my life since I have thought of it as "the hour in the boathouse." I sat on the high bench where Isidri had sat. The rain fell and the river roared and the early night came on. When at last I moved, I turned on a light, and began to try to defend my purpose, my planned future, from the ter-

rible plain reality. I began to build up a screen of emotions and evasions and versions; to look away from what Isidri had shown me; to
look away from Isidri's eyes.

By the time I went up to the house for dinner I was in control of
myself. By the time I went to bed I was master of my destiny again,
sure of my decision, almost able to indulge myself in feeling sorry for
Isidri — but not quite. Never did I dishonor her with that. I will say
that much for myself. I had had the pity that is self-pity knocked out
of me in the hour in the boathouse. When I parted from my family
at the muddy little station in the village, a few days after, I wept, not
luxuriously for them, but for myself, in honest, hopeless pain. It was
too much for me to bear. I had had so little practice in pain! I said to
my mother, "I will come back. When I finish the course — six years,
maybe seven — I'll come back, I'll stay a while."

"If your way brings you," she whispered. She held me close to her,
and then released me.

So, then: I have come to the time I chose to begin my story, when
I was twenty-one and left my home on the ship *Terraces of Darranda* to
study at the Schools on Hain.

Of the journey itself I have no memory whatever. I think I remember entering the ship, yet no details come to mind, visual or kinetic; I
cannot recollect being on the ship. My memory of leaving it is only of
an overwhelming physical sensation, dizziness. I staggered and felt
sick, and was so unsteady on my feet I had to be supported until I had
taken several steps on the soil of Hain.

Troubled by this lapse of consciousness, I asked about it at the
Ekumenical School. I was told that it is one of the many different ways
in which travel at nearlightspeed affects the mind. To most people it
seems merely that a few hours pass in a kind of perceptual limbo; others have curious perceptions of space and time and event, which can
be seriously disturbing; a few simply feel they have been asleep when
they "wake up" on arrival. I did not even have that experience. I had
no experience at all. I felt cheated. I wanted to have felt the voyage,
to have known, in some way, the great interval of space: but as far as
I was concerned, there was no interval. I was at the spaceport on O,

and then I was at Ve Port, dizzy, bewildered, and at last, when I was able to believe that I was there, excited.

My studies and work during those years are of no interest now. I will mention only one event, which may or may not be on record in the ansible reception file at Fourth Beck Tower, EY 21-11-93/1645. (The last time I checked, it was on record in the ansible transmission file at Ran'n, ET date 30-11-93/1645. Urashima's coming and going was on record, too, in the Annals of the Emperors.) 1645 was my first year on Hain. Early in the term I was asked to come to the ansible center, where they explained that they had received a garbled screen transmission, apparently from O, and hoped I could help them reconstitute it. After a date nine days later than the date of reception, it read:

les oku n hide problem netru emit it hurt di it may not be salv devir

The words were gapped and fragmented. Some were standard Hainish, but *oku* and *netru* mean "north" and "symmetrical" in Sio, my native language. The ansible centers on O had reported no record of the transmission, but the Receivers thought the message might be from O because of these two words and because the Hainish phrase "it may not be salvageable" occurred in a transmission received almost simultaneously from one of the Stabiles on O, concerning a wave-damaged desalinization plant. "We call this a creased message," the Receiver told me, when I confessed I could make nothing of it and asked how often ansible messages came through so garbled. "Not often, fortunately. We can't be certain where or when they originated, or will originate. They may be effects of a double field — interference phenomena, perhaps. One of my colleagues here calls them ghost messages."

Instantaneous transmission had always fascinated me, and though I was then only a beginner in ansible principle, I developed this fortuitous acquaintance with the Receivers into a friendship with several of them. And I took all the courses in ansible theory that were offered.

When I was in my final year in the school of temporal physics, and considering going on to the Cetian Worlds for further study — after my promised visit home, which seemed sometimes a remote, irrelevant daydream and sometimes a yearning and yet fearful need — the first reports came over the ansible from Anarres of the new theory of transilience. Not only information, but matter, bodies, people might be transported from place to place without lapse of time. "Churten technology" was suddenly a reality, although a very strange reality, an implausible fact.

I was crazy to work on it. I was about to go promise my soul and body to the School if they would let me work on churten theory when they came and asked me if I'd consider postponing my training as a Mobile for a year or so to work on churten theory. Judiciously and graciously, I consented. I celebrated all over town that night. I remember showing all my friends how to dance the fen'n, and I remember setting off fireworks in the Great Plaza of the Schools, and I think I remember singing under the Director's windows, a little before dawn. I remember what I felt like next day, too; but it didn't keep me from dragging myself over to the Ti-Phy building to see where they were installing the Churten Field Laboratory.

Ansible transmission is, of course, enormously expensive, and I had only been able to talk to my family twice during my years on Hain; but my friends in the ansible center would occasionally "ride" a screen message for me on a transmission to O. I sent a message thus to Ran'n to be posted on to the First Sedoretu of Udan Farmhold of Derdan'nad Village of the hill district of the Northwest Watershed of the Saduun, Oket, on O, telling them that "although this research will delay my visit home, it may save me four years' travel." The flippant message revealed my guilty feeling; but we did really think then that we would have the technology within a few months.

The Field Laboratories were soon moved out to Ve Port, and I went with them. The joint work of the Cetian and Hainish churten research teams in those first three years was a succession of triumphs, postponements, promises, defeats, breakthroughs, setbacks, all happening so fast that anybody who took a week off was out-of-date.

"Clarity hiding mystery," Gvonesh called it. Every time it all came clear it all grew more mysterious. The theory was beautiful and maddening. The experiments were exciting and inscrutable. The technology worked best when it was most preposterous. Four years went by in that laboratory like no time at all, as they say.

I had now spent ten years on Hain and Ve, and was thirty-one. On O, four years had passed while my NAFAL ship passed a few minutes of dilated time going to Hain, and four more would pass while I returned: so when I returned I would have been gone eighteen of their years. My parents were all still alive. It was high time for my promised visit home.

But though churten research had hit a frustrating setback in the Spring Snow Paradox, a problem the Cetians thought might be insoluble, I couldn't stand the thought of being eight years out-of-date when I got back to Hain. What if they broke the paradox? It was bad enough knowing I must lose four years going to O. Tentatively, not too hopefully, I proposed to the Director that I carry some experimental materials with me to O and set up a fixed double-field auxiliary to the ansible link between Ve Port and Ran'n. Thus I could stay in touch with Ve, as Ve stayed in touch with Urras and Anarres; and the fixed ansible link might be preparatory to a churten link. I remember I said, "If you break the paradox, we might eventually send some mice."

To my surprise my idea caught on; the temporal engineers wanted a receiving field. Even our Director, who could be as brilliantly inscrutable as churten theory itself, said it was a good idea. "Mouses, bugs, gholes, who knows what we send you?" she said.

So, then: when I was thirty-one years old I left Ve Port on the NAFAL transport *Lady of Sorra* and returned to O. This time I experienced the near-lightspeed flight the way most people do, as an unnerving interlude in which one cannot think consecutively, read a clockface, or follow a story. Speech and movement become difficult or impossible. Other people appear as unreal half presences, inexplicably there or not there. I did not hallucinate, but everything seemed hallucination. It is like a high fever — confusing, miserably boring, seeming endless, yet very difficult to recall once it is over, as if it were an episode outside one's life, encapsulated. I wonder now if its resemblance to the "churten experience" has yet been seriously investigated.

I went straight to Ran'n, where I was given rooms in the New Quadrangle, fancier than my old student room in the Shrine Quadrangle, and some nice lab space in Tower Hall to set up an experimental transilience field station. I got in touch with my family right away and talked to all my parents; my mother had been ill, but was fine now, she said. I told them I would be home as soon as I had got things going at Ran'n. Every tenday I called again and talked to them and said I'd be along very soon now. I was genuinely very busy, having to catch up the lost four years and to learn Gvonesh's solution to the Spring Snow Paradox. It was, fortunately, the only major advance in theory. Technology had advanced a good deal. I had to retrain myself, and to train my assistants almost from scratch. I had had an idea about an aspect of double-field theory that I wanted to work out before I left. Five months went by before I called them up and said at last, "I'll be there tomorrow." And when I did so, I realized that all along I had been afraid.

I don't know if I was afraid of seeing them after eighteen years, of the changes, the strangeness, or if it was myself I feared.

Eighteen years had made no difference at all to the hills beside the wide Saduun, the farmlands, the dusty little station in Derdan'nad, the old, old houses on the quiet streets. The village great tree was gone, but its replacement had a pretty wide spread of shade already. The aviary at Udan had been enlarged. The yama stared haughtily, timidly at me across the fence. A road gate that I had hung on my last visit home was decrepit, needing its post reset and new hinges, but the weeds that grew beside it were the same dusty, sweet-smelling summer weeds. The tiny dams of the irrigation runnels made their multiple, soft click and thump as they closed and opened. Everything was the same, itself. Timeless, Udan in its dream of work stood over the river that ran timeless in its dream of movement.

But the faces and bodies of the people waiting for me at the station in the hot sunlight were not the same. My mother, forty-seven when

I left, was sixty-five, a beautiful and fragile elderly woman. Tubdu had lost weight; she looked shrunken and wistful. My father was still handsome and bore himself proudly, but his movements were slow and he scarcely spoke at all. My otherfather Kap, seventy now, was a precise, fidgety, little old man. They were still the First Sedoretu of Udan, but the vigor of the farmhold now lay in the Second and Third Sedoretu.

I knew of all the changes, of course, but being there among them was a different matter from hearing about them in letters and transmissions. The old house was much fuller than it had been when I lived there. The south wing had been reopened, and children ran in and out of its doors and across courtyards that in my childhood had been silent and ivied and mysterious.

My sister Koneko was now four years older than I instead of four years younger. She looked very like my early memory of my mother. As the train drew in to Derdan'nad Station, she had been the first of them I recognized, holding up a child of three or four and saying, "Look, look, it's your Uncle Hideo!"

The Second Sedoretu had been married for eleven years: Koneko and Isidri, sister-germanes, were the partners of the Day. Koneko's husband was my old friend Sota, a Morning man of Drehe Farmhold. Sota and I had loved each other dearly when we were adolescents, and I had been grieved to grieve him when I left. When I heard that he and Koneko were in love I had been very surprised, so self-centered am I, but at least I am not jealous: it pleased me very deeply. Isidri's husband, a man nearly twenty years older than herself, named Hedran, had been a traveling scholar of the Discussions. Udan had given him hospitality, and his visits had led to the marriage. He and Isidri had no children. Sota and Koneko had two Evening children, a boy of ten called Murmi, and Lasako, Little Isako, who was four.

The Third Sedoretu had been brought to Udan by Suudi, my brother-germane, who had married a woman from Aster Village; their Morning pair also came from farmholds of Aster. There were six children in that sedoretu. A cousin whose sedoretu at Ekke had broken had also come to live at Udan with her two children; so the coming and going and dressing and undressing and washing and slamming and running and shouting and weeping and laughing and eating was prodigious. Tubdu would sit at work in the sunny kitchen courtyard and watch a wave of children pass. "Bad!" she would cry. "They'll never drown, not a one of 'em!" And she would shake with silent laughter that became a wheezing cough.

My mother, who had after all been a Mobile of the Ekumen, and had traveled from Terra to Hain and from Hain to O, was impatient to hear about my research. "What is it, this churtening? How does it work, what does it do? Is it an ansible for matter?"

"That's the idea," I said. "Transilience: instantaneous transference of being from one s-tc point to another."

"No interval?"

"No interval."

Isako frowned. "It sounds wrong," she said. "Explain."

I had forgotten how direct my soft-spoken mother could be; I had forgotten that she was an intellectual. I did my best to explain the incomprehensible.

"So," she said at last, "you don't really understand how it works."

"No. Nor even what it does. Except that — as a rule — when the field is in operation, the mice in Building One are instantaneously in Building Two, perfectly cheerful and unharmed. Inside their cage, if we remembered to keep their cage inside the initiating churten field. We used to forget. Loose mice everywhere."

"What's *mice*?" said a little Morning boy of the Third Sedoretu, who had stopped to listen to what sounded like a story.

"Ah," I said in a laugh, surprised. I had forgotten that at Udan mice were unknown, and rats were fanged, demon enemies of the painted cat. "Tiny, pretty, furry animals," I said, "that come from Grandmother Isako's world. They are friends of scientists. They have traveled all over the Known Worlds."

"In tiny little spaceships?" the child said hopefully.

"In large ones, mostly," I said. He was satisfied, and went away.

"Hideo," said my mother, in the terrifying way women have of passing without interval from one subject to another because they have them all present in their mind at once, "you haven't found any kind of relationship?"

I shook my head, smiling.

"None at all?"

"A man from Alterra and I lived together for a couple of years," I said. "It was a good friendship; but he's a Mobile now. And...oh, you know...people here and there. Just recently, at Ran'n, I've been with a very nice woman from East Oket."

"I hoped, if you intend to be a Mobile, that you might make a couple-marriage with another Mobile. It's easier, I think," she said. Easier than what? I thought, and knew the answer before I asked.

"Mother, I doubt now that I'll travel farther than Hain. This churten business is too interesting; I want to be in on it. And if we do learn to control the technology, you know, then travel will be nothing. There'll be no need for the kind of sacrifice you made. Things will be different. Unimaginably different! You could go to Terra for an hour and come back here: and only an hour would have passed."

She thought about that. "If you do it, then," she said, speaking slowly, almost shaking with the intensity of comprehension, "you will...you will shrink the galaxy — the universe? — to..." and she held up her left hand, thumb and fingers all drawn together to a point.

I nodded. "A mile or a light-year will be the same. There will be no distance."

"It can't be right," she said after a while. "To have event without interval... Where is the dancing? Where is the way? I don't think you'll be able to control it, Hideo." She smiled. "But of course you must try."

And after that we talked about who was coming to the field dance at Drehe tomorrow.

I did not tell my mother that I had invited Tasi, the nice woman from East Oket, to come to Udan with me and that she had refused, had, in fact, gently informed me that she thought this was a good time for us to part. Tasi was tall, with a braid of dark hair, not coarse, bright black like mine but soft, fine, dark, like the shadows in a forest. A typical ki'O woman, I thought. She had deflated my protestations of love skillfully and without shaming me. "I think you're in love with somebody, though," she said. "Somebody on Hain, maybe. Maybe the man from Alterra you told me about?" No, I said. No, I'd never been in love. I wasn't capable of an intense relationship, that was clear by now. I'd dreamed too long of traveling the galaxy with no attachments anywhere, and then worked too long in the churten lab, married to a damned theory that couldn't find its technology. No room for love, no time.

But why had I wanted to bring Tasi home with me?

Tall but no longer thin, a woman of forty, not a girl, not typical, not comparable, not like anyone anywhere, Isidri had greeted me quietly at the door of the house. Some farm emergency had kept her from coming to the village station to meet me. She was wearing an old smock and leggings like any field worker, and her hair, dark beginning to grey, was in a rough braid. As she stood in that wide doorway of polished wood she was Udan itself, the body and soul of that thirty-century-old farmhold, its continuity, its life. All my childhood was in her hands, and she held them out to me.

"Welcome home, Hideo," she said, with a smile as radiant as the summer light on the river. As she brought me in, she said, "I cleared the kids out of your old room. I thought you'd like to be there — would you?" Again she smiled, and I felt her warmth, the solar generosity of a woman in the prime of life, married, settled, rich in her work and being. I had not needed Tasi as a defense. I had nothing to fear from Isidri. She felt no rancor, no embarrassment. She had loved me when she was young, another person. It would be altogether inappropriate for me to feel embarrassment, or shame, or anything but the old affectionate loyalty of the years when we played and worked and fished and dreamed together, children of Udan.

So, then: I settled down in my old room under the tiles. There were new curtains, rust and brown. I found a stray toy under the chair, in the closet, as if I as a child had left my playthings there and found them now. At fourteen, after my entry ceremony in the shrine, I had carved my name on the deep window jamb among the tangled patterns of names and symbols that had been cut into it for centuries. I looked for it now. There had been some additions. Beside my careful, clear *Hideo*, surrounded by my ideogram, the cloudflower, a younger child had hacked a straggling *Dohedri*, and nearby was carved a delicate three-roofs ideogram. The sense of being a bubble in Udan's river, a moment in the permanence of life in this house on this land on this quiet world, was almost crushing, denying my identity, and profoundly reassuring, confirming my identity. Those nights of my visit home I slept as I had not slept for years, lost, drowned in the waters of sleep and darkness, and woke to the summer mornings as if reborn, very hungry.

The children were still all under twelve, going to school at home. Isidri, who taught them literature and religion and was the school planner, invited me to tell them about Hain, about NAFAL travel, about temporal physics, whatever I pleased. Visitors to ki'O farmholds are always put to use. Evening-Uncle Hideo became rather a favorite among the children, always good for hitching up the yamacart or taking them fishing in the big boat, which they couldn't yet handle, or telling a story about his magic mice who could be in two places at the same time. I asked them if Evening-Grandmother Isako had told them about the painted cat who came alive and killed the demon rats — "And his mouf was all BLUGGY in the morning!" shouted Lasako, her eyes shining. But they didn't know the tale of Urashima.

"Why haven't you told them 'The Fisherman of the Inland Sea'?" I asked my mother.

She smiled and said, "Oh, that was your story. You always wanted it."

I saw Isidri's eyes on us, clear and tranquil, yet watchful still.

I knew my mother had had repair and healing to her heart a year before, and I asked Isidri later, as we supervised some work the older children were doing, "Has Isako recovered, do you think?"

"She seems wonderfully well since you came. I don't know. It's damage from her childhood, from the poisons in the Terran biosphere; they say her immune system is easily depressed. She was very patient about being ill. Almost too patient."

"And Tubdu — does she need new lungs?"

"Probably. All four of them are getting older, and stubborner.... But you look at Isako for me. See if you see what I mean."

I tried to observe my mother. After a few days I reported back that she seemed energetic and decisive, even imperative, and that I hadn't seen much of the patient endurance that worried Isidri. She laughed.

"Isako told me once," she said, "that a mother is connected to her child by a very fine, thin cord, like the umbilical cord, that can stretch light-years without any difficulty. I asked her if it was painful, and she said, 'Oh, no, it's just there, you know, it stretches and stretches and never breaks.' It seems to me it must be painful. But I don't know. I have no child, and I've never been more than two days' travel from my mothers." She smiled and said in her soft, deep voice, "I think I love Isako more than anyone, more even than my mother, more even than Koneko...."

Then she had to show one of Suudi's children how to reprogram the timer on the irrigation control. She was the hydrologist for the village and the oenologist for the farm. Her life was thick-planned, very rich in necessary work and wide relationships, a serene and steady succession of days, seasons, years. She swam in life as she had swum in the river, like a fish, at home. She had borne no child, but all the children of the farmhold were hers. She and Koneko were as deeply attached as their mothers had been. Her relation with her rather fragile, scholarly husband seemed peaceful and respectful. I thought his Night marriage with my old friend Sota might be the stronger sexual link, but Isidri clearly admired and depended on his intellectual and spiritual guidance. I thought his teaching a bit dry and disputatious; but what did I know about religion? I had not given worship for years, and felt strange, out of place, even in the home shrine. I felt strange, out of place, in my home. I did not acknowledge it to myself.

I was conscious of the month as pleasant, uneventful, even a little boring. My emotions were mild and dull. The wild nostalgia, the romantic sense of standing on the brink of my destiny, all that was gone with the Hideo of twenty-one. Though now the youngest of my generation, I was a grown man, knowing his way, content with his work, past emotional self-indulgence. I wrote a little poem for the house album about the peacefulness of following a chosen course. When I had to go, I embraced and kissed everyone, dozens of soft or harsh cheek touches. I told them that if I stayed on O, as it seemed I might be asked to do for a year or so, I would come back next winter for another visit. On the train going back through the hills to Ran'n, I thought with a complacent gravity how I might return to the farm next winter, finding them all just the same; and how, if I came back after another eighteen years or even longer, some of them would be gone and some would be new to me and yet it would be always my home, Udan with its wide dark roofs riding time like a dark sailed ship. I always grow poetic when I am lying to myself.

I got back to Ran'n, checked in with my people at the lab in Tower Hall, and had dinner with colleagues, good food and drink — I brought them a bottle of wine from Udan, for Isidri was making splendid wines, and had given me a case of the fifteen-year-old Kedun. We talked about the latest breakthrough in churten technology, "continuous-field sending," reported from Anarres just yesterday on the ansible. I went to my rooms in the New Quadrangle through the summer night, my head full of physics, read a little, and went to bed. I turned out the light and darkness filled me as it filled the room. Where was I? Alone in a room among strangers. As I had been for ten years and would always be. On one planet or another, what did it matter? Alone, part of nothing, part of no one. Udan was not my home. I had no home, no people. I had no future, no destiny, any more than a bubble of foam or a whirlpool in a current has a destiny. It is and it isn't. Nothing more.

I turned the light on because I could not bear the darkness, but the light was worse. I sat huddled up in the bed and began to cry. I could not stop crying. I became frightened at how the sobs racked and shook me till I was sick and weak and still could not stop sobbing. After a long time I calmed myself gradually by clinging to an imagination, a childish idea: in the morning I would call Isidri and talk to her, telling her that I needed instruction in religion, that I wanted to give worship at the shrines again, but it had been so long, and I had never listened to the Discussions, but now I needed to, and I would ask her, Isidri, to help me. So, holding fast to that, I could at last stop the terrible sobbing and lie spent, exhausted, until the day came.

I did not call Isidri. In daylight the thought which had saved me from the dark seemed foolish; and I thought if I called her she would ask advice of her husband, the religious scholar. But I knew I needed help. I went to the shrine in the Old School and gave worship. I asked for a copy of the First Discussions, and read it. I joined a Discussion group, and we read and talked together. My religion is godless, argumentative, and mystical. The name of our world is the first word of its first prayer. For human beings its vehicle is the human voice and mind. As I began to rediscover it, I found it quite as strange as churten theory and in some respects complementary to it. I knew, but had never understood, that Cetian physics and religion are aspects of one knowledge. I wondered if all physics and religion are aspects of one knowledge.

At night I never slept well and often could not sleep at all. After the bountiful tables of Udan, college food seemed poor stuff; I had no appetite. But our work, my work went well — wonderfully well.

"No more mouses," said Gvonesh on the voice ansible from Hain. "Peoples."

"What people?" I demanded.

"Me," said Gvonesh.

So our Director of Research churtened from one corner of Laboratory One to another, and then from Building One to Building Two — vanishing in one laboratory and appearing in the other, smiling, in the same instant, in no time.

"What did it feel like?" they asked, of course, and Gvonesh answered, of course, "Like nothing."

Many experiments followed; mice and gholes churtened halfway around Ve and back; robot crews churtened from Anarres to Urras, from Hain to Ve, and then from Anarres to Ve, twenty-two light-years. So, then, eventually the *Shoby* and her crew of ten human beings churtened into orbit around a miserable planet seventeen light-years from Ve and returned (but words that imply coming and going, that imply distance traveled, are not appropriate) thanks only to their intelligent use of entrainment, rescuing themselves from a kind of chaos of dissolution, a death by unreality, that horrified us all. Experiments with high-intelligence life forms came to a halt.

"The rhythm is wrong," Gvonesh said on the ansible (she said it "rithkhom.") For a moment I thought of my mother saying, "It can't be right to have event without interval." What else had Isako said? Something about dancing. But I did not want to think about Udan. I did not think about Udan. When I did I felt, far down deeper inside me than my bones, the knowledge of being no one, no where, and a shaking like a frightened animal.

My religion reassured me that I was part of the Way, and my physics absorbed my despair in work. Experiments, cautiously resumed, succeeded beyond hope. The Terran Dalzul and his psychophysics took everyone at the research station on Ve by storm; I am sorry I never met him. As he predicted, using the continuity field he churtened without a hint of trouble, alone, first locally, then from Ve to Hain, then the great jump to Tadkla and back. From the second journey to Tadkla, his three companions returned without him. He died on that far world. It did not seem to us in the laboratories that his death was in any way caused by the churten field or by what had come to be known as "the churten experience," though his three companions were not so sure.

"Maybe Dalzul was right. One people at a time," said Gvonesh; and she made herself again the subject, the "ritual animal," as the Hainish say, of the next experiment. Using continuity technology she churtened right round Ve in four skips, which took thirty-two seconds because of the time needed to set up the coordinates. We had taken to calling the non-interval in time/real interval in space a "skip." It sounded light, trivial. Scientists like to trivialize.

I wanted to try the improvement to double-field stability that I had been working on ever since I came to Ran'n. It was time to give it a test; my patience was short, life was too short to fiddle with figures forever. Talking to Gvonesh on the ansible I said, "I'll skip over to

Ve Port. And then back here to Ran'n. I promised a visit to my home farm this winter." Scientists like to trivialize.

"You still got that wrinkle in your field?" Gvonesh asked. "Some kind, you know, like a fold?"

"It's ironed out, ammar," I assured her.

"Good, fine," said Gvonesh, who never questioned what one said. "Come."

So, then: we set up the fields in a constant stable churten link with ansible connection; and I was standing inside a chalked circle in the Churten Field Laboratory of Ran'n Center on a late autumn afternoon and standing inside a chalked circle in the Churten Research Station Field Laboratory in Ve Port on a late summer day at a distance of 4.2 light-years and no interval of time.

"Feel nothing?" Gvonesh inquired, shaking my hand heartily. "Good fellow, good fellow, welcome, ammar, Hideo. Good to see. No wrinkle, hah?"

I laughed with the shock and queerness of it, and gave Gvonesh the bottle of Udan Kedun '49 that I had picked up a moment ago from the laboratory table on O.

I had expected, if I arrived at all, to churten promptly back again, but Gvonesh and others wanted me on Ve for a while for discussions and tests of the field. I think now that the Director's extraordinary intuition was at work; the "wrinkle," the "fold" in the Tiokunan'n Field still bothered her. "Is unaesthetical," she said.

"But it works," I said.

"It worked," said Gvonesh.

Except to retest my field, to prove its reliability, I had no desire to return to O. I was sleeping somewhat better here on Ve, although food was still unpalatable to me, and when I was not working I felt shaky and drained, a disagreeable reminder of my exhaustion after the night which I tried not to remember when for some reason or other I had cried so much. But the work went very well.

"You got no sex, Hideo?" Gvonesh asked me when we were alone in the Lab one day, I playing with a new set of calculations and she finishing her box lunch.

The question took me utterly aback. I knew it was not as impertinent as Gvonesh's peculiar usage of the language made it sound. But Gvonesh never asked questions like that. Her own sex life was as much a mystery as the rest of her existence. No one had ever heard her mention the word, let alone suggest the act.

When I sat with my mouth open, stumped, she said, "You used to, hah," as she chewed on a cold varvet.

I stammered something. I knew she was not proposing that she and I have sex, but inquiring after my well-being. But I did not know what to say.

"You got some kind of wrinkle in your life, hah," Gvonesh said. "Sorry. Not my business."

Wanting to assure her I had taken no offense I said, as we say on O, "I honor your intent."

She looked directly at me, something she rarely did. Her eyes were clear as water in her long, bony face softened by a fine, thick, colorless down. "Maybe is time you go back to O?" she asked.

"I don't know. The facilities here — "

She nodded. She always accepted what one said. "You read Harraven's report?" she asked, changing one subject for another as quickly and definitively as my mother.

All right, I thought, the challenge was issued. She was ready for me to test my field again. Why not? After all, I could churten to Ran'n and churten right back again to Ve within a minute, if I chose, and if the Lab could afford it. Like ansible transmission, churtening draws essentially on inertial mass, but setting up the field, disinfecting it, and holding it stable in size uses a good deal of local energy. But it was Gvonesh's suggestion, which meant we had the money. I said, "How about a skip over and back?"

"Fine," Gvonesh said. "Tomorrow."

So the next day, on a morning of late autumn, I stood inside a chalked circle in the Field Laboratory on Ve and stood —

A shimmer, a shivering of everything — a missed beat — skipped — in darkness. A darkness. A dark room. The lab? A lab — I found the light panel. In the darkness I was sure it was the laboratory on Ve. In the light I saw it was not. I didn't know where it was. I didn't know where I was. It seemed familiar yet I could not place it. What was it? A biology lab? There were specimens, an old subparticle microscope, the maker's ideogram on the battered brass casing, the lyre ideogram.... I was on O. In some laboratory in some building of the Center at Ran'n? It smelled like the old buildings of Ran'n, it smelled like a rainy night on O. But how could I have not arrived in the receiving field, the circle carefully chalked on the wood floor of the lab in Tower Hall? The field itself must have moved. An appalling, an impossible thought.

I was alarmed and felt rather dizzy, as if my body had skipped that beat, but I was not yet frightened. I was all right, all here, all the pieces in the right places, and the mind working. A slight spatial displacement? said the mind.

I went out into the corridor. Perhaps I had myself been disoriented and left the Churten Field Laboratory and come to full consciousness somewhere else. But my crew would have been there; where were they? And that would have been hours ago; it should have been just past noon on O when I arrived. A slight temporal displacement? said the mind, working away. I went down the corridor looking for my lab, and that is when it became like one of those dreams in which you cannot find the room which you must find. It was that dream. The building was perfectly familiar: it was Tower Hall, the second floor of Tower, but there was no Churten Lab. All the labs were biology and biophysics, and all were deserted. It was evidently late at night. Nobody around. At last I saw a light under a door and knocked and opened it on a student reading at a library terminal.

"I'm sorry," I said. "I'm looking for the Churten Field Lab — "

"The what lab?"

She had never heard of it, and apologized. "I'm not in Ti Phy, just Bi Phy," she said humbly.

I apologized too. Something was making me shakier, increasing my sense of dizziness and disorientation. Was this the "chaos effect" the crew of the *Shoby* and perhaps the crew of the *Galba* had experienced? Would I begin to see the stars through the walls, or turn around and see Gvonesh here on O?

I asked her what time it was. "I should have got here at noon," I said, though of course that meant nothing to her.

"It's about one," she said, glancing at the clock on the terminal. I looked at it too. It gave the time, the tenday, the month, the year.

"That's wrong," I said.

She looked worried.

"That's not right," I said. "The date. It's not right." But I knew from the steady glow of the numbers on the clock, from the girl's round, worried face, from the beat of my heart, from the smell of the rain, that it was right, that it was an hour after midnight eighteen years ago, that I was here, now, on the day after the day I called "once upon a time" when I began to tell this story.

A major temporal displacement, said the mind, working, laboring.

"I don't belong here," I said, and turned to hurry back to what seemed a refuge, Biology Lab 6, which would be the Churten Field Lab eighteen years from now, as if I could re-enter the field, which had existed or would exist for .004 second.

The girl saw that something was wrong, made me sit down, and gave me a cup of hot tea from her insulated bottle.

"Where are you from?" I asked her, the kind, serious student.

"Herdud Farmhold of Deada Village on the South Watershed of the Saduun," she said.

"I'm from downriver," I said. "Udan of Derdan'nad." I suddenly broke into tears. I managed to control myself, apologized again, drank my tea, and set the cup down. She was not overly troubled by my fit of weeping. Students are intense people, they laugh and cry, they break down and rebuild. She asked if I had a place to spend the night: a perceptive question. I said I did, thanked her, and left.

I did not go back to the biology laboratory, but went downstairs and started to cut through the gardens to my rooms in the New Quadrangle. As I walked the mind kept working; it worked out that somebody else had been/would be in those rooms then/now.

I turned back towards the Shrine Quadrangle, where I had lived my last two years as a student before I left for Hain. If this was in fact, as the clock had indicated, the night after I had left, my room might still be empty and unlocked. It proved to be so, to be as I had left it, the mattress bare, the cyclebasket unemptied.

That was the most frightening moment. I stared at that cyclebasket for a long time before I took a crumpled bit of outprint from it and carefully smoothed it on the desk. It was a set of temporal equations scribbled on my old pocketscreen in my own handwriting, notes from Sedharad's class in Interval, from my last term at Ran'n, day before yesterday, eighteen years ago.

I was now very shaky indeed. You are caught in a chaos field, said the mind, and I believed it. Fear and stress, and nothing to do about it, not till the long night was past. I lay down on the bare bunk mattress, ready for the stars to burn through the walls and my eyelids if I shut them. I meant to try and plan what I should do in the morning, if there was a morning. I fell asleep instantly and slept like a stone till broad daylight, when I woke up on the bare bed in the familiar room, alert, hungry, and without a moment of doubt as to who or where or when I was.

I went down into the village for breakfast. I didn't want to meet any colleagues — no, fellow students — who might know me and say, "Hideo! What are you doing here? You left on the *Terraces of Darranda* yesterday!"

I had little hope they would not recognize me. I was thirty-one now, not twenty-one, much thinner and not as fit as I had been; but my half-Terran features were unmistakable. I did not want to be recognized, to have to try to explain. I wanted to get out of Ran'n. I wanted to go home.

O is a good world to time-travel in. Things don't change. Our trains run on the same schedule to the same places for centuries. We sign for payment and pay in contracted barter or cash monthly, so I did not have to produce mysterious coins from the future. I signed at the station and took the morning train to Saduun Delta.

The little suntrain glided through the plains and hills of the South Watershed and then the Northwest Watershed, following the ever-widening river, stopping at each village. I got off in the late afternoon at the station in Derdan'nad. Since it was very early spring, the station was muddy, not dusty.

I walked out the road to Udan. I opened the road gate that I had re-hung a few days/eighteen years ago; it moved easily on its new hinges. That gave me a little gleam of pleasure. The she-yamas were all in the nursery pasture. Birthing would start any day; their woolly sides stuck out, and they moved like sailboats in a slow breeze, turning their elegant, scornful heads to look distrustfully at me as I passed. Rain clouds hung over the hills. I crossed the Oro on the humpbacked wooden bridge. Four or five great blue ochid hung in a backwater by the bridgefoot; I stopped to watch them; if I'd had a spear... The clouds drifted overhead trailing a fine, faint drizzle. I strode on. My face felt hot and stiff as the cool rain touched it. I followed the river road and saw the house come into view, the dark, wide roofs low on the tree-crowned hill. I came past the aviary and the collectors, past the irrigation center, under the avenue of tall bare trees, up the steps of the deep porch, to the door, the wide door of Udan. I went in.

Tubdu was crossing the hall — not the woman I had last seen, in her sixties, grey-haired and tired and fragile, but Tubdu of The Great Giggle, Tubdu at forty-five, fat and rosy-brown and brisk, crossing the hall with short, quick steps, stopping, looking at me at first with mere recognition, there's Hideo, then with puzzlement, is that Hideo? and then with shock — that can't be Hideo!

"Ombu," I said, the baby word for othermother, "Ombu, it's me, Hideo, don't worry, it's all right, I came back." I embraced her, pressed my cheek to hers.

"But, but — " She held me off, looked up at my face. "But what has happened to you, darling boy?" she cried, and then, turning, called out in a high voice, "Isako! Isako!"

When my mother saw me she thought, of course, that I had not left on the ship to Hain, that my courage or my intent had failed me; and in her first embrace there was an involuntary reserve, a withholding. Had I thrown away the destiny for which I had been so ready to throw away everything else? I knew what was in her mind. I laid my cheek to hers and whispered, "I did go, mother, and I came back. I'm thirty-one years old. I came back — "

She held me away a little just as Tubdu had done, and saw my face. "Oh Hideo!" she said, and held me to her with all her strength. "My dear, my dear!"

We held each other in silence, till I said at last, "I need to see Isidri."

My mother looked up at me intently but asked no questions. "She's in the shrine, I think."

"I'll be right back."

I left her and Tubdu side by side and hurried through the halls to the central room, in the oldest part of the house, rebuilt seven centuries ago on the foundations that go back three thousand years. The walls are stone and clay, the roof is thick glass, curved. It is always cool and still there. Books line the walls, the Discussions, the discussions of the Discussions, poetry, texts and versions of the Plays; there are drums and whispersticks for meditation and ceremony; the small, round pool which is the shrine itself wells up from clay pipes and brims its blue-green basin, reflecting the rainy sky above the skylight. Isidri was there. She had brought in fresh boughs for the vase beside the shrine, and was kneeling to arrange them.

I went straight to her and said, "Isidri, I came back. Listen — "

Her face was utterly open, startled, scared, defenseless, the soft, thin face of a woman of twenty-two, the dark eyes gazing into me.

"Listen, Isidri: I went to Hain, I studied there, I worked on a new kind of temporal physics, a new theory — transilience — I spent ten years there. Then we began experiments, I was in Ran'n and crossed over to the Hainish system in no time, using that technology, in no time, you understand me, literally, like the ansible — not at lightspeed, not faster than light, but in no time. In one place and in another place instantaneously, you understand? And it went fine, it worked, but coming back there was...there was a fold, a crease, in my field. I was in the same place in a different time. I came back eighteen of your years, ten of mine. I came back to the day I left, but I didn't leave, I came back, I came back to you."

I was holding her hands, kneeling to face her as she knelt by the silent pool. She searched my face with her watchful eyes, silent. On her cheekbone there was a fresh scratch and a little bruise; a branch had lashed her as she gathered the evergreen boughs.

"Let me come back to you," I said in a whisper.

She touched my face with her hand. "You look so tired," she said. "Hideo... Are you all right?"

"Yes," I said. "Oh, yes. I'm all right."

And there my story, so far as it has any interest to the Ekumen or to research in transilience, comes to an end. I have lived now for eighteen years as a farmholder of Udan Farm of Derdan'nad Village of the hill region of the Northwest Watershed of the Saduun, on Oket, on O. I am fifty years old. I am the Morning husband of the Second Sedoretu of Udan; my wife is Isidri; my Night marriage is to Sota of Drehe, whose Evening wife is my sister Koneko. My children of the Morning with Isidri are Latubdu and Tadri; the Evening children are Murmi and Lasako. But none of this is of much interest to the Stabiles of the Ekumen.

My mother, who had had some training in temporal engineering, asked for my story, listened to it carefully, and accepted it without question; so did Isidri. Most of the people of my farmhold chose a simpler and far more plausible story, which explained everything fairly well, even my severe loss of weight and ten-year age gain overnight. At the very last moment, just before the spaceship left, they said, Hideo decided not to go to the Ekumenical School on Hain after all. He came back to Udan, because he was in love with Isidri. But it had made him quite ill, because it was a very hard decision and he was very much in love.

Maybe that is indeed the true story. But Isidri and Isako chose a stranger truth.

Later, when we were forming our sedoretu, Sota asked me for that truth. "You aren't the same man, Hideo, though you are the man I always loved," he said. I told him why, as best I could. He was sure that Koneko would understand it better than he could, and indeed she listened gravely, and asked several keen questions which I could not answer.

I did attempt to send a message to the temporal physics department of the Ekumenical Schools on Hain. I had not been home long before my mother, with her strong sense of duty and her obligation to the Ekumen, became insistent that I do so.

"Mother," I said, "what can I tell them? They haven't invented churten theory yet!"

"Apologize for not coming to study, as you said you would. And explain it to the Director, the Anarresti woman. Maybe she would understand."

"Even Gvonesh doesn't know about churten yet. They'll begin telling her about it on the ansible from Urras and Anarres about three years from now. Anyhow, Gvonesh didn't know me the first couple of years I was there." The past tense was inevitable but ridiculous; it would have been more accurate to say, "she won't know me the first couple of years I won't be there."

Or *was* I there on Hain, now? That paradoxical idea of two simultaneous existences on two different worlds disturbed me exceedingly. It was one of the points Koneko had asked about. No matter how I discounted it as impossible under every law of temporality, I could not keep from imagining that it was possible, that another I was living on Hain, and would come to Udan in eighteen years and meet myself. After all, my present existence was also and equally impossible.

When such notions haunted and troubled me I learned to replace them with a different image: the little whorls of water that slid down between the two big rocks, where the current ran strong, just above the swimming bay in the Oro. I would imagine those whirlpools forming and dissolving, or I would go down to the river and sit and watch them. And they seemed to hold a solution to my question, to dissolve it as they endlessly dissolved and formed.

But my mother's sense of duty and obligation was unmoved by such trifles as a life impossibly lived twice.

"You should try to tell them," she said.

She was right. If my double transilience field had established itself permanently, it was a matter of real importance to temporal science, not only to myself. So I tried. I borrowed a staggering sum in cash from the farm reserves, went up to Ran'n, bought a five-thousand-word ansible screen transmission, and sent a message to my director of studies at the Ekumenical School, trying to explain why, after being accepted at the School, I had not arrived — if in fact I had not arrived.

I take it that this was the "creased message" or "ghost" they asked me to try to interpret, my first year there. Some of it is gibberish, and some words probably came from the other, nearly simultaneous transmission, but parts of my name are in it, and other words may be fragments or reversals from my long message — problem, churten, return, arrived, time.

It is interesting, I think, that at the ansible center the Receivers used the word "creased" for a temporally disturbed transilient, as Gvonesh would use it for the anomaly, the "wrinkle" in my churten field. In fact, the ansible field was meeting a resonance resistance, caused by the ten-year anomaly in the churten field, which did fold the message back into itself, crumple it up, inverting and erasing. At that point, within the implication of the Tiokunan'n Double Field, my existence on O as I sent the message was simultaneous with my existence on Hain when the message was received. There was an I who sent and an I who received. Yet, so long as the encapsulated field anomaly existed, the simultaneity was literally a point, an instant, a crossing without further implication in either the ansible or the churten field.

An image for the churten field in this case might be a river winding in its floodplain, winding in deep, redoubling curves, folding back upon itself so closely that at last the current breaks through the double banks of the s and runs straight, leaving a whole reach of the water aside as a curving lake, cut off from the current, unconnected. In this analogy, my ansible message would have been the one link, other than my memory, between the current and the lake.

But I think a truer image is the whirlpools of the current itself, occurring and recurring, the same? Or not the same?

I worked at the mathematics of an explanation in the early years of my marriage, while my physics was still in good working order. See the "Notes toward a Theory of Resonance Interference in Doubled Ansible and Churten Fields," appended to this document. I realize that the explanation is probably irrelevant, since, on this stretch of the river, there is no Tiokunan'n Field. But independent research from an odd direction can be useful. And I am attached to it, since it is the last temporal physics I did. I have followed churten research with intense interest, but my life's work has been concerned with vineyards, drainage, the care of yamas, the care and education of children, the Discussions, and trying to learn how to catch fish with my bare hands.

Working on that paper, I satisfied myself in terms of mathematics and physics that the existence in which I went to Hain and became a temporal physicist specializing in transilience was in fact encapsulated (enfolded, erased) by the churten effect. But no amount of theory or proof could quite allay my anxiety, my fear — which increased after my marriage and with the birth of each of my children — that there was a crossing point yet to come. For all my images of rivers and whirlpools, I could not prove that the encapsulation might not reverse at the instant of transilience. It was possible that on the day I churtened from Ve to Ran'n I might undo, lose, erase my marriage, our children, all my life at Udan, crumple it up like a bit of paper tossed into a basket. I could not endure that thought.

I spoke of it at last to Isidri, from whom I have only ever kept one secret.

"No," she said, after thinking a long time, "I don't think that can be. There was a reason, wasn't there, that you came back — here."

"You," I said.

She smiled wonderfully. "Yes," she said. She added after a while, "And Sota, and Koncko, and the farmhold.... But there'd be no reason for you to go back there, would there?"

She was holding our sleeping baby as she spoke; she laid her cheek against the small silky head.

"Except maybe your work there," she said. She looked at me with a little yearning in her eyes. Her honesty required equal honesty of me.

"I miss it sometimes," I said. "I know that. I didn't know that I was missing you. But I was dying of it. I would have died and never known why, Isidri. And anyhow, it was all wrong — my work was wrong."

"How could it have been wrong, if it brought you back?" she said, and to that I had no answer at all.

When information on churten theory began to be published I subscribed to whatever the Center Library of O received, particularly the work done at the Ekumenical Schools and on Ve. The general progress of research was just as I remembered, racing along for three years, then hitting the hard places. But there was no reference to a Tiokunan'n Hideo doing research in the field. Nobody worked on a theory of a stabilized double field. No churten field research station was set up at Ran'n.

At last it was the winter of my visit home, and then the very day; and I will admit that, all reason to the contrary, it was a bad day. I felt waves of guilt, of nausea. I grew very shaky, thinking of the Udan of that visit, when Isidri had been married to Hedran, and I a mere visitor.

Hedran, a respected traveling scholar of the Discussions, had in fact come to teach several times in the village. Isidri had suggested inviting him to stay at Udan. I had vetoed the suggestion, saying that though he was a brilliant teacher there was something I disliked about him. I got a sidelong flash from Sidi's clear dark eyes: *Is he jealous?* She suppressed a smile. When I told her and my mother about my "other life," the one thing I had left out, the one secret I kept, was my visit to Udan. I did not want to tell my mother that in that "other life" she had been very ill. I did not want to tell Isidri that in that "other life" Hedran had been her Evening husband and she had had no children of her body. Perhaps I was wrong, but it seemed to me that I had no right to tell these things, that they were not mine to tell.

So Isidri could not know that what I felt was less jealousy than guilt. I had kept knowledge from her. And I had deprived Hedran of a life with Isidri, the dear joy, the center, the life of my own life.

Or had I shared it with him? I didn't know. I don't know.

That day passed like any other, except that one of Suudi's children broke her elbow falling out of a tree. "At least we know she won't drown," said Tubdu, wheezing.

Next came the date of the night in my rooms in the New Quadrangle, when I had wept and not known why I wept. And a while after that, the day of my return, transilient, to Ve, carrying a bottle of Isidri's wine for Gvonesh. And finally, yesterday, I entered the churten field on Ve, and left it eighteen years ago on O. I spent the night, as I sometimes do, in the shrine. The hours went by quietly; I wrote, gave worship, meditated, and slept. And I woke beside the pool of silent water.

So, now: I hope the Stabiles will accept this report from a farmer they never heard of, and that the engineers of transilience may see it as at least a footnote to their experiments. Certainly it is difficult to verify, the only evidence for it being my word, and my otherwise almost inexplicable knowledge of churten theory. To Gvonesh, who does not know me, I send my respect, my gratitude, and my hope that she will honor my intent.

Kissing Frogs

Jaye Lawrence

This modern revisiting of "The Frog Prince" was immediately recognized, by both the jury and the editors, as a pleasing after-dinner mint of a story, the perfect way to end an anthology and send you home.

> **Single Green Frog** seeks his princess. Do you believe in fairy tales? One kiss and it's happily ever after. No smokers, please. PETA members preferred.

We met near a pond, of course.

"I loved your ad," I said after we'd finished our introductions. Sharon, meet Jerry. Frog, meet human. "But I have to admit I wasn't expecting an actual amphibian."

My companion shrugged what would have been his shoulders, if only he'd had some. The result was a rippling quiver of the skin just behind his sleek green head. Jerry was an attractive frog, really. Striking. He had iridescent green skin dappled with bronze, and a splendid crimson vocal sac below his broad froggy smile. Behind each golden eye was a perfectly round black spot, which I took to be purely decorative until a hazy memory surfaced from junior high. We'd dissected frogs in eighth grade biology. *Tympanums*, I thought. *My date has tympanums.*

"I wasn't expecting a genuine PETA member either," Jerry said. "That was just a bit of frog humor." He didn't croak. His voice was a smooth and pleasant baritone, surprisingly low for a creature the size of my fist, and his diction was perfect. The red vocal sac swelled to impressive proportions as he spoke.

I looked down at the Starbucks cups between us on the picnic table. I'd brought two vanilla lattes to our rendezvous, gambling that my date would be a coffee drinker. He wasn't. "I'm not a member anymore," I confessed. "I stopped contributing after they asked the town of Hamburg, Pennsylvania, to change its name to Veggieburg."

"You're joking."

"No, it's true. Years back they asked a town called Fishkill to change its name to Fishsave, but that didn't get as much publicity." I shut up and sipped my coffee, embarrassed by my own babbling. It strikes me like that on first dates sometimes, even with my own species. Glib to gibbering in two seconds flat.

After a moment's awkward silence I forced myself to meet Jerry's shining eyes again. They were bulging, but kind. He smiled. I smiled back. "So how did it happen? If you don't mind me asking."

He waved a forefoot in a dismissive gesture. His front feet had four toes each, while the heavily webbed hind feet had five. "I find it unnatural if someone doesn't. It suggests either an excess of politeness or an appalling lack of curiosity, wouldn't you say?"

He hopped a few lengths away from me along the tabletop, pausing to stare out across the water. Following his gaze, I noticed the lily pads for the first time: a flotilla of round emerald leaves, a scattered few captained by luminous white flowers. I wondered how they looked through Jerry's jewel-like eyes. A promised land? A prison?

"I was married, once upon a time," he said in his fine, fluid voice. Like a child I closed my eyes to listen. "To a rich man's daughter. When we met she had everything and I had nothing, and that attracted us both madly. We were polar opposites."

"Like magnets," I murmured.

"Magnets in love?" He sounded amused. "But you know what happens to magnets when the polarity of one is reversed."

In place of attraction, repulsion. Yes, I knew.

"She loved me. I do believe that. But she'd never lacked for anything in her life, and she wanted all the luxuries she was accustomed to — things I couldn't afford to give her on a middle manager's salary. So she'd take them as gifts from her father, against my wishes, or run up our credit cards impossibly high, and then we'd argue. Bitter fights half the night sometimes. We didn't leave any marks, but we didn't take any prisoners either.

"With every argument I felt smaller in her eyes, less of a man. And with every shiny, expensive thing she wanted that I couldn't give her, I felt her drawing farther away. At the end she would physically recoil from me in bed at night, as though she'd touched something horrible and slimy."

I opened my eyes. "She left you because you became a frog?"

"Oh no," he said with surprise. "I became a frog because she left me."

Now there's a self-esteem problem, I thought. But it happens to us all, doesn't it? Whether you're a beauty or a beast, when someone you love rejects you, your mirror turns mean. You stand in front of it crying, "Mirror, mirror, what's wrong with me? Why wasn't I good enough for him to love?" And the damn mirror shows you. Suddenly every line and flaw is magnified, suddenly every year shows. Those extra ten pounds, that too prominent Adam's apple, the ass too flat, the boobs too small — the cold glass reflects it all. Jerry probably started out as a nice presentable guy with eyes that bulged just a little, before his wife and his self-confidence disappeared through the looking glass.

"But at least you're getting out there now," I said finally, in what I hoped Jerry would consider an encouraging tone. To my own ears it sounded appallingly like my mother's voice, trying to cheer me up after my disastrous senior prom. "Dating. Trying to get back to normal."

Jerry's green head bobbed in a nod. "Trying, yes," he said. "But not succeeding very well so far. It's difficult enough for normal, attractive people to find love these days, Sharon, never mind a guy who's …well, not exactly Prince Charming."

I snorted. "Nobody is Prince Charming, Jerry. Prince Charming doesn't exist, and ugly stepsisters need love too. Are you sure you don't want some of this latte?"

"No, you go ahead and have it. Caffeine makes me jumpy." He winked one golden eye.

Laughing, I toasted him with the Starbucks cup. "You don't know what you're missing. I've got to have my coffee every day or I'm absolutely Grimm."

Jerry groaned and that *did* come out as a croak, a silly wavering croak that broke in the middle like a pubescent boy's. We both succumbed to a fit of the giggles then, human laughter mingling with bursts of frog song. The first shared laugh with someone new is always a shining moment, an instant of connection that warms you inside even if you're not wildly attracted to your date. Sometimes I get from a first date to a second on laughs alone. That's not such a bad thing, either; it beats the hell out of getting there on desperation. I've done that too, I'm sorry to say.

"That's better!" I said. "You've got to keep laughing in this world, Jerry, that's why your ad caught my eye: it was funny and optimistic."

He hopped closer and looked up intently into my eyes. His pupils weren't vertical or horizontal like most frogs' eyes, they were round like a person's. It gave him a wide-eyed, earnest look. "Is that what made you answer it?"

"I suppose so. It certainly wasn't because I believe in fairy tales." A rueful smile turned up the corners of my mouth. "Not the ones with happy endings, anyway. But I was impressed that a guy who described himself as a 'frog' still had the confidence to hope for a happily-ever-after. It sounded a little naive, maybe, but sweet. And I figured a sweet guy who didn't consider himself a handsome prince might overlook me not being much of a princess."

Jerry's vocal sac swelled and deflated, swelled and deflated. I took this to be the froggy equivalent of being at a loss for words.

"It's okay, Jerry," I said. "I know I'm no beauty." It was the truth. When I work at it, as I'd worked at it that day, I clean up well. I'm tall and slender; my hair is a glossy natural auburn; I've been told I have a lovely smile. But no amount of expensive tailoring or makeup can disguise the fact that my shoulders are too broad, my cheekbones too flat, my jaw square, my nose long. I'm a handsome woman when I try, but it would take more than plastic surgery to make me a beautiful one.

Jerry's eyes distended; he looked alarmed. "Sharon, don't say that. For pity's sake, I'm a *frog* — you can't believe I'm sitting here making judgments about your appearance! I'm grateful, so deeply grateful, that you're still here speaking with me at all. You're — you're the most beautiful woman I've dated in seven months!"

My eyebrows raised. "Jerry."

The red balloon of his vocal sac emptied in a sigh. "All right, I confess you're also the only one. But believe me when I tell you that you look lovely to me. Certainly much more attractive than I must look to you."

I felt my cheeks grow pink. "Uh, well, you're very — "

"Sharon."

It was my turn to sigh. "Okay. As a frog you're drop-dead gorgeous, hon, but as a guy you just aren't my type."

I ached for him as the words registered. His whole body seemed to shrink with disappointment. He looked so small and miserable, so crushed.

The strange thing about not fitting the world's narrow definition of beauty is that you never quite accept it inside. No matter how squarely you face facts in front of your own bathroom mirror, no matter how hard you struggle to make peace with yourself and live happily inside your own skin, it still hurts like hell to see your homeliness reflected in another person's eyes. Why? God only knows. It's just how we're made. We can't tickle ourselves, and we can't deal our own egos a mortal blow. Not like another person can.

At least we can pleasure ourselves. There'd be a lot more suicide in lonely apartments if we couldn't.

"I'm sorry, Jerry," I said softly. Leaning closer to him, I was stricken to see his eyes welling up with tears. "Oh, Jerry! Don't — please, it's not worth it, *please* don't — "

His mouth opened, but not to speak: to sing. Not in laughter this time, but in pain.

The sound was larger than Jerry, larger than both of us. Its mournfulness echoed across the park, its longing rippled across the water. My ears were filled with it. My bones ached with it. Each note reverberated with all the misery his small green body had borne for months, the loneliness and loss flowing from his lipless mouth in a wordless, universal song of sorrow. Wordless, yet it spoke.

I am a stranger alone in a strange land, his song said to me. *I am a beautiful creature trapped behind other eyes. I love but am not allowed to love, I long for all I cannot have, I lust with loins that never cool, I love! I love! I love!*

It was his song, but it could have been mine. By the time he sang the final notes, tears were streaming down my face. When the final echoes faded, I picked Jerry up in trembling hands and brought his mouth to mine.

Hands still shaking, I set him gently down again.

He was unchanged.

I put my head down on the picnic table and sobbed as though my heart were breaking. It was.

"Sharon." Jerry's cool, moist head nudged my bare arm. "Shhh, Sharon, it's all right. Please don't cry anymore."

My breath came in ragged gasps. "My name isn't Sharon, it's Stephen."

"Oh." There was a moment's silence. "Stephen, then. Please don't cry, Stephen. You did a marvelous thing for me."

I raised my head reluctantly. I knew I had to be a mess with my nose all red and runny, eyes swollen, foundation streaked. More than that, I felt exhausted emotionally and physically, aching from my head to my size eleven Prada pumps.

"You're still a frog, Jerry," I said miserably. "I didn't do a thing except hurt you. I'm so sorry."

But Jerry didn't look hurt. His golden eyes were alight with a new glow, and when he spoke his voice was jubilant. "You kissed me! Even though I'm a slimy amphibian; Sharon — Stephen — you kissed me!"

I sniffed and dabbed at my face with a Starbucks napkin. "So what? Two minutes more of that song and I probably would've slept with you too, for all the good it would do. *You're still a frog, Jerry*. I'm not your princess. I'm nobody's princess. I'm just a freak in women's clothing, dreaming of the day he gets his willy lopped off."

Jerry winced a little at that, but not as much as a man would have. Frogs don't have penises. "If you're a freak," he said gently, "then what am I? Stephen, you gave me the first ray of hope I've had in seven months. You kissed me. You weren't the right one to transform me — you said it yourself, I'm not your type — but you did kiss me. That means it's not hopeless after all. I'm not so repulsive that no one will ever touch me again.

"Don't you understand? I've been terrified that even if I did meet the right woman, my princess, she would only run from me. But you didn't run from me, you kissed me!"

I shook my head in disbelief. "Jerry, I'm glad I made your day. But if your idea of a successful relationship is your date not running away screaming — " I stopped as my own words registered. "Hmm. Come to think of it, that's my idea of a good date too."

For the second time that afternoon we laughed together, but I was still weighed down with the sorrow of his song. My head was aching, and my Wonderbra was digging sharply into my chest in a way that felt anything but wonderful. All I wanted was to go home, put on pajamas, and drown my sorrows in a pint of Cherry Garcia. I gathered up the Starbucks litter and took it to a nearby trash barrel, then returned to the picnic table to make my farewells to Jerry.

He was still beaming from tympanum to tympanum. "It's been a pleasure, Sharon."

I picked up my handbag from the bench seat. "You don't have to call me Sharon anymore. But thank you."

"You *are* Sharon," he replied, "and you are beautiful. I'll never forget you."

I smiled wryly. "I have to say you're going to stick in my mind for a while too, hon. Thank you for a very…memorable date." I bent down and gave him one more for the road, right on top of his dappled green head. "You take care now. I hope you find your princess."

"And you your prince, sweet Sharon."

———

Still haunted by his beautiful, terrible song, I was all the way home and halfway naked before I discovered why my padded bra had suddenly gotten so uncomfortable.

Mirror, mirror, on the wall. I had breasts.

winners and short lists

The Tiptree Award process does not call for a list of nominees from which a winner is chosen, because we feel that creates an artificial set of "losers." Instead, each panel releases a winner (or winners) and a "short list" of fiction which the jurors consider especially worthy of readers' attention. In some years, the jurors publish a "long list" of books they also found interesting in the course of their reading.

Below are the winners and short lists from all years of the award, as well as the long list from 2004. Entries in boldface are represented in this volume. For more information on all of these works, please visit our website — at www.tiptree.org — for all of the annotated lists.

You are encouraged to join the not-so-secret Secret Feminist Cabal and forward recommendations for novels and short fiction works that explore and expand gender. You'll find a recommendation form on the website. The wider our network of supporters, the more good candidates the jurors see every year.

2004 WINNERS
Joe Haldeman, *Camouflage* (Ace 2004)
Johanna Sinisalo, *Not Before Sundown* (Peter Owen, UK 2003);
    also as *Troll: A Love Story* (Grove Press, US 2004). Originally
    published in Finnish in 2000 as *Ennen päiävanlaskua ei voi*

2004 SHORT LIST
A.S. Byatt, *Little Black Book of Stories* (Chatto and Windus 2003; Knopf 2004)

L. Timmel Duchamp, *Love's Body, Dancing in Time* (Aqueduct Press 2004)

Carol Emshwiller, "All of Us Can Almost..." (*Sci Fiction*, 17 November 2004)

Nancy Farmer, *Sea of Trolls* (Atheneum 2004)

Eileen Gunn, *Stable Strategies and Others* (Tachyon Press 2004)

Gwyneth Jones, *Life* (Aqueduct Press 2004)

Jaye Lawrence, "Kissing Frogs" (*Fantasy & Science Fiction*, May 2004)

2004 LONG LIST

Christopher Barzak, "The Other Angelas" (www.pindeldyboz.com/cbangelas.htm)

Elizabeth Bear, "This Tragic Glass" (*SciFiction* 04.07.04)

Glenn Grant, "Burning Day" (*Island Dreams: Montreal Writers of the Fantastic*, ed. Claude Lalumiere, Vehicule Press 2004)

Victoria Elisabeth Garcia, *Unspeakable Vitrine* (Clawfoot Bathdog Press 2004)

Hiromi Goto, *Hopeful Monsters* (Arsenal Pulp Press 2004)

Elizabeth Hand, *Mortal Love* (HarperCollins 2004)

Anne Harris, *Inventing Memory* (Tor 2004)

Marie Jakober, *Even the Stones* (Edge 2004)

Ian McDonald, *River of Gods* (Simon & Schuster UK 2004)

Kat Meads, *Sleep* (Livingston Press 2004)

Terry Pratchett, *Monstrous Regiment* (HarperCollins 2003)

Tom Purdom, "Romance for Augmented Trio" (*Asimov's* SF, February 2004)

Victoria Somegyi & Kathleen Chamberlain, "Time's Swell" (*Strange Horizons*, 15 November 2004)

Peter Verhehst, *Tonguecat* (Farrar Straus & Giroux 2004)

N. Lee Wood, *Master of None* (Warner Aspect 2004)

2004 SPECIAL MENTION

Samuel R. Delany, *Stars in My Pocket Like Grains of Sand*, (Wesleyan University Press, 2004) (20th anniversary edition)

Will Roscoe, *Changing Ones: Third and Fourth Genders in Native North America* (St Martin's 1998)

2003 WINNER
Matt Ruff, *Set This House in Order: A Romance of Souls*

2003 SHORT LIST
Kim Antieau, *Coyote Cowgirl*
Richard Calder writing as Christina X, "The Catgirl Manifesto: An Introduction"
Kara Dalkey, "The Lady of the Ice Garden"
Carol Emshwiller, "Boys"
Nina Kiriki Hoffman, *A Fistful of Sky*
Kij Johnson, *Fudoki*
Sandra McDonald, "The Ghost Girls of Rumney Mill"
Ruth Nestvold, "Looking through Lace"
Geoff Ryman, "Birth Days"
Tricia Sullivan, *Maul*

2002 WINNERS
M. John Harrison, *Light*
John Kessel, "Stories for Men"

2002 SHORT LIST
Eleanor Arnason, "Knapsack Poems"
Ted Chiang, "Liking What You See: A Documentary"
John Clute, *Appleseed*
Karen Joy Fowler, "What I Didn't See"
Gregory Frost, "Madonna of the Maquiladora"
Shelley Jackson, *The Melancholy of Anatomy*
Larissa Lai, *Salt Fish Girl*
Peter Straub, editor, *Conjunctions 39: The New Wave Fabulists*

2001 WINNER
Hiromi Goto, *The Kappa Child*

2001 SHORT LIST
Joan Givner, *Half Known Lives*
Hugh Nissenson, *The Song of the Earth*
Ken MacLeod, *Dark Light*
Sheri S. Tepper, *The Fresco*

2000 WINNER
Molly Gloss, *Wild Life*

2000 SHORT LIST
Michael Blumlein, "Fidelity: A Primer"
James L. Cambias, "A Diagram of Rapture"
David Ebershoff, *The Danish Girl*
Mary Gentle, *Ash: A Secret History*
Camille Hernandez-Ramdwar, "Soma"
Nalo Hopkinson, "The Glass Bottle Trick"
Nalo Hopkinson, *Midnight Robber*
China Miéville, *Perdido Street Station*
Pamela Mordecai, "Once on the Shores of the Stream Senegambia"
Severna Park, *The Annunciate*
Tess Williams, *Sea as Mirror*

1999 WINNER
Suzy McKee Charnas, *The Conqueror's Child*

1999 SHORT LIST
Judy Budnitz, *If I Told You Once*
Sally Caves, "In the Second Person"
Graham Joyce, "Pinkland"
Yumiko Kurahashi, *The Woman with the Flying Head and other stories*
Penelope Lively, "5001 Nights"
David E. Morse, *The Iron Bridge*
Kim Stanley Robinson, "Sexual Dimorphism"

1998 WINNER
Raphael Carter, "Congenital Agenesis of Gender Ideation"

1998 SHORT LIST
Eleanor Arnason, "The Gauze Banner"
Octavia Butler, *Parable of the Talents*
Ted Chiang, "Story of Your Life"
Stella Duffy, *Singling Out the Couples*
Karen Joy Fowler, *Black Glass*
Maggie Gee, *The Ice People*
Carolyn Ives Gilman, *Halfway Human*
Phyllis Gotlieb, *Flesh and Gold*
Nalo Hopkinson, *Brown Girl in the Ring*
Gwyneth Jones, "La Cenerentola"
James Patrick Kelly, "Lovestory"
Ursula K. Le Guin, "Unchosen Love"
Elizabeth A. Lynn, *Dragon's Winter*
Maureen F. McHugh, *Mission Child*
Karl-Rene Moore, "The Hetairai Turncoat"
Rebecca Ore, "Accelerated Grimace"
Sara Paretsky, *Ghost Country*
Severna Park, *Hand of Prophecy*
Kit Reed, "The Bride of Bigfoot"
Kit Reed, *Weird Women, Wired Women*
Robert Reed, "Whiptail"
Mary Rosenblum, "The Eye of God"
Joan Slonczewski, *The Children Star*
Martha Soukup, "The House of Expectations"
Sean Stewart, *Mockingbird*
Sarah Zettel, *Playing God*

1997 WINNERS
Candas Jane Dorsey, *Black Wine*
Kelly Link, "Travels with the Snow Queen"

1997 SHORT LIST
Storm Constantine, "The Oracle Lips"
Paul Di Filippo, "Alice, Alfie, Ted and the Aliens"
Emma Donoghue, *Kissing the Witch: Old Tales in New Skins*
L. Timmel Duchamp, "The Apprenticeship of Isabetta di Pietro Cavazzi"
Molly Gloss, *The Dazzle of Day*
M. John Harrison, *Signs of Life*
Gwyneth Jones, "Balinese Dancer"
Ian McDonald, *Sacrifice of Fools*
Vonda N. McIntyre, *The Moon and the Sun*
Shani Mootoo, *Cereus Blooms at Night*
Salman Rushdie, "The Firebird's Nest"
Paul Witcover, *Waking Beauty*

1996 WINNERS
Ursula K. Le Guin, "Mountain Ways"
Mary Doria Russell, *The Sparrow*

1996 SHORT LIST
Fred Chappell, "The Silent Woman"
Suzy McKee Charnas, "Beauty and the Opera, or The Phantom Beast"
L. Timmel Duchamp, "Welcome, Kid, to the Real World"
Alasdair Gray, *A History Maker*
Jonathan Lethem, "Five Fucks"
Pat Murphy, *Nadya*
Rachel Pollack, *Godmother Night*
Lisa Tuttle, *The Pillow Friend*
Tess Williams, "And She Was the Word"
Sue Woolfe, *Leaning Towards Infinity*

1995 WINNERS
Elizabeth Hand, *Waking the Moon*
Theodore Roszak, *The Memoirs of Elizabeth Frankenstein*

1995 SHORT LIST
Kelley Eskridge, "And Salome Danced"
Kit Reed, *Little Sisters of the Apocalypse*
Lisa Tuttle, "Food Man"
Terri Windling, editor, *The Armless Maiden, and Other Stories for Childhood's Survivors*

1994 WINNERS
Ursula K. Le Guin, "The Matter of Seggri"
Nancy Springer, *Larque on the Wing*

1994 SHORT LIST
Eleanor Arnason, "The Lovers"
Suzy McKee Charnas, *The Furies*
L. Warren Douglas, *Cannon's Orb*
Greg Egan, "Cocoon"
Ellen Frye, *Amazon Story Bones*
Gwyneth Jones, *North Wind*
Graham Joyce & Peter F. Hamilton, "Eat Reecebread"
Ursula K. Le Guin, *A Fisherman of the Inland Sea*
Ursula K. Le Guin, "Forgiveness Day"
Rachel Pollack, *Temporary Agency*
Geoff Ryman, *Unconquered Countries*
Melissa Scott, *Trouble and Her Friends*
Delia Sherman, "Young Woman in a Garden"
George Turner, *Genetic Soldier*

1993 WINNER
Nicola Griffith, *Ammonite*

1993 SHORT LIST
Eleanor Arnason, *Ring of Swords*
Margaret Atwood, *The Robber Bride*
Sybil Claiborne, *In the Garden of Dead Cars*
L. Timmel Duchamp, "Motherhood"

R. Garcia y Robertson, "The Other Magpie"
James Patrick Kelly, "Chemistry"
Laurie J. Marks, *Dancing Jack*
Ian McDonald, "Some Strange Desire"
Alice Nunn, *Illicit Passage*
Paul Park, *Coelestis*

1992 WINNER
Maureen McHugh, *China Mountain Zhang*

1992 SHORT LIST
Carol Emshwiller, "Venus Rising"
Ian MacLeod, "Grownups"
Judith Moffett, *Time, Like an Ever-Rolling Stream*
Kim Stanley Robinson, *Red Mars*
Sue Thomas, *Correspondence*
Lisa Tuttle, *Lost Futures*
Élisabeth Vonarburg, *In the Mothers' Land*

1991 WINNERS
Eleanor Arnason, *A Woman of the Iron People*
Gwyneth Jones, *White Queen*

1991 SHORT LIST
John Barnes, *Orbital Resonance*
Karen Joy Fowler, *Sarah Canary*
Mary Gentle, *The Architecture of Desire*
Greer Ilene Gilman, *Moonwise*
Marge Piercy, *He, She and It*

RETROSPECTIVE AWARD WINNERS
Suzy McKee Charnas, *Motherlines* (1978)
Suzy McKee Charnas, *Walk to the End of the World* (1974)
Ursula K. Le Guin, *The Left Hand of Darkness* (1969)

Joanna Russ, *The Female Man* (1975)
Joanna Russ, "When It Changed" (1972)

RETROSPECTIVE AWARD SHORT LIST
Margaret Atwood, *The Handmaid's Tale* (1986)
Iain Banks, *The Wasp Factory* (1984)
Katherine Burdekin, *Swastika Night* (1937)
Octavia Butler, *Wild Seed* (1980)
Samuel R. Delany, *Babel-17* (1966)
Samuel R. Delany, *Triton* (1976)
Carol Emshwiller, *Carmen Dog* (1990)
Sonya Dorman Hess, "When I Was Miss Dow" (1966)
Elizabeth A. Lynn, *Watchtower* (1979)
Vonda McIntyre, *Dreamsnake* (1978)
Naomi Mitchison, *Memoirs of a Spacewoman* (1962)
Marge Piercy, *Woman on the Edge of Time* (1976)
Joanna Russ, *The Two of Them* (1978)
Pamela Sargent, editor, *Women of Wonder* (1974), *More Women of Wonder* (1976) and *The New Women of Wonder* (1977)
John Varley, "The Barbie Murders" (1978)
Kate Wilhelm, *The Clewiston Test* (1976)
Monique Wittig, *Les Guerillères* (1969)
Pamela Zoline, "The Heat Death of the Universe" (1967)

about the authors

RAPHAEL CARTER is the author of the novel *The Fortunate Fall* (Tor Books, 1996). Raphael lives in Minneapolis, Minnesota.

L. TIMMEL DUCHAMP is the author of *Alanya to Alanya*, the first novel in a series, and *Love's Body, Dancing in Time*, a collection of her short fiction, both from Aqueduct Press in Seattle. Her thoughts about narrative, a complete bibliography of her work, and several of her stories can be found on her website, ltimmel.home.mindspring.com.

CAROL EMSHWILLER grew up in France and Ann Arbor, Michigan. She was a housewife with three children through all the big middle part of her life and had to struggle for every little moment of writing time she could get. She now lives in New York City in the winter, where she teaches at New York University School of Continuing and Professional Studies, and spends the summers in a shack in the California Sierras. Her young adult novel, *Mr. Boots*, has just been released by Viking and her short story collection, *I Live With You* is available from Tachyon Publications. *Carmen Dog* and *The Mount* were also both reprinted in 2005.

EILEEN GUNN won the 2005 Nebula Award for "Coming to Terms," a story that appears, along with this volume's "Nirvana High," in her collection, *Stable Strategies and Others*, from Tachyon Publications.

JOE HALDEMAN was born in 1943 in Oklahoma City, and grew up mostly in Anchorage, Alaska and Bethesda, Maryland. He has a B.S.

in physics & astronomy and an MFA in writing. He was a Vietnam draftee in 1968 and received the Purple Heart for being wounded in action. He has been a part-time professor at the Massachusetts Institute of Technology since 1983. He has won four Hugo Awards (two for Best Novel), three Nebula Awards (one for Best Novel), and one World Fantasy Award, as well as the Rhysling Award for science fiction poetry and the Ditmar Award for the best science fiction novel published in Australia.

NALO HOPKINSON has so far published a collection of short stories, some plays, two novels, and an anthology or two. She has lived in Toronto, Canada since 1977, but spent most of her first sixteen years in the Caribbean, where she was born. Her writing reflects her hybrid reality. More details can be found on her website, www.sff.net/people/nalo.

GWYNETH JONES is a writer and critic of science fiction and fantasy, who also writes for teenagers under the name Ann Halam. Among other honors, she's won two World Fantasy Awards, the British Science Fiction Award, the Dracula Society's Children of the Night Award, the Philip K. Dick Award, and shared the first Tiptree Award, in 1992, with Eleanor Arnason. *Bold As Love*, the first novel of a fantasy sequence set in the near future, won the Arthur C. Clarke Award for 2001. Her collected critical writings and essays, *Deconstructing the Starships*, have been published by the Liverpool University Press. She lives in Brighton, UK, with her husband and son, plus two cats called Ginger and Frank, practices yoga, has done some extreme tourism in her time, likes old movies and cooking, and enjoys playing with her websites: http://www.boldaslove.co.uk and http://homepage.ntlworld.com/gwynethann.

JAYE LAWRENCE lives in Minnesota with her husband Theo, two daughters, three cats, and one fat, nervous rabbit. By day she is Director of Web Communications for Carleton College. Her short stories have appeared in *The Magazine of Fantasy & Science Fiction* and *Great River Review.*

URSULA K. LE GUIN has published six books of poetry, twenty novels, over a hundred short stories (collected in eleven volumes), four collections of essays, eleven books for children, and four volumes of translation. Her work includes realistic fiction, science fiction, fantasy, young children's books, books for young adults, screenplays, essays, verbal texts for musicians, and voicetexts for performance or recording. Her awards include a National Book Award, five Hugo Awards, five Nebula Awards, SFWA's Grand Master designation, the Kafka Award, a Pushcart Prize, the Howard Vursell Award of the American Academy of Arts and Letters, the *Los Angeles Times*'s Robert Kirsch Award, the PEN/Faulkner Award for short stories, and the ALA's Margaret A. Edwards Award for Young Adult fiction. She is also a two-time winner of the James Tiptree, Jr. Award and a winner of the Tiptree Retrospective Award.

Just before this anthology went to press, JONATHAN LETHEM received a 2005 MacArthur Foundation Fellowship, the prize colloquially known as the "genius grant." He is the author of six novels, including *Motherless Brooklyn*. He studied at Bennington College (1982-84) and immersed himself in the culture of literature by working as a bookseller at numerous bookshops in New York City and in Berkeley, California.

JULIE PHILLIPS is the author of the forthcoming biography of Alice Sheldon from St. Martin's Press. She lives in the Netherlands.

ALICE SHELDON/JAMES TIPTREE, JR., needs no introduction here, because she is introduced repeatedly throughout the book.

JOHANNA SINISALO was born in Finnish Lapland in 1958. Even before publication of her first novel, which won the prestigious Finlandia Prize, she had won the Aurora Prize for best Finnish science fiction or fantasy story six times, and the Kemi National Comic Strip Contest three times. *Troll: A Love Story* (or *Not Before Sundown*) is her first novel to be published in English.

LESLIE WHAT won a Nebula Award in 1999 for her story "The Cost of Doing Business," which can be found in her short story collection, *The Sweet and Sour Tongue*, published by Wildside Press. She also wrote the novel *Olympic Games*, available from Tachyon Publications. She lives in Eugene, Oregon.

about the editors

Karen Joy Fowler is the *New York Times* best-selling author of *The Jane Austen Book Club*. Her previous novel, *Sister Noon*, was a finalist for the PEN/Faulkner award. Her first novel, *Sarah Canary*, won the Commonwealth Medal for best first novel by a Californian in 1991. Her short story collection *Black Glass* won the World Fantasy Award in 1999; her first two novels were both *New York Times* notable books in their year. She is a Founding Mother of the Tiptree Award. She lives with her husband in Davis, California.

Pat Murphy has won numerous awards for her science fiction and fantasy writing. In 1987, she won the Nebula, an award presented by the Science Fiction Writers of America, for both her second novel, *The Falling Woman*, and her novelette "Rachel in Love." Her novel *There and Back Again* won the 2002 Seiun Award for best foreign science fiction novel translated into Japanese. Her most recent novel is *Adventures in Time and Space with Max Merriwell*. When she is not writing science fiction, Pat writes for the Exploratorium, San Francisco's museum of science, art, and human perception. She is a Founding Mother of the James Tiptree, Jr. Award and a member of the award's Motherboard.

Debbie Notkin is an editor and nonfiction writer. She edited *Flying Cups & Saucers*, the first collection of Tiptree-recognized short fiction, published by Edgewood Press in 1998. She edited and wrote the text for photographer Laurie Toby Edison's two books, *Women En Large: Images of Fat Nudes*, and *Familiar Men: A Book of Nudes*. She is the chair of the James Tiptree, Jr. Award Motherboard and an advisor to Broad Universe, an organization with the primary goal of promoting science fiction, fantasy, and horror written by women. She has been an editor and consulting editor for Tor Books and Prima Publishing. Her essays on body image and on science fiction have been widely published and she has spoken on these topics all over the United States and in Japan.

JEFFREY D. SMITH was a friend of James Tiptree's and is the literary trustee of her estate. He is a member of the James Tiptree, Jr. Award Motherboard. He edited "Women in Science Fiction," a groundbreaking 1975 symposium, and *Meet Me at Infinity*, a posthumous collection of Tiptree's stories and essays.